Out at the
Old Ball Game

Out at the Old Ball Game

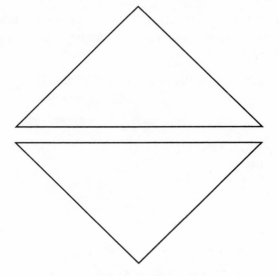

A NOVEL

Bernie Bookbinder

Bridge Works Publishing Co.
Bridgehampton, New York

All rights reserved under International and Pan-American Copyright Conventions. Published 1995 in the United States by Bridge Works Publishing Co., Bridgehampton, New York. Distributed in the United States by National Book Network, Lanham, Maryland.

This book is a work of fiction. Names, characters, places and incidents are either products of the author's imagination or are used fictitiously.

Library of Congress Cataloging-in-Publication Data

Bookbinder, Bernie.
    Out at the old ball game : a novel / Bernie Bookbinder. — 1st ed.
.   p.   cm.
    ISBN 1-882593-09-X
    I. Title.
PS3552.06433097   1995
813'.54 — dc20   94-37578
                                         CIP

10 9 8 7 6 5 4 3 2 1

Book and jacket design by Edith Allard

Printed in the United States of America

FIRST EDITION

This book is dedicated to the gay men and lesbians who are struggling —
within themselves and against a hostile society —
to come to terms with their sexuality.

Acknowledgments

The author is grateful for the generous assistance and support of his sons, Ronald, Joseph, and Jack; his wife, Marilyn; his friends Stan Isaacs and Chuck Hitchcock; those at Long Island Association for AIDS Care; and his editor, Barbara Phillips.

Out at the Old Ball Game

7

In recent years, as the cheers and crowds dwindled, Scrappy found himself spending more and more time with his memories and less and less with his baseball team. Administrative duties, once his bane, took on a certain appeal, if only as an alternative to watching the Gents invent new strategies for losing. He even appreciated the boredom of the off-season for its respite from defeat.

Now, on a chill winter's day in the catacombs beneath once-grand Gents Stadium, his bearlike arms cradling a shifting pyramid of mail, Scrappy kicked open, with customary viciousness, the door labeled

SCRAPPY SCHWRTZNBRGR
OWNER-MANAGER
THE NEW YORK GENTS
PRIVATE

and grunted with the guilt-free satisfaction derived from attacking something inanimate. He dumped the letters onto a vast messy desk whose disorder was so extensive as to seem calculated.

The office seemed unnecessarily large, like a sparsely filled ballpark. The desk was jammed into one corner, protecting Scrappy from all but a frontal assault, while the remaining space contained only a television set, a blackboard, a few uncomfortable chairs, a miniature refrigerator, and a bedpan that served as a cuspidor. Windowless, the office offered a huge amount of wall space, nearly filled with framed photographs of teams, players, and show business and political celebrities. One wall, however, displayed only a single picture. It was a tinted portrait of a bald man with a broad smile. A metal plate identified the subject simply as "UNCLE MANNY — A REAL GENT."

The Gents' team photographs, no two of which hung parallel, proved, on scrutiny, to include boyish-looking versions of Scrappy, initially with a fielder's glove or a bat, and later with thick arms crossed over a barrel chest. This display, which seemed to follow a generally chronological pattern from left to right, featured a substantial number of individual "action" pictures of Scrappy, similar to those appearing on baseball cards. Examining Scrappy's likenesses more closely, a discerning viewer would recognize an unfolding saga not only of aging but also of disappointment, disillusion, and, ultimately, despair. As the years had sapped his youthfulness, so, the camera indicated, had his team's decline drained his zest.

In the early scenes, his strength and well-being somewhat concealed by a droopy Gents uniform, Scrappy posed confidently at the plate, daring a nonexistent pitcher to challenge him. Subsequent photos outlined the beginnings of physical indifference while Scrappy's face reflected more hope than defiance. Most recently, devoid of bat and glove but still outfitted as a Gent, he looked like a disenchanted survivor, a leftover athlete tired of trying to resurrect his former glory.

As a young, stubby sandlotter in the 1940s, he had learned to substitute bluster for skill. A big mouth, he had found, was as good as a big bat, particularly for a chronic .230 singles hitter. While his young friends idolized shy, introverted, homerun-hitting Mel Ott, Scrappy's hero was snarling, umpire-baiting Leo Durocher.

Reasoning early that his own fears were common, if not universal, ten-year-old Scrappy disdained such routine infield chatter as "There's no hitter up there!" in favor of urging his pitcher to "Hit 'em in the nuts!"

Such advice tended to stimulate the few aged retirees who, in a pre–Little League era, were about the only adults concerned with kids' games. Few plays, good or bad, seemed to engage these half-hearted spectators. But they were quick to react to arguments, impending fights, and, most of all, examples of poor sportsmanship, which confirmed their conviction that morality and decency were deteriorating further with each generation. To that end, Scrappy was invaluable; his unscrupulousness and naked drive to win embodied all their worst fears.

Scrappy's awareness of his spectators' scorn served only to exacerbate his truculent behavior. Once, irritated by a persistent heckler who shouted, "You can't hit! You can't hit! You can't hit!" each time he came to bat, Scrappy waited patiently at his right field position for the appropriate ball and, ignoring the hitter and base runners, threw it hard at the old man, who was seated on a bench along the first base line. "Can't throw neither," Scrappy snarled sarcastically, as a half-dozen spectators rushed to minister to the bruised target. Scrappy quickly apologized—not to his victim, but to his teammates, for the two runs that scored on his errant play.

Being shrewd and nasty, two qualities that had given Scrappy a significant advantage in his career as a professional athlete, now seemed irrelevant. His team, the New York Gents, had passed through all the stages of decline: from a nonthreat to a perennial cellar-dweller to, during the past few years, a joke. They had lost their confidence, their pride and, worst of all, their attendance. Fans no longer turned out even to express contempt. Finally, the Gents had become the first team in major league history to have its games *de*televised.

Prospects had grown dimmer with each season. The 1994 strike had almost delivered the *coup de grace*. Now, in 1996, Scrappy's desire to win had been supplanted by his desire to get out of the business. He had scrutinized the books, and his cousin Norman, the accountant, had examined them with prosecutorial zeal. Their conclusions had been identical: sell the Gents and retire to North Miami Beach.

Scrappy thought of Dick (Rootie) Toote, the Gents' first baseman, without whom it might have been impossible to find a buyer. Toote had carried the Gents for so many years that a sportswriter had nicknamed him Atlas. It was not only an appropriate metaphor, it was also an accurate physical description, and one that Scrappy noted reverentially each time he passed Rockefeller Center. Toote's mammoth shoulders, swelling biceps, and sculptured chest tapered to a fat-free waist, flat hips, keglike thighs, and bulging calves. His physique, immortalized by artists and featured in underwear ads, was no less extraordinary than his reflexes, his coordination, his anticipation, his intelligence, and his ability to pound and retrieve a baseball. Toote was the best hitter and fielder in the majors, had been named to the All-Star team every season, including his rookie year, and four times had been designated the league's Most Valuable Player. Respectfully dubbed "Mister Baseball" by the *New York Times,* he was, with the possible exception of Central Park, New York's most valuable property.

He was also an attractive person. Honest and humor-ously self-deprecatory in interviews, supportive of his teammates on the field and off, cooperative with the press, and knowledgeable and thoughtful beyond the sporting scene, he even disdained to employ an agent or to endorse products he didn't use.

Scrappy shared the universal regard for Toote and, indeed, appreciated him as only an heir values a bene-factor, yet he always felt vaguely uneasy in the ball-player's presence. In Scrappy's world, there were only good guys and bastards, and, being one of them, he much preferred the latter.

The jangling ring of the telephone drew Scrappy's attention from the hill of letters he had contemplated opening.

"Yeah?" he answered.

"Scrappy? Mann. What's doing with Toote?"

The caller was a *Post* sportswriter whose column, "Mann to Man," was read, according to readership studies commissioned by the paper's business manager, almost as much as "Dear Abby" and "Doonesbury."

"Waddayuh talkin' about?" Scrappy asked.

"Toote. The press conference. Didn't he tell you?"

"Look, Stan," Scrappy said, "I can't talk about *that*

right now." Then, feigning a remark to an invisible guest, he added, "Y'know what I mean?"

"You got somebody with you? OK, I've got a little time. But get back to me, OK? Something's going on and I don't want to read about it in the *News*." The phone clicked off.

Scrappy sucked in his breath. Visions of headlines announcing premature retirement or linking his star with drug abuse made him gasp. "Oh, no!" he wailed to his empty office. "Is Toote gonna fuck me up?" He pulled a water glass and a bottle of vodka from the tiny refrigerator near his desk, half-filled the glass and drained it with a sustained swallow. "What *is* it?" Scrappy asked himself. "I bet it's cocaine. Oh, shit, there goes *everything*."

Taped to the wall behind Scrappy's desk was a stain-smeared sheet, crisscrossed with penciled arrows, notations, and deletions, that listed the phone numbers of everyone essential to his existence. He found Toote's number and dialed.

"Dick!" he grunted, barely waiting to hear who answered. "What the hell's goin' on?"

The rasp Toote heard was distinctive. "Scrappy?"

"Right, right. It's me." Scrappy was unable to control the sound of his fear. "What the hell is this all about? A press conference? You got a problem, we can talk. Just like always. What's going on? You gonna drop something on me?"

"Easy," Toote said in his gentle, modulated voice. "It's something that's been on my mind for a long time. A *real* long time. This is how I want to handle it."

"Jesus, Dick. I mean, you're leavin' me bare-assed here. I gotta know what's goin' on."

"I'm sorry," Toote said softly. "I guess I just wasn't thinking about *you*. Look, I don't want to discuss this on the phone. Can you meet me?"

"Sure, sure. Where? When?"

"Well . . ." Toote paused, then resumed slowly. "There's a quiet place I know in the Village where nobody will bother us. Could you make it there in, say, an hour?" Toote's tone seemed reassuring, contagious.

"Yeah, right," Scrappy said. "I need to know what's goin' on. Where's it at? You say the Village?"

"That's right," Toote replied. "It's called The Velvet Glove. It's on Bleecker, just west of Seventh Avenue. See you there in about an hour."

Scrappy hung up the receiver and took another drink. Jesus, what's Toote up to? The feeling of uncertainty was familiar. His wives, his friends, his coaches, his ballplayers had all learned not to look to him for understanding. It was not a quality Scrappy had sought to develop.

He hadn't been to Greenwich Village lately and was somewhat surprised by the proliferation of menswear stores and leather clothing boutiques that lined the route his cabdriver was taking. It keeps getting worse, he thought, recalling how the narrow, winding streets and antiquated buildings had once evoked a more serene New York, while the offbeat shops and unconventional-looking people seemed to foretell trends still unformed. But in recent years, Scrappy felt, the counterculture had become *too* aggressive and flamboyant: racially mixed and same-sex couples seemed to be more prevalent and far more bold, walking arm in arm or embracing in doorways.

He remembered his first visit to the Village as a

high school senior seeking excitement. On that occasion, he and his teammates had wandered into a jazz club. Fascinated with a seductive-looking blonde at the bar, after a few drinks Scrappy attempted a pickup. He was astonished by his success until his eager hand found its way to the blonde's lap and felt an unmistakable bulge. Red-faced, he had pushed the transvestite off the bar stool and run away into the narrow, winding street.

The cab braked, abruptly ending his reverie. The Velvet Glove identified itself with a sedate nameplate. It looked sophisticated and expensive.

Scrappy was blinded by the darkness when he entered and blinked rapidly to adjust to the dim surroundings. Everything was decorated in shades of gray, even the substantial bar that took up most of one wall.

"Scrappy," a soft voice called. The Gents owner-manager turned and saw the huge frame of Dick Toote at his elbow. "Let's go over to a booth."

As they moved away from the bar, Scrappy noted some men sitting together. He thought he saw two of them holding hands.

"Hey, Dick," Scrappy said seriously as they slid into seats against the wall, "this place—I think this is a *queer* joint."

"You think so?" Toote replied, nodding indulgently. "Tell me, Scrappy, suppose it was. Then what?"

Scrappy squinted through the darkness at Toote, as if a clearer vision of his star ballplayer might provide greater insight. "Well, shit, Dick, I been around. I mean, what the hell does it matter where we talk?"

"It could matter a lot," Toote replied. "That's why we're here."

Scrappy felt uncomfortable. Something unsettling, almost frightening, was going on.

"Look, Dick," Scrappy said. "The place is fine. I mean, you wanna talk here, that's OK with me. I gotta know what's goin' on, though. What's this crap about a press conference? You know Ruby sets those up. The club takes care of that bullshit." Irwin Rubinstein had been the Gents' director of public relations for more than 30 years.

"This is different. This is personal, very personal," Toote said in measured tones. "It has to do with feelings." He paused. "It has to do with sex."

"Oh, shit," Scrappy exclaimed with relief. "And I thought it had to do with dope."

Toote seemed annoyed with Scrappy's reaction. "No," he said, shaking his head. "It's not like that. It's nothing the club has had to deal with before." He hesitated. "Nothing baseball has had to deal with."

"Dick," Scrappy said. "Don't look so worried. Y'know, we've all been around. I mean, I don't care what your thing is." Scrappy grinned. "So you like to jerk off giraffes. You're not the first." Scrappy reconsidered. "Well, maybe you would be . . ."

Toote managed a weak smile. "I don't think you understand, Scrappy." Toote gestured toward the bar. "This is the kind of place I'd like to hang out in. These are the kinds of people I want to be with."

Scrappy froze. "What're you sayin'? What're you tellin' me?"

Toote looked very tired. "I don't expect you to understand, Scrappy. In fact, I don't think you can. Hell, I'm not even sure *I* understand. But that really doesn't matter. What matters is that it's true. I'm homosexual.

It's been true for a long time. I knew it in high school; even earlier. But I didn't want to believe it. And until now I couldn't admit it. Certainly not to anyone who wasn't like me." The ballplayer took a deep breath, swelling his massive chest. "But it's true. I know it, and I can't lie about it anymore. No matter what."

Scrappy shook his head. "Jeezus, you don't know what you're talkin' about. I know you, for Crissakes," the manager insisted. "I've been in the clubhouse with you — in the showers. We've even stayed in hotel rooms together. You never tried *nothin'*. It's crazy." Scrappy stared at Toote incredulously. "You're an *athlete*," he bellowed. "You *can't* be a fairy."

Toote laughed derisively. "Yeah, Scrappy, sure. Look, I'm not going to argue with you about *what* I am. I think *I* ought to know. The point is that I plan to *do* something about it. Or, at least, *say* something about it. And while we're at it, the word we use is *'gay.'* "

"I can't believe this shit," Scrappy replied. "This is just a gag, right? You're puttin' me on? The guys are gonna come in here in a minute and laugh at me, right? Like when 'Iron Man' Murphy put his arm in a fake cast just before the '72 playoffs." Scrappy stopped. He knew it was no joke. "It's unbelievable, unbelievable," he muttered.

A life in baseball and a lifetime of womanizing had prepared Scrappy for surprises. But not for this one. Not Toote. Sure, he thought, kids, boys, fool around with each other. Who hadn't? And the first time you do it with a girl might not be as terrific as everybody makes it out to be. But to do it with a man — with *men?* The idea of it was repulsive. An image of Toote embracing a man flashed through his mind and he recoiled reflexively.

Scrappy could not reconcile that image with the person seated across from him in the booth. He shrugged, inducing his sense of practicality to take control. Suddenly, his face brightened. "Look, Dick. I see what you're sayin'. OK, so you're queer, I mean, gay— whatever you wanna call it. It's your business, right? I mean, so what? Who cares? So why tell th' whole world? Y'know, I got a secret, too. And you're the first one I'm tellin'. Know what? I wanna sell the club, the Gents. I wanna get my dough out and go down to Florida and lay around by the pool with a vodka tonic and remember the good times. Know what I mean?"

"Sure," Toote said. "I can understand that."

"You understand that?" Scrappy said, his face reddening as his voice rose. "I'm not sure you do. You understand that without you the Gents are like, what? Like a stud without balls, y'know what I mean? Y'know what's gonna happen when you tell people you're a fag? You think they're gonna cheer? Y'think they're gonna say, 'Boy, that Dick Toote's terrific'? Y'know what they're gonna say? They're gonna say, 'Get rid of that faggot! He don't belong in a baseball uniform, put that fairy in a ballet dress!' "

Scrappy reached across the table and grasped Toote's thick right arm. "Y'know what the Gents'll be worth if you make your speech? *Bupkis,* that's what! Zero! Y'know what you're gonna do to me? Y'know what'll happen now? Sell? For Crissakes, I won't get a cent for the club! It'll be a joke. You and me and the Gents'll be a fuckin' laugh. You understand? It'll all go down the drain. Your career will be finished. I won't be able to *give* the team away. Nobody'll want to have nothin' to do with the Gents, with us. Jeezus, Dick, I wish to hell I could stop you. I want you to think about it some more. Think about what it's gonna do to you, to the team, to the game. Think of what the hell it's gonna do to me!"

Shaking his head, Scrappy rose awkwardly and walked through the illusory half-light of the bar into the glare of the afternoon's reality.

Back at his office in Gents Stadium, Scrappy disconsolately received a message that Stan Mann had called again, poured himself an inch of ice-cold vodka, and directed Irwin Rubinstein to join him.

Ruby entered without knocking. He was wearing a green plaid sport jacket, a yellow striped shirt, and gold pants. His off-white hair, retrieved from somewhere behind his ears, was painstakingly arranged forward and across a bald pate. He sucked a Tums.

"You talked to Toote?" Ruby asked. His years in the business had established Ruby as *the* repository of baseball information; his memory was legendary, his contacts legion. There was a saying among New York sportswriters: "If you want to know what happened, read the *Times;* if you want to know what didn't happen, read the *Post;* if you want to know what's going to happen, call Ruby."

"Hell, yeah," Scrappy said. "But I don't think you're ready for it."

"That bad?" Ruby asked.

"The worst. I still can't believe it."

"Well, whatever it is, we're gonna have to do some-

thin' about it," Ruby said impatiently. Being unin-
formed about anything irritated him.

"*You're* not gonna believe it, either."

"Try me."

"He's a *queer,*" Scrappy said. "Dick Toote is a fairy.
The All-American Boy is a faggot. Our hero, 'The Franchise,' is — let me use the correct word — *gay.* And what's
more, he wants the whole fuckin' world to know it!"

"That's crazy," Ruby said. "I can't believe that.
Scrappy, you got it wrong."

"No Ruby, it's goddam true."

"C'mon, c'mon. A guy like Toote? Big strong fella like
that? Hey, Scrappy, it's a gag. He's just pullin' your
chain."

"Wrong. It *is* true. I know it's true. And how about you
try using a different expression?"

"You can make jokes? Wait'll you try selling the ball
club, you'll see how much a major league homo is going
for."

"That's why we're talking," Scrappy said. "There's
gotta be something we can do. He's the only thing I got. I
can't sell *him,* I might as well go bankrupt."

Ruby bit down on his bottom lip. "You could fix him up
with a broad. Maybe he just needs a good *schtup.*"

"That's stupid. Look, Ruby, the guy knows what he
needs. We just gotta figure out some way to protect
ourselves."

"Let's take it logically," Ruby said. "Who knows about
this besides you?"

"Shit, you got me. But he's gonna hold a press conference. When is it?"

"Next week. Not till next week, Mann told me. He
said Toote sent out a press release. It didn't say any-

thing except that he had somethin' very important to announce. But we got a week."

"We could have forever," Scrappy said forlornly. "He's not gonna change his mind. I could tell the way he was talkin'."

"Maybe not," Ruby said, as the approximation of a smile crept across his face. "But *Donald* doesn't know anything about this yet, does he?"

"Holy shit!" Scrappy shouted gleefully, instantly grasping Ruby's meaning. "Y'think it could work? Y'think we could get away with it?" Even the remote possibility of outwitting his Bronx counterpart sent shivers of pleasure through Scrappy. And here, just maybe, was the chance of hitting a superjackpot.

"Hell, he's been after Toote ever since Steinbrenner sold him the club, right?" Ruby said. "Donald would throw in his houses, his boat, maybe even his wife to get him. You play it cool, you're out of the woods."

"Yeah, terrific," Scrappy said, savoring the prospect. Then, pensively, he added, "The only thing might be the other club owners. You know what they think about them kinda deals."

"Forget that," Ruby said. "This is business. Besides, everybody wants to see Donald Bigg get screwed."

"You're right," Scrappy said as he scanned the phone list for his rival owner's private number and then dialed it.

"Donald? This is Scrappy. How's it hangin'?"

"Scrappy? Scrappy? What's a Scrappy?"

"It's a man with a deal, Donald? You interested?"

"Oh, that Scrappy. That's the one who only knows how to say, 'No.' I'd like to do business with the Scrappy who is reasonable and intelligent and appreciates reality."

"You can bag the bullshit, Donald. I've decided to cut Toote loose. If the numbers are right."

"Well, how 'bout that, as Mel used to say. Sure, I might be interested."

"I can see you drooling from here. Look, I need the bucks. But I'm talkin' big ones. And I need them soon. I wouldn't even be thinkin' about nothin' like this if I wasn't bein' squeezed. I want to get it over with. Fast. We can even work it out on the phone."

"I didn't hang up. Yet."

"OK." Scrappy inhaled deeply. "He's got three to go on a five-year deal. That'll cost you 20 million. And to get him . . . to get him will cost you 15."

"You just heard me hang up."

"Twelve."

"Beep. Beep. Beep."

"This is it, Donald. Ten."

"I'll get back to you."

"Make it this afternoon."

Scrappy slammed down the phone excitedly. "Ruby, I think we just bought ourselves a condo."

"You got it, Scrappy. Money don't mean that much to Donald. It's getting what he wants. That's the button to push. And he really wants Toote." Ruby paused. "What *about* Toote? What do y'think he'll have to say?"

"I dunno. Prob'ly he'll be happy to get with a winner for a change. Who wouldn't? But it don't really matter. He ain't been up in the majors long enough to kill a deal. Anyways, once we got Donald's money, who gives a shit?"

Ruby looked through Scrappy's open office door into the empty clubhouse. Nothing as quiet as a stadium during the off-season. Or as superfluous. The peeling lockers were accumulating dust and grime. Ruby's eyes were drawn to the one marked TOOTE, and he recalled the familiar sight of the ballplayer quietly dressing for games, encouraging teammates, graciously accepting congratulations. The news of Toote's homosexuality was shocking enough, Ruby mused. But his decision to reveal it was incredible. What kind of a nut would do that? Maybe it wasn't true. But what would be the point of making up something like that? Even a conniver like me wouldn't go that far, Ruby acknowledged.

The phone jangled, and Scrappy let it ring a few times before he picked it up. No sense letting Donald know just *how* eager he was. But it wasn't Donald, it was Stan Mann.

"What's the story, Scrappy? What's going down?"

"About what? Oh, you mean Toote?"

"Yeah, Toote. What the hell is he calling a press conference for? He won't tell me a goddam thing."

"I'd like to help you, Stan, but, y'know, it's *his* thing."

"You know what it's about? I don't know where to begin. Some other guy, you figure it's coke or something, but Toote? *Mister Baseball?* He'd confess if he accidentally inhaled some pot smoke in the stands. I don't get it, unless he wants to jump ship. And who'd blame him for that?"

"Look, Stan, maybe we ain't pennant contenders this season but I got a few ideas. We're gonna be buildin'. It may take a few years—"

"Building the pyramids would be quicker. I don't have time for that bullshit now, I'm on deadline. You got something to tell me, tell me. Otherwise, I'll see you around."

"I'll try to help you, but this time I dunno. What can I tell you? Look, I'll do the best I can."

"You been doing that for years. Try something else." The sports columnist hung up.

"That sonuvabitch," Scrappy growled. "It won't be long now when I can tell 'em all to take a flyin' fuck." Ruby wished he could share Scrappy's enthusiasm for retirement. For himself, it seemed empty, frightening. Baseball had filled his life. Hanging out with the ballplayers, the executives, the sportswriters was his joy. And theirs. On the road, in Cincinnati and St. Louis and Atlanta, he was the best show in town. He was liked and, for a PR man, respected. It wouldn't be the same without the Gents. Without Scrappy. And until now, he had never thought about it coming to an end.

Scrappy's phone rang again, and this time it *was* Donald.

"What're you trying to pull?"

"What do you mean?"

"Don't give me that crap! I mean his press conference!"

"Oh, that. Donald, I heard about that. What're you worried about? Believe me, *I'm* not worried. What's the big deal? He announces his retirement, you get your money back."

"It's not his retirement I'm worried about. What's he gonna announce?"

"If I told you, you'd laugh. It's no big deal. It's just somethin' he wants to handle by himself. I told him, 'Sure, go ahead.' He asked me not to tell nobody, so I says, 'OK, whatever you want.' "

"There's nothing to it?"

"Would I con *you*, Donald?"

"Every chance you get. Look, *maybe* we'll talk about Toote again. *After* his press conference."

Scrappy stared at the phone in frustration. "Balls!" he shouted. But Donald had already hung up. "I should of figured. He heard about the press conference. He won't deal until he finds out what Toote's up to. Jeezus, he's got us by the short hairs."

Ruby shook his head, then shrugged. "You could try Toote again. Maybe you can change his mind. If not, maybe you can get him to hold off on everything for a while. It gets close to opening day and he hasn't talked, Donald might take a chance. What've you got to lose?"

Scrappy nodded, but his expression reflected his pessimism. Toote hadn't indicated any misgivings about his decision to make the crucial announcement. If anything, he had conveyed a sense of eagerness to get it done. Scrappy felt desperately weary. There had been enough for one day. The future could wait until tomorrow.

That night, even his favorite hooker couldn't help. "C'mon, coach, you can make it," she urged, trying to rouse him into action.

"It's no good," Scrappy said. "I got too much on my mind. Look, you wanna stay the night? I . . . I'll make it worth your while."

"Not tonight, coach," she said, kissing his cheek as she climbed off the bed. "Get some sleep and keep in touch."

"You know," Scrappy said with annoyance, "it could be *you*."

* * *

When he walked into The Bagelry for breakfast the next morning, Scrappy's first move was to reach for a house copy of the *Post* and turn to the sports section. "ROOTIE TOOTE WANTS MORE LOOT?" asked the headline beneath the "Mann to Man" logo and an absurdly youthful photo of columnist Stan Mann.

"All *right!*" Scrappy murmured with satisfaction as he scoured the column without finding any reference to the actual subject of Toote's upcoming press conference. In the timeworn manner of a reporter who has not yet picked up the scent, Mann simply speculated, hoping to seem informed while knowing he hadn't the slightest clue. He'd settled on the likelihood that the All Star was looking for more money, and he went on to suggest that to seek it from Scrappy was tantamount to expecting the Gents to reduce ticket prices. "The last thing Scrappy gave away was a bad check," Mann's column concluded.

"Better you should have chicken soup, the way you look." The accented voice belonged to a small, middle-aged woman with reddish-orange hair who placed a cup of black coffee and a bagel with smoked salmon and cream cheese in front of Scrappy.

"If I needed medical advice, Sophie," Scrappy said, "I wouldn't take it from a waitress."

"Plenty doctors listen to me," Sophie said, fluffing her hair. "Also," she continued, eyeing Mann's column, which she had already read, "plenty newspapermen."

"*That* I can believe," he said with a wink. "Considerin' the crap they write."

"They write, I serve, you play games." Sophie sighed. "We do what we do."

Scrappy savored the bland smoothness of the cream cheese, the faintly salty delicacy of the smoked salmon,

the chewy texture of the bagel. Each morning he anticipated breakfast the way a smoker does the day's first
cigarette. He had been going to The Bagelry since it
opened a dozen years ago; always the same order, the
same taste, the same delight. Not like when the Gents
were on the road. Out of town, even in cities like Chicago and Los Angeles, nobody knew from lox or bagels
like New York.

It made Scrappy wonder whether he'd get decent food
in North Miami Beach. It was Jewish, all right, but he
remembered on his last visit being served lox and bagels adorned with raw onion, lettuce, and tomatoes.
Clearly not New York. But maybe he wouldn't be down
there so fast, anyhow. If he didn't swing the deal with
Donald, he'd be stuck with the Gents for who knows
how long. It used to be so different, he mused, when he
bought the franchise years ago with the money Uncle
Manny had left him. Now *there* was a businessman.
Made a fortune from gefilte fish. Pushed carp, mullet,
whitefish through a sieve and came up with a slogan:
"Don't strain *yourself!*" Helluva guy.

Scrappy's wandering thoughts came back to rest on
his immediate problem: a talk with Toote. "Let's go,
Schwartzie," he said to himself as he left a too-generous
tip for Sophie and walked out of the restaurant.

He decided to be as direct as possible. "Dick," he said
when Toote answered the phone. "This is Scrappy. I
gotta talk to you again, right away."

"You got me at a bad time. I'm on my way out."

"It's *really* important. It won't take long."

"Well ... I've got ... uh, a date, an appointment.
Soon."

"Hey, c'mon," Scrappy cajoled. "I'll make it quick.
Meet you wherever you say."

"I don't know. Look, if you can make it right away and keep it short, OK. But you'll have to meet me in the Village again. And it may be a little, uh, offbeat."

"Hey, Dick, it'll be quick. It's real important to *you*, too."

"All right. The place is called The Different Drummer. It's on Christopher Street. Number 34. You'd better leave now."

"Gotcha."

Scrappy found a cab the instant he reached the street. It was, he thought, a good omen. Traffic was light at that hour, and only minutes later he found himself on Christopher Street. The Different Drummer identified itself with a picture of a Revolutionary War drummer boy wearing a skirt. The sign was lavender and so was the door that Scrappy opened.

The interior was dark, very dark. He made out comfortably upholstered booths lit by flickering bulbs in reproductions of eighteenth-century sconces. At the rear there appeared to be an open space, possibly a dance floor, surrounded by small tables and chairs. A few of the booths were taken, and perhaps a half-dozen men occupied stools at the bar. The men had shortish haircuts, and several wore black leather vests.

Scrappy walked to the bar and was struggling to read some signs on the wall behind it when a voice asked, "Help you, mister?"

"Oh," Scrappy replied, "it's OK. I'm looking for, um, Dick."

"Aren't we all?" one of the customers replied.

"Oh, y'know'im?" Scrappy asked.

"My God," one of the patrons said, shaking his head. "Can you believe it?" His companions grinned.

Oblivious, Scrappy was finally able to make out the signs behind the bar. One said: A HARD MAN IS GOOD TO FIND; another: I NEVER LIKED FLIES UNTIL I STARTED OPENING THEM; a third, under a picture of a closet with its door ajar: OUT FOR A GOOD TIME; and still another, over a photograph of a tightly uniformed ballplayer: SEX IS A GAME OF INCHES.

"Times sure have changed," Scrappy muttered. "They used to say that about baseball."

"Don't say I didn't warn you," a voice behind Scrappy said lightly. It was Toote. Scrappy followed him to a booth.

"I'm not going to apologize for this place," Toote said firmly. "You said it was *very important* to talk. What's up?"

Scrappy looked straight at Toote for a few seconds. "I want you to call off your press conference. Well, not call it off really, just hold it off."

"C'mon, Scrappy. You know I can't do that. I told you what it's all about. And I told you what it means to me."

"Sure," Scrappy said, "but there's been developments. Like big ones. Can you imagine what it'd be like on a team that put it all together? It's like nothin' else. Playin' for a contender. Havin' a shot at the series. Listen to me, Dick. I'm talkin' New York Yankees!"

"What are you telling me?"

"I'm tellin' you that Donald wants to pick up your contract. And I'm tellin' you that it's all right with me. But I'm also tellin' you that if you make your little announcement next week, you can forget it. Donald won't want you. Nobody will."

"We went all through that. I told you, I've got to do this."

"Sure you do. And I'm not askin' you not to. I'm just askin' you to wait a while. You call off your press conference and you'll be a Yankee next week. Once you're under contract to Donald, you do whatever you want. You hold your conference, you make your announcement. Just like that."

"You think so, Scrappy? You think it's simple? You know how long I've thought about this? What it's taken to get me this far? This isn't some kind of publicity stunt. It's my *life* we're talking about. What kind of credibility do you think I'd have if I pulled a sleazy stunt like that? You don't know me, do you Scrappy? You don't know anything about me."

"I know one thing, for Crissakes! I know you're gonna be one sorry pansy if you shoot off your mouth. You think people are gonna *understand?* Like shit they will! You think you're gonna get support? Forget it! The sportswriters will cut you to pieces. The fans will run the other way. You know what they'll say? They'll say, 'I don't want my kids seein' queers playin' baseball!'"

"But they *do*, Scrappy," Toote replied. "The point is they *do*."

"Bullshit!" Scrappy said. "What kind of crap you feedin' me? You tellin' me people *want* their kids to see fairy ballplayers?"

"No," Toote said with annoyance. "I mean they *are* seeing gay ballplayers. You think I'm the *only* one? Look, they say maybe 10 percent of all men are gay—one in ten. You think they're all ballet dancers and hairdressers? With six hundred, seven hundred ballplayers in the major leagues, there could be thirty, forty, fifty gays playing any day."

Scrappy sat numbly. "Look, you told me about yourself. OK, I gotta believe it 'cause *nobody's* gonna make that up about himself. I mean, you could be weird but you ain't stupid. Look, you're talkin' to somebody who's been in baseball all of his life. We're talkin' 40 years. And you're tellin' me I been playin' with fairies and coachin' fairies and managin' fairies and ownin' fairies and not knowin' nothin' about it. Jeezus, Dick, don't jerk me off!"

Toote smacked the table with his huge fist. "Dammit, you don't know anything about it! You don't know what it's like! Making believe! Watching what we say! Hiding our feelings! Our selves! It's not just *me,* you know. It's Rhino Romanski! And Dave Ripp! And Jughead Jackson! And Chico Santiago! And Zipper Zeeman! And Speedy Gonzalez! And Tony Mike! And Gigolo Johnson! And Mickey Mayo!"

Scrappy was stunned. These weren't ballplayers, they were superstars. Pitchers, hitters, fielders. Some were powerful, others were fast, heady, solid. The names came straight off the All-Star lineup. They were the best.

"Holy crap!" Scrappy shouted. Several closely cropped heads turned. "It ain't true. It can't be. Nobody'd believe it. The whole game would go down the bowl. What you're tellin' me is true and I'll kiss an ump's ass at home plate."

"My, aren't we getting inventive?" a voice said from the direction of the bar.

Scrappy, unhearing, continued. "You're talkin' about giants, heroes. Christ, every kid in America wants to be like 'em. It's unbelievable, unbelievable. If it's true, for Crissakes, you know what would happen if it got out?

The country would come apart. I mean, it's like sayin' George Washington was a homo."

Toote looked shaken. "Look, Scrappy, forget what I said. You just got me going. I had no right—I mean, you're right, it's not true. Those guys, they're not gay. They're as straight as you."

Scrappy shrugged and nodded in agreement. The discussion had gotten out of hand. He felt very tired. He wanted to get away. "Yeah, Dick, whatever you say. Look, I thought maybe you'd wait on your announcement. It means a helluva lot to me. Just think about it, OK? That's all I ask. Maybe you can see your way clear to work this out for both of us, huh? Well, I guess that's it. I guess we got nothin' more to talk about now."

Toote nodded and remained seated as Scrappy, for the second time in two days, dejectedly walked out of a gay bar to confront the dazzling afternoon sun.

Will it never end, Dick Toote asked himself, preparing
for his most public "coming out" party. With Scrappy's
fierce reaction reverberating in his mind, he wondered
if you ever stop revealing yourself to the straight world,
admitting your sexuality as if you were baring some
long-buried criminal conviction. He mechanically removed his razor, shaving cream, aftershave lotion and
deodorant from the medicine cabinet, placed them
neatly on the shelf under the wall-to-wall bathroom
mirror, and sighed deeply. Being gay did not necessarily
mean feeling lighthearted.

Because of his ostensible virility, his power, Toote's
homosexuality had been his secret to retain or reveal. In
rare moments of anxiety and depression, he envied his
effeminate soulmates whose speech and mannerisms
sent an unmistakable message. For him, life was a con-
stant subterfuge, an ongoing sequence of shameful lies
lurking just beneath the surface of his existence. How
much simpler it would be, he thought, to be relieved of
the need to play the daily game of make-believe. Finally
to relieve his anxiety, to come out, even in a world of
hostility and oppression. It was time to do it, past time.

He wasn't quite sure when he first suspected that he might be gay; understandable, his psychotherapist had assured him: "Do you think heterosexuals remember?" What *did* matter, Dr. Goodkind had said authoritatively, were his dreams at the onset of puberty of naked men, the strange excitement he experienced in the locker room with his classmates. Of less interest to the therapist, Toote remembered somewhat disappointedly, was an incident at Boy Scout camp that the ballplayer had starred in his mental memory book.

He had celebrated his twelfth birthday and found himself admiring a tall, lean, 17-year-old counselor who played first base with the grace and range of a shortstop. Sitting alone together before a smoldering campfire, the older boy asked Toote if he had a "bush." Toote had looked at him quizzically. "Hair," the counselor said with a slight tone of annoyance. "Do you have hair around your pecker?" Aroused, but confused and embarrassed, he feigned ignorance. The older youth promptly unzipped his own pants, pulled down his undershorts and pointed proudly to a thick crown of pubic hair. "See? C'mere, give me your hand," the older youth directed. While Toote quivered with excitement, he allowed the counselor to take his right hand and place it firmly on what the youngster saw was a growing and, to him, enormous penis. The incident, which culminated in mutual masturbation, left Toote gratified, ashamed, worried. He felt unsure of the meaning of what had happened, but had little doubt of his enjoyment.

In his college sessions with Dr. Goodkind, Toote learned that the episode was a commonplace expression of adolescent sexual curiosity that furnished no evidence of orientation. Toote recollected somewhat amusedly his initiation into the mysteries of heterosexual sex two years later. It was the end of the 1983 baseball season during his freshman year in high school and Grace Anderson, subsequently known as Amazing Grace, was a senior, a cheerleader, and the school's self-described "Number One Fan," a distinction she decided to confirm by "giving it" to every member of the undefeated team's starting lineup — in succession.

On a moonless June night, she took the ballplayers to the darkened diamond and directed them to await her at their positions. Almost as proud of her baseball expertise as she was of her carnal knowledge, Grace proceeded to screw the team in the numerical order ascribed by scorekeeping tradition: first the pitcher, next the catcher, then the first baseman, and so on. It was Toote's misfortune to be the right fielder, designated the last position, and so the anxious 14-year-old looked up from his grassy bed to see Grace, nakedly and unsteadily advancing toward him, accompanied by his eight sated but still-curious teammates. It did nothing for his confidence, moreover, to hear them loudly betting on his imminent performance.

No one was more surprised than he to see his body respond eagerly to Grace's deft handling. Like the passive partner in a ballroom dance team, Dick felt himself led onto her perspiring body and between her slithery legs. He emulated her movements, erupted in a spasmodic orgasm to the cheers of his predecessors, struggled to his feet and graciously tipped the cap he had never removed.

Slathering shaving cream on his cheeks, Toote recalled the conflict that had gripped him as a teenager, of the struggle between wanting to be like his friends yet fearing that he wasn't. Years later, when his therapy had enabled him to recognize — and accept — the fact of his gayness, Dr. Goodkind helped him realize that his desire for intimacy with men did not preclude having — and even enjoying — sex with women.

While the therapeutic sessions had been painful, Toote now regarded them fondly. As he examined his lathered face in the mirror, the recollection of those discussions triggered another flashback: growing up in a Christian fundamentalist household. One of his earliest memories was of driving with his parents from their Ohio farm to California in a Ford pickup with a broken radio. He remembered how they alternately recited psalms and sang hymns while he prayed silently — for the radio's resurrection. The popular Twenty-third Psalm, "Our Father, which art in heaven, hallowed be Thy name . . ." was a family favorite. As their strong voices broke out in "The Old Rugged Cross" and begged Jesus for mercy and forgiveness, young Dick sat soundlessly between them, keeping count of unfamiliar license plates and wondering why he lacked their spirit and had no use for their faith.

Once settled in southern California, the religious fervor of his parents took on even greater intensity, prompting him to spend as little time with them as possible. More than a normal childish rebellion, he felt an alienation from his parents and their spiritual preachings. That estrangement, and the eternal springlike climate, coaxed him onto the ballfields. He found first solace and then satisfaction in developing batting and fielding skills. He devised his own fitness routine, rising at dawn to run miles through the foothills of the Santa Ana Mountains before school, and driving himself with sit-ups and push-ups before collapsing into sleep at night.

Socially, however, he remained a loner, protecting himself from the need to confide and risk sharing the confusing feelings that would not go away. In high school, as his classmates began pairing off, Dick's anxiety about his sexuality became more discomforting. On the diamond, he felt in control; off it, at a loss. He postponed dating as long as possible. With stirring sexual feelings, his strong attraction to some of the other boys made him wonder if he somehow might develop the same impulses toward girls.

During his adolescence in the mideighties, he recalled, his attitude toward the gay world had been ambivalent and his approach hesitant. He began to acknowledge to himself that he was "different," but the result was more a fear of discovery than a desire to immerse himself in the gay life. That world's most obvious inhabitants, the drag queens and swishy dandies, struck him, then as now, as unappealing. And while the memory of his Boy Scout encounter still stirred him, he was afraid to initiate any further physical contact with his male schoolmates. Instead, he spent hours at bookstores and libraries reading everything he could find about homosexuality. What he learned fanned his interest but did not overcome his apprehensions. After high school graduation, on a visit to Los Angeles, he spent a few hours in the gay mecca of West Hollywood. On the streets there he admired the tanned, well-coiffed men but turned away embarrassed when they made eye contact.

His razor poised in midair, Dick remembered, as though it were last night, his first real homosexual encounter. The week before he entered Stanford on an athletic scholarship, at a bar in Palo Alto, he allowed himself to be picked up by a fortyish sociology professor, fed drinks for three hours, taken to the academic's campus home, and made love to. He awoke the next morning to find himself alone in a king-size bed in a ranch-style house. A note on the dresser said: "Loved it; liked you." The next time he saw the professor was on the plaza near the bookstore. The professor did not meet his eyes.

There were several casual contacts and short-lived relationships during the next four years, including at least one that he was certain would last forever. And there was one, during his senior year, that involved a woman.

The setting, appropriately if accidentally, was the zoology lab, where he had remained after class one rainy winter afternoon to familiarize himself with primate reproductive processes. As Toote began examining models of monkey genitalia, he was interrupted by the arrival of Lizbeth Meacham, a stern graduate assistant into whose lab section the alphabet had delivered him.

With her metal-rimmed glasses, mouse-brown hair worn in a tight bun, and drab, shapeless dresses, Miss Meacham, as she was known even to her peers, was the target of countless student jokes. "How do you make out with Miss Meacham?" one version went. "With a broom," was the response. "Why a broom?" the gag continued. "To sweep away the cobwebs," came the punchline.

If she knew of such sophomoric cruelty, Lizbeth Meacham gave no indication it mattered. She was brisk, precise, and businesslike on campus, and what she did on her own time or in the confines of the efficiency apartment she occupied off campus she did not disclose. Both her unadorned appearance and prosaic manner seemed totally appropriate to the dreary, ill-lit laboratory, with its long, slablike black tables and gray walls decorated with diagrams of amphibian, reptilian, and mammalian innards.

"Hello. It's, er, refreshing to see a student here voluntarily," she said convivially. "You *are* a student?"

"Yes, that's right, Miss Meacham," he replied. "Toote, Dick Toote. I'm in the Tuesday section."

She had come quite close to him now, and Dick felt an unexpected openness; not warmth, exactly, but a familiarity that seemed totally out of keeping with her usual classroom demeanor. Looking at her closely for the first time, really, he became aware that she was far more attractive than she allowed herself to appear. It was as if, like a nun, she sought to repudiate her physical appeal by hiding any suggestion of beauty or sexuality. He imagined, for example, that her body, normally undetected within a swirl of fabric, appeared to be taking shape now as she attempted to unknot the string that closed the front of the stained white lab coat.

"It's my nails," she said. "I cut them short. It makes working in the lab a lot easier. And cleaner."

Toote looked befuddled.

"My nails," she repeated. "That's why I have trouble with knots."

He understood now and nodded in agreement.

"Do you think maybe you could give me a hand?" she asked. "This coat is filthy. Even the pickled monkeys will be avoiding me."

Dick stood in front of her and tried to undo the string,

but the knot was tight and resisted. Seconds and then minutes seemed to pass without any perceptible success, and he began to feel awkward and nervous. There was no sound, except for the ticking of a large wall clock.

"I'm, um, sorry," he mumbled, "but I don't seem to be getting it."

"That's for sure," she said, quickly adding, "maybe if you tried from behind?"

He looked at her uncertainly, shrugged, stood behind her and reached around her waist. "Like this?" he asked.

She nodded and he suddenly felt the pressure of her buttocks against his thighs. It couldn't be accidental, he told himself, as he struggled with the ends of the stubborn drawstring. The firmness and warmth of her body were stirring, but he wasn't certain she was aware of what she was doing and the effect it was having on him. To test her, he moved back out of contact. It was only an instant before she pressed back against his groin.

Dick felt himself getting hard as the knot started to give way. "That's better," he said. "It's working."

"I can tell," she said, putting her hands on his to help loosen the tie. As the string came undone, she turned toward him and the lab coat fell open. Although she was wearing a plain cotton dress, she clutched at the coat as if an intimacy had been revealed.

"Let's see," she said. "Maybe I can help *you*. Have you covered sexual characteristics?"

He nodded.

"Perhaps you'd like to review them," she said.

He took a deep breath and, uncertain as to whether it was from fear of rebuke or curiosity about his own nature, nodded his head affirmatively.

"Well," she said, "one of the most obvious secondary characteristics, of course, involves voice. A male voice is deeper."

Dick feigned a soprano. "Yes, Miss Meacham," he squeaked.

She laughed. "Call me," she said huskily, "Ishmael, er, I mean, Lizbeth." She moved closer and touched his cheek with her fingertips. "Now that," she said, "is another. Your beard."

Momentarily distracted, Dick mechanically drew the razor across his face; he felt once more the odd mixture of excitement and unease that had marked the episode. His thoughts turned back to the zoology lab and Lizbeth, who had taken one of his hands and placed it gently on her own cheek. "See," she said, continuing to hold his hand. "No beard."

He felt the softness of her skin and saw her lips part slightly, revealing the tip of a pink tongue. Lizbeth smiled encouragement, moved her hands down to his neck and began unbuttoning his shirt. When it was open to his waist, she ran her fingers across his broad bare chest. His nipples tightened and sent an instantaneous message to his groin.

"This is another secondary characteristic," she purred, scraping him gently with her nails. "Body hair. It's far more prevalent in males."

As she stroked his chest, Lizbeth's lab coat fell open again. She took it off, then unzipped her dress and allowed it to fall to her feet. Her nipples outlined themselves inside her bra. A few brown hairs stood out from the almost invisible down that edged from her navel toward the top of her panties.

"Here," she said, taking both his hands and leading

them to the catch on her bra, "give me a hand." Dick felt his heart racing as he fidgeted with the catch. Caught up in the excitement, he felt helpless. He had no sense of how his body might respond. And he knew he could not utter the words that would release him. He was standing very close to her when the catch released. Lizbeth took his hands and placed them under the bra. As his fingers brushed her nipples he felt them harden, and he cupped his palms around them.

She began breathing more heavily. "Some students forget that breasts are *secondary* characteristics," she said. "They confuse them with primaries."

Lizbeth moved closer and, through his underwear and pants, Dick felt her body. She draped her arms around his neck, drawing herself closer, and slid her pelvis against him. "Mmmm," Lizbeth purred, "you're progressing very well."

Suddenly, her fingers were at his waist, deftly unbuckling his belt and drawing down his pants zipper with a quick hiss. Another flick and his boxer shorts were below his hips. "Oh, yesss," she said, gripping him with both hands. "*This* is a primary."

Lizbeth dropped to her knees so quickly Dick thought for an instant that she had collapsed. "You look good enough to eat," she said, as he instinctively grasped her head between his hands and watched in fascination as her tongue slipped out, snakelike, and caressed him. "Oh, oh, oh," he began to groan as the warm wetness of her tongue sent a shockwave through him.

But it was images of men — with tanned, glistening, muscular bodies — that flashed through his mind as Lizbeth adroitly manipulated him with her fingers, tongue and lips. He felt huge, swollen beyond belief. And as her head bobbed back and forth below him, he suddenly was drawn into a rushing river, carried along by a current he couldn't control, and didn't want to.

And then it was over. "Oh, my God," he moaned.

"Oh, shit!" Lizbeth exploded. She coughed and spat. Her face was twisted with frustration and anger.

Dick looked down and reddened. "I'm, I'm sorry," he stammered. "I couldn't help—"

Lizbeth was not placated. "You've got a lot to learn," she snapped. "This time, you get an F. Next time, I hope *you* get an incomplete." He sought to touch her arm, but she pulled away. "Class," Lizbeth said with finality, "is over."

In the weeks that followed, the incident lingered in Toote's mind. He was upset by Lizbeth's outrage, but far more distressing was his confusion. To be sure, his body had responded to her; yet he had not felt any desire for a repetition. Not with Lizbeth nor with any woman. What was he? Toote agonized. Was he gay? Was he straight? Was he both? The weight of his uncertainty became oppressive. He found it difficult to sleep, impossible to study.

He had finished shaving, he realized, but had forgotten to turn off the water in the sink. He twisted the tap and patted his face dry with a towel.

He squirmed as he remembered how in those college days the anxiety had even followed him to the ball field, previously an impenetrable sanctuary. When he committed three errors and struck out four times in a critical game against Arizona, Toote's coach asked him, "What the hell's going on?" He merely shrugged. The next day he sought out the student counseling office, which quickly arranged an appointment with Dr. Goodkind.

Just the opportunity to reveal his doubts and confusion lifted Toote's spirits immensely. In subsequent sessions he sought to comprehend his sexual nature and, in the months that followed, to come to terms with it. As he accepted his homosexuality, became comfortable with it, Toote's need to divulge it grew. But the pressures to remain closeted were formidable. Although gays were tolerated on campus, from the athletes they met with only contempt and ridicule. It had taken him five long years to gain enough strength and confidence to make his sexuality public. But, damn it, at last he was going to do it. And in little more than an hour.

Actually, he had first come out to a fellow patient of Dr. Goodkind's at Stanford, a soft-spoken student who dismissed Toote's mumbled admission matter-of-factly. "I never would have guessed," he said. "But I appreciate your telling me. I mean that you trusted me enough."

The extraordinary sense of relief and liberation that followed encouraged him to consider telling his parents. It was, he felt certain, an appropriate decision, but he was hardly optimistic about their reaction. With the passage of time, the gap between child and parents had widened significantly in terms of values, politics, social issues, and, most certainly, religious commitment. While Dick had been off at Stanford mixing with students of every background and being exposed in class to diverse philosophic and political positions, his parents' fundamentalist Christian beliefs were narrowing through their involvement with the burgeoning religious right movement. The broader his horizons became, the more he realized how narrow theirs were. They were quite surprised and very pleased when he called to tell them he wanted to spend the next weekend at home. As Dick stepped under his shower, the memory of that long-ago visit struck him with similar force. When he drove up to his parents' house, neighborhood youngsters had materialized at the curb. It took him a few moments to realize that the attraction was his white Mercedes convertible, the gift of a wealthy alumnus, grateful for the star first baseman's leading role in delivering a national intercollegiate championship.

When the excitement had settled, his parents emerged from the front door and greeted him with the tense embraces that passed for affection in his family. He reached into the backseat and extracted his luggage, a monogrammed weekend case made of hand-tooled leather, courtesy of another appreciative and successful Stanford graduate. As he walked through the house to his old bedroom, he noticed that the interior was less tidy than he had remembered. Stacks of newspapers and magazines, heaps of envelopes, and two new metal filing cabinets now filled the living room.

Unlike the house, his parents appeared no older; in truth, they seemed more vibrant than he recalled, exuding an unfamiliar energy and purpose. Grinning, he gestured toward the material scattered around the living room, the piles of religious and right-wing literature, posters, signs, and bumper stickers depicting ravaged fetuses, wolfish communists, and predatory homosexuals.

"What's going on here," he asked, "a mail-order business?"

His father laughed. "You might say 'male' business, son. M-A-L-E. We're in the business of keeping males male. It's a full-time job, I'll tell you. 'Specially here in

California, with all the perverts and degenerates. Right now your mother and I are doing our best for Anita Bryant and her crusade against those who would violate God's law and corrupt our children."

His father placed a unifying arm around his mother's shoulders and smiled. "Son, your folks are making a name for themselves."

Dick winced at the mention of Anita Bryant, the former pop singer whose relentless campaign to rescind a Dade County, Florida, gay-rights ordinance had triggered homophobic attitudes from coast to coast. "But, but," he stammered, struggling for control, "but it's terrible what she's doing. Attacking innocent people."

His father smiled indulgently. "Not so innocent, son. Not innocent at all. Not innocent of defying God's will. Not innocent of recruiting children into their ranks. Not innocent—"

Toote's mother interrupted. "You see, dear, they can't procreate their kind as the Lord intended, and so they have to perpetuate themselves by corrupting the young. Innocent? I'd say that they're anything but."

He shook his head vigorously. "You don't know what you're saying! You don't know what you're talking about!" He was shouting now, letting the words and feelings pour out. "You talk about perverts! You talk about degenerates! Well, you *should* know about them! You've got one for a son! You've got a dirty faggot for a son! You've got me—" His voice broke.

His father stared at him incredulously. His mother put her hands to her ears, trying to shut out what already had been heard. Then, "No! No!" she screamed, slapping her son across the face.

As the color flamed into his cheek, they glared at each

other. No one spoke. Then he turned and walked past them out of the house.

He drove to his old high school, parked, climbed into the empty grandstand, and stared out across the playing field that he had once graced. He was nauseous, drained, empty. He had not expected support, but he had not anticipated such raw hostility. He got back in his car and drove home, or at least to what had been home. Despite the tension, he felt better than he had in a long time. The relief that came with disclosure was unbelievably soothing. And so he was totally unprepared to find, when he pulled up in front of the house, that only his valise was waiting for him on the steps outside the front door.

The shower brought him back to the present, and Dick relished the sensation of being cleansed. He hadn't thought about his parents for some time. What was it, now, five years since then, since the last contact? None of his letters to them had been answered; they had, in fact, been returned unopened. When he phoned, the only response was the click of a receiver laid in its cradle.

In the intervening years, he had sought vainly to comprehend the origin of his gayness. All he knew for certain was that being homosexual was not a conscious act, any more, say, than being heterosexual. It was a conclusion brought about by his therapy sessions with Dr. Goodkind. But the rejection by his parents had been traumatic enough to dissuade him, until now, from revealing his sexuality to other straights. It was only among gay men and lesbians that he was open, in gay bars and at gay parties, and, of course, with his lovers — from occasional one-night stands to consuming affairs that lasted for months.

Now, as he readied himself for his public unmasking, Toote mentally reviewed again the questions the reporters would surely raise and the answers he must be ready to give. No American president or contender had ever rehearsed more diligently before meeting the press.

He had taken great care to preserve the secrecy of his imminent disclosure, not to maximize its impact, which in fact would be the effect, but because he wanted to explain himself, to come out, in his own terms and in his own words.

The result had been the press release, brief but painstakingly crafted and dispatched. After carefully selecting a conservative regimental stripe tie, he looked at the copy on his dresser.

To: Members of the news media

From: Dick Toote

Subject: Press Conference

There is something of considerable importance to me that I believe may interest you as well. I will be present at Gallagher's Steak House at two o'clock Wednesday to make a statement and to respond to your questions. Gallagher's is located at 228 West 52nd Street.

Shaved, showered and dressed, Toote reminded himself that, as a professional athlete, he had faced and handled what were deemed critical situations almost daily during the season. Time and again he had picked up his stumbling teammates with a key hit, a fielding gem, a stolen base, or simply the strength of his confidence. But he wasn't certain that sports heroics were transferable to "real-life" circumstances. Outsiders might think in such general terms, but athletes were trained to deal in specifics. He recalled a column by Ira Berkow of the *New York Times* about Yankee Hall of Famer Lefty Gomez, when the 80-year-old pitcher lay on his deathbed. The doctor had said, "Lefty, picture yourself on the mound and rate the pain from 1 to 10." And Lefty looked at him and said, "Who's hitting, Doc?"

Well, Toote thought, as he hailed a cab for the ride to Gallagher's, you're up.

From his desk at the New York *Post,* sports columnist Stan Mann once told his wife, Marti, he was close enough to smell the nearby Fulton Fish Market if his newspaper didn't stink so badly itself. "You should leave," she said. He knew he should, but he knew he wouldn't. He tried to explain to Marti that his age and salary made him unmarketable any place else. In truth, he was afraid.

After—what was it now, almost 30 years?—he was trapped by his ego and insecurities and by the *Post*'s benefits. "My future," he confided to a colleague, "is in the past." In his late fifties, the seductive appeal of a comfortable pension had succeeded, beyond any personnel director's fondest hopes, in binding Stan to the newspaper company.

Paradoxically, the security supposedly conferred by the corporation's retirement program caused him only anxiety. He began to worry that some impulsive act of disloyalty or momentary lapse into negligence might cancel his benefits. Such thoughts had never occurred to him during the 20 years he had worked and campaigned to rise from reporting to writing a column. The whole point then had been to extend his journalistic freedom and expand his influence. He had had a lot to say about sports, most of it unconventional.

Sports, he had always insisted, should be fun. From the beginning, he liked to ridicule the pomposity, materialism, and hypocrisy of the sports establishment. At every opportunity, Stan disclosed how money, rather than grace or sportsmanship, was driving the teams and athletes. He had been among the first to write about professional sports figures as people, with problems and passions, rather than as idols. His description of a typical road trip, including the boozing and sexual escapades with groupies, had become the classic revelation. And he had been among the first to probe baseball's political and social consciousness.

Although Stan had arrived on the sports scene after Jackie Robinson had broken the color barrier, he immediately recognized and described the racism that remained rampant in the front offices, even as it appeared to fade on the field. His column tracing the declining proportion of nonwhites from the players' level to the upper echelons of management became the subject of countless college sociology lectures. When a Midwestern team threw a clubhouse birthday party in the early 1960s for its star black center fielder and served watermelon while wearing white sheets, the *Post* was the only paper to run the story, because Stan was the only writer to report it. Predictably he got the silent treatment from the team, including its birthday celebrant.

Stan had also made a point of involving himself with many nonwhite ballplayers, blacks and Latinos, on and off the field. Such enterprise was generally rewarded with offbeat stories about growing up in ghetto gangs or in dusty, impoverished Central American villages. For such efforts over the years, Stan had gained the emnity of some of his subjects, the criticism of many of his editors, and the envy of most of his colleagues. Many reporters began to follow his lead; he was the ground-breaker for a new kind of sportswriting.

But as times changed and competition from televi-sion and all-sports radio sent editors scampering off in pursuit of low-cost ways to retain readers, they quickly discovered that gray masses of statistics — not carefully researched articles that explored trends and foibles — were sufficient to satisfy the sports-hungry fanatics. Stan regarded such developments with bemused dis-taste and parodied them. He staged competitions for Greediest Owner, Most Devious Manager, and Dullest Sports Pages, inviting readers to respond. While the columns engaged Stan's readers, they infuriated his editor.

Once a beacon of liberalism, the *Post* had gradually become a model of sensationalism. To Stan, it pandered to appetites for the "two big Cs: crime and cunt," repre-senting all the values Stan had formerly reviled. When he began to satirize the paper's obsession with gaining readers at any cost, irritated corporate officers and ranking editors had to work to restrain their displea-sure, because readership surveys showed "Mann to Man" was a major attraction.

Stan knew to keep his touch light, his imagination whimsical. His column became required reading in journalism courses, and its author, a cult figure in American sportswriting. A favorite speaker on cam-puses, he stressed his contention that sports was only a game, and that journalism, too, should be fun. His closing line became so familiar that student audiences chimed in: "When you stop enjoying it, hang up your jock. But be good to yourself. Take it off first."

Now, sitting in front of a blank screen on his word processor, Stan felt an echo of the joy that once had infused his work. The Toote story had stimulated his curiosity. Here was a touch of the old enthusiasm that had once sent him rushing off to work each day, believing that what he wrote would make a difference.

It took him back to the youthful journalism school graduate whose credo had been the traditional exhortation to "comfort the afflicted and afflict the comfortable." He recalled little else from those courses, but his diploma had gotten him a job with the onetime Binghamton *Sun* in upstate New York. Hired as a news reporter, he soured quickly on the paper's commitment to feeding its readers' conservative biases, and eagerly jumped at an opening in the sports department. He soon was assigned to cover the Triplets, a New York Yankees' farm team in the Eastern League. And although he found the pace of baseball boring, the time lapses between pitches, plays, and innings provided opportunities to think and observe.

Wandering in the grandstand and bleachers, Stan readily discovered that the fans were far more interesting than his colleagues, and certainly more than most of the players, who struck him as primarily concerned with getting paid, getting laid, and getting their names in the paper.

It was a sultry night during a meaningless game in July when Stan met Marti. It was not accidental; he had seen her before, sitting in the same field box along the third baseline, next to the same older man, probably her father. And he felt the same charge of excitement when she flipped her long auburn hair away from the back of her neck.

The night was suffocating; even the familiar breeze that right-handed pull hitters blessed had vanished. Looking over the crowd, Stan estimated that the sale of programs had set a record: everyone seemed to be fanning himself. Even with the particularly thin turnout, vendors would run out of beer by the third inning and soda by the fifth.

When her companion left, Stan almost tripped as he rushed down to her field-level box. "Hi!" he said. "I'm with the *Sun*."

She looked at him with curiosity, and he marveled at the emerald greenness of her eyes. Her mouth was wider than he had thought, and her bottom lip was seductively full. He noticed it curled slightly when she said, "Who's minding the Father and the Holy Ghost?"

"Um," he stammered. "I guess they can take care of themselves. That's, um, that's pretty funny. Nobody ever said that to me before."

"I'm not surprised," she said, adding, "around *here*." Her manner was not discouraging. Her voice was soft and did not betray any geographic origins, although Binghamton appeared to be clearly ruled out.

Stan, emboldened, had smiled convivially. "You, too? I thought I was the only captive."

She contorted her face in mock anger. "You're knocking *Binghamton*? The *Triple Cities*? *God's* country? Don't you know how *wonderful* it is here? How *fortunate* you are? You know, you could be deported to . . ."

she paused and affected the flat, country accent of upstate New York, "Paris, France, or London, England, or—" and now she feigned horror—*"New York, New York."*

"Oh, please," Stan said, clasping his hands in front of him. *"Please, please* . . . make it *any* of them."

Now he glanced anxiously at the clock on his office wall at the *Post.* For the moment, he had done all he could with Toote; the next development would have to emerge from the upcoming press conference. Still, he needed a column. And soon. He began tapping out an uninspired string of comic baseball anecdotes. Fortunately, he mused, when necessary he could rely on his memory to grind out three columns a week.

He allowed his mind to wander back to that time he met Marti. He recalled the encouragement in her laughter just as the public address system announced the imminent playing of the national anthem. He remembered noting with satisfaction that he was a few inches taller than she and that she wore no ring.

The recording ended to cheers from the crowd and the sounds and movements of a few thousand spectators sitting down to an evening of minor league baseball. The field, as always, looked crisp and green in the glare of the stadium lights. The dirt base paths were untrod, the foul lines gleamed whitely. It was always the same: the hint of excitement, of unpredictability, of possibilities; a blank canvas awaiting the touch of a master's brush. Stan took a seat in the box and, to justify himself, pulled some sheets of folded copy paper out of his back pocket. She looked at him mischievously and asked: "You're in charge of the *Sun?*"

"Well, not in charge, exactly," he said. "They're sort of

preparing me. For now, I'm kind of familiarizing myself with the area and its people. Now, you, for example. Can you tell me a little about yourself? Uh, you know, name, address, *phone number* — no, I mean occupation, how often you come out here, why you do, and so on?"

"Are you sure this is for the newspaper?"

"Well, it depends," Stan hedged. "I could keep it to myself."

"Say," she said, with exaggerated seriousness. "Are you *sure* you're with the newspaper? Daddy says we have to be very careful these days, what with Korea and, you know, the Russians and the Chinese and everything. He says you can't trust *anyone,* and it's a good thing Senator McCarthy has been finding out about commies and pinkos in the State Department and the Army and God knows where else."

"Your dad? He *likes* McCarthy?"

"*Likes* him? Daddy is *crazy* about him. So are all of Daddy's friends. And probably even Mommy, although with her you can't really tell. They think it's about time that somebody had the guts to go after those traitors."

"And *you?*" Stan asked anxiously. "What do you think about him?"

She grinned. "I think he's a disaster. Don't *you?*"

"Yes, yes, yes," Stan said with relief. "Look, as long as you know enough to have me deported, don't you think I'm entitled to know your *name?*"

"Marti," she said. "With an *i.* It stands for Martine."

"Oh. I thought maybe it stood for martini."

"Bite your tongue," Marti said. "If Daddy ever heard you say that, you *would* be deported."

"I don't get it."

"He's with IBM. To them, to *him,* drinking is almost as bad as using an abacus. Come on, you must know that."

Do I *ever* know, Stan thought, as he recalled his first week at the *Sun,* when he had accompanied a veteran reporter on his rounds. In Endicott, where IBM had a plant, one of the stops on the beat was the village police station. As the reporter took down some information about a drunk driving arrest, a voice called out from one of the cells at the rear.

"Please, please don't put my name in the *paper.* They'll can me. I've got a family. Give me a break, *please.*"

Stan looked questioningly at the other reporter. "He works for IBM," the reporter said. "He's right. They find out you've been arrested for DWI, they bounce you."

"What do *you* do?"

"*Me?* I write the story. Around here that's news. It's bigger news if the guy works for IBM, 'cause everybody knows it means his job."

"But," Stan protested, "suppose he gets acquitted? Suppose he's innocent?"

"Then I guess it's between him and them. Hell, I can't worry about *what* I write, about what *happens* to people I write about. If I think it's news, I write it. And if I write it, they'll probably run it. That's my job. *Our* job. You worry about what *happens* after you write it, you might not write *anything.* What happens to news after it gets printed is somebody else's job. We got enough trouble getting it right."

The incident had bothered Stan. These weren't "comfortable" people he'd be "afflicting." He had never considered the consequences of having the power to hurt the helpless. Now he saw Marti looking at him expectantly. Stan nodded. "Yes, I *do* know."

As if on cue, a male voice interrupted. "Well, how are *you?* Malcolm Wyatt. I'm Marti's father," he said, offering a hand which Stan shook enthusiastically. "I'm Stan Mann." Then, looking in her direction, "A friend of Marti's."

As the game progressed, the heat began to erode the pitchers' skills. In the sixth inning, a cocky, freewheeling rookie shortstop named Schwartzenberger climaxed a Triplet rally by rocketing a hanging curve over the left-field fence for a grand-slam home run. To the delight of the hometown fans, and the contempt of the visiting Elmira Pioneers, Schwartzenberger jumped up and down a half-dozen times on each sack as he rounded the bases. For his arrogance, the barrel-chested rookie had to dive across the plate to avoid being hit by the first pitch thrown to him at his next time up, a challenge that sent him sprinting to the mound with an upraised bat. He and the pitcher were separated before anyone was injured, but the incident, which resulted in a $25 fine cheerfully paid by the Triplets, gave the club a genuine attraction and ensured Schwartzenberger a secure place in its lineup.

"How come you didn't hit him?" Stan asked the shortstop during the postgame interview. Schwartzenberger just winked in reply. In the next morning's *Sun,* Stan's piece enthusiastically described Binghamton's instant hero, the scrappy little guy who knew how to enliven ball games and newspapers. By August, the Triplets' brazen infielder had become involved in so many confrontations that he adopted the adjective "scrappy" as his first name and legally shortened his last to conform to the box score spelling: "Schwr-tznbrgr." Stan made sure the story went out on the Associated Press sports wire.

Except for the near fight, the game itself had provided little more excitement, enabling Marti's father to air his political views. He said to Stan, "As a member of the Fourth Estate, I'm sure you're aware of the threat that international communism poses, and of the patriotic efforts of some to expose and confront that threat. And of the indifference and, even, opposition that such patriots must endure."

Stan had felt his stomach tighten. The last thing he needed was a political argument with the father of the girl with whom he was falling in love. "Well, sir," he said airily, "in the sports department we get to deal with the *critical* events, like whether the Triplets win or lose."

But Mr. Wyatt was not deflected. "I understand the limits of the milieu you're functioning in currently. But you *do* recognize what our country is up against? And how we must protect it?"

"I think I know very well what we're up against," Stan agreed. "And I know what I'd *like* to do to protect us."

Mr. Wyatt nodded with satisfaction. "Of course, the *Sun* tries, but it hardly has the resources to participate significantly in this vital battle. And as for most of the press, well, should I say pink might be the appropriate color for their ink? What we need are more forceful writers like Westbrook Pegler, and more courageous newspapers like the New York *Journal-American*."

Stan hoped his wince was not detected. Westbrook Pegler, once described as a "champion of the upperdog," was a former sportswriter whose political gossip-mongering represented the antithesis of Stan's concept of journalistic integrity.

"Have you ever thought of working for the *Journal?*" Mr. Wyatt asked.

"I've thought of what it would be *like,*" Stan replied noncommittally.

"You were terrific!" Marti said later when her father had left for the men's room.

"I, well, I wish I had been more honest," Stan said. "You know, about the politics and stuff."

"No, you were fine. Really. Anybody could've called him a fat-cat fascist or whatever. And gotten written off." Marti took his hand. "I thought you handled him just right."

Stan checked the word count of his anecdotal column and was surprised to discover he was finished. He read it through indifferently, and hit the key of his word processor that sent it to the sports copy desk for editing. Then he reached back into the past once more, shaking his head at the recollection of his youthful idealism.

"It's lousy not to be able to speak up," he recalled having said. "Oh, I don't mean just to your father. It's this whole area up here. The narrow minds, the conformity. I figured that when I began covering sports I'd avoid having to get involved in reactionary politics. But that's not the answer. I didn't intend to make a speech but, you know, Marti, we can't just stand *by* when things go wrong, when the country gets off-track. We've got to stand *up*. Stand up and, if we can, sound off. I'm sure as hell not going to be able to do that at the *Sun*."

Marti had looked at him admiringly. "You're right,

you're right," she had said. "But what would you *do?* Where would you *go?*"

"The one paper that's really standing up to McCarthy is the New York *Post,*" Stan had replied. "They've got the resources *and* the guts. That's where I *should* be."

"Then go," Marti said.

And he did.

"The way you look, I won't ask how you feel," Ruby said.

"Look," Scrappy said, "there's no way he's gonna call off that announcement. It's like the biggest thing in his life right now. Like a cause, or somethin'. I don't know what gets into these people."

"What gets into 'em is each other," Ruby quipped.

"Forgive me if I don't laugh," Scrappy snorted. "Like the end of my life is coming fast and you're makin' stupid jokes. There's no way I'll be able to unload Toote. By this time next week I won't be able to give the team away. It's just unbelievable that a ballplayer as good as him could be a fairy. Jeezus."

Scrappy took the bottle of vodka out of the refrigerator and poured himself a drink. Ruby waved him off, although Scrappy hadn't offered him any.

"Well," Ruby said, "it's not the first time in sports, you know. Bill Tilden was queer as they come, and Billie Jean and those dykey women tennis players—"

"That's *tennis*," Scrappy said disgustedly. "What the hell has *tennis* got to do with baseball?"

"Well, *baseball* then," Ruby continued. "That umpire,

y'know, Dave Pallone. Even wrote a *book* about it."

"Ruby, I'm talkin' *athletes,* you give me a fuckin' *umpire.* What would you expect from *them,* anyway?"

"OK, OK. Then there was that pro football player a couple years back," Ruby persisted. "He also wrote a book. I think he said there were others like him, too."

"Yeah, that's what they all say. Like Toote. He was tryin' to tell me that guys like Dave Ripp and Romanski are gay. Can you beat that? They just don't want to sound like they're the *only* ones."

"Ripp and Romanski?" Ruby repeated. "He picked some pretty hot ballplayers."

"That's what I told him. It was like an All-Star team."

"He said they were *fairies?*" Ruby started to chuckle.

"Yeah. Also Mickey Mayo and Gonzalez and Tony Mike. And get this: Gigolo Johnson, the biggest cocksman in the majors."

Ruby was laughing openly. "What a gag. The best goddam ballplayers in the league are fags. I guess it helps. Jeez, Scrappy, no wonder you never *really* made it."

The first traces of the vodka were beginning to reach Scrappy's brain cells. He poured himself another drink and, fishing a stain-speckled glass out of a desk drawer, poured one for Ruby.

"That would make some fuckin' team," Scrappy said.

"Wrong," Ruby shot back. "A *no* fuckin' team."

They burst into laughter.

"Can you imagine?" Scrappy chortled, "a *team* of fairies?"

"Sure, sure," Ruby said, entering the fantasy. "They could wear pink uniforms."

"No, not pink. *Lavender*. Don't you know what's *in?*"

"Well, I guess I'd know *who's* in. That's about as much as I'd *wanna* know."

"Instead of a trainer," Scrappy continued, "we could have a hairdresser."

"Yeah, and the spikes could have high heels."

They paused and as the sound of laughter died, the mood began to evaporate. Scrappy poured them some more vodka and they sipped their drinks silently, each staring vacantly, fashioning his own chain of thoughts.

"Scrappy," Ruby said abruptly. "What if—now hang in here—what if Toote is right. I mean, what if those guys really *are* fairies?"

"So?"

"Well, they *would* make a helluva ball club. I mean, those guys are *terrific*."

"So?"

"So suppose somebody put them together. They'd be, maybe, *unbeatable*."

"Yeah," Scrappy agreed, "They'd be *sensational*. But who would watch them? Who'd pay to see a bunch of fags? Even if they would, who could afford them? You're talkin' some of the top-paid guys in baseball. You're talkin' millions. Nobody's got that kind of money. Not even Donald. It's like sayin' you're gonna buy up every guy in the All-Star lineup."

"I understand that," Ruby continued, "but what's the selling price of an All-Star *faggot?*"

Scrappy's eyes narrowed. "Sonuvabitch!" he shouted as Ruby's idea took shape. Scrappy bolted out of his chair and pounded the publicist's shoulder. "What an idea! What a crazy idea! You're a genius! A fuckin' genius!"

Ruby grinned. "OK, OK, it's a great idea. But it's got plenty, plenty problems. Like you said, 'Who'd pay to see faggots?'"

Scrappy thought for a moment. "Ruby," he said, "who paid to see Liberace? Millions, that's who. And what about that Michael Jackson kid, whatever he is? Millions and millions. They'll even pay to see ya if they hate ya. Go take Mohammed Ali. They *hated* him for an uppity nigger and they made him a multimillionaire. What Americans want is a winner. A winner can be *anything*."

Scrappy felt the euphoria returning. "You're incredible, Ruby. I knew you were worth whatever it is I'm payin' you."

Seizing the moment, Ruby quickly poured himself some vodka. "Yeah. What you ain't payin'. You know when Ozzie Smith got two million three in '88, I figured out I didn't make half that. And I'm talkin' over 30 years," Ruby said. "Now let's come down to earth here and try to work this out. First thing, you gotta be certain these guys really *are* fairies. They're not fairies, you got nothin'. What did Toote say about them? How did he say it?"

"He was mad," Scrappy recalled. "I hardly ever saw him like that. He was real pissed. And it just sort of poured out. You know, I figured he was only shootin' off his mouth to make a point. But I'm thinkin' now: Why would he pick *those* guys? And then, he sort of pulled back, y'know? Like he'd said somethin' wrong. He even said that, like, 'Forget it, Scrappy, I shouldn't of told you that.' Y'know, the more I think of it, the more I gotta believe it. It's true, Ruby. I feel it."

"Well, OK," Ruby said, "I think you're probably right.

A guy like Toote wouldn't come up with somethin' like that so fast. But you *still* got plenty problems. Nobody knows these guys are fairies."

"An' you think *that's* a problem?" Scrappy grinned slyly. "I don't think that's any problem at all. Like I wish all my problems were that tough."

"Wuddayuh mean?" Ruby often found Scrappy's mind surprisingly agile. And unreadable.

"What kind of public relations man *are* you?" Scrappy chided. "I mean there's dozens, hey, hundreds, of newspaper and TV guys out there just prayin' to get their mitts on a story like this. One phone call is all it takes."

"Jeezus, Scrappy, I dunno. That's dangerous stuff. Libel, slander. You can't run around spreadin' stories about people."

"*Spreadin'*?" Scrappy feigned innocence. "Who's *spreadin'*? If anybody's spreadin', it's a guy name of Toote. Me? I'm just maybe *passin'* it along. I mean, Toote's so hot to tell the world about himself, these guys are probably just as hot. You know, Ruby, it's sorta doin' them a favor."

Ruby shook his head. Scrappy's rationalizations sometimes made him uneasy. "You think *that's* a favor, don't do me any, OK?"

"You'll see. Things work out, they'll all be playin' ball together. They'll be as happy as pigs in shit." Scrappy gulped some more vodka and warmed to the prospects. "Sonuvabitch, that's gonna be some kind of clubhouse!"

"Not to mention the showers."

Scrappy roared with laughter. "It'll be like a zoo, like a circus."

"They may never wanna go out on the field."

"Now there you go," Scrappy said, convulsed. "That'll be the *problem*."

Scrappy poured them both another drink. It had been a long time since he had felt so upbeat. Years, probably. Enthusiasm was running through him along with the vodka. It was still little more than an idea, a glimmer. But it had possibilities, and that, Scrappy thought, is what life's all about. Possibilities, hopes, dreams, whatever you want to call them. It keeps you going. It's what kept *him* going, Scrappy recalled. There certainly was nothing else: no caring parents, no older brothers or sisters, no interested teachers, nobody concerned enough to put him on the right track, to give support, to raise expectations. There was only Uncle Manny and that was later, years later, after Scrappy had made a name for himself. But hope, that's what keeps you alive, he thought. It's even better than vodka. Like Ruby said, there *were* plenty of problems. But they could be dealt with. To begin, there had to be a plan.

"First thing, Ruby, we gotta keep this quiet. Nobody knows but us. We gotta work things out very careful, the two of us. Now, where do we start?"

"Well, it's gotta get out that these guys are queers. Once that happens, their clubs'll drop 'em fast. Nobody'll want to *touch* 'em," Ruby chuckled at his unintended pun. "If you get what I mean."

Scrappy shared the laugh, then stopped abruptly. "Whatsamatter?" Ruby asked, "you look sick."

"Sick. Yeah, sick," Scrappy replied slowly. "That's the word. Sick, like with AIDS. Maybe Toote's got it. Maybe *that's* what this is all about."

"Jeez, Scrappy, maybe you're right."

Scrappy scowled. There was always a down side. Always something to wreck the plans, threaten the future. It had always been this way for him. "It could be even worse, Ruby. Any of those guys could have it. Or get it. You're really lucky, you get maybe ten good years tops out of a ballplayer. These guys? Who knows? It's a hell of a risk. We got enough to worry about already. I don't know, Ruby. We need *that* hangin' over us?"

Ruby shook his head sadly. Not even a lifetime's exposure had inured him to Scrappy's capacity for cynicism and ruthlessness. The sonuvabitch is worried *he'll* lose money if some poor bastard gets AIDS, Ruby thought. He wondered why Scrappy was so shabby. What prompted the selfishness, the greed? On a few drunken occasions, Scrappy had confided how lonely he had felt as a child, that his parents, consumed by making a living from their drygoods store, were rarely at home. He had complained he felt orphaned, left to shift for himself, without guidance or support or encouragement. Ruby had felt sorry for Scrappy then, but such speculation made him uncomfortable. It forced him to reconsider his ready acceptance of Scrappy's sleaziness.

Another swallow of the vodka enabled Ruby to reject the sense of self-loathing that had crept into his consciousness and allow him to confront Scrappy's latest need. "Look, Scrappy, it ain't all bad. It gets out that some of these guys maybe got AIDS, their clubs will be payin' *you* to take 'em. You know, damaged goods. But you don't *have* to take 'em. That's the beauty part. We test 'em before we buy 'em. You know, the deal's subject to a physical. And the physical will include an AIDS test. They come up positive, screw 'em." Ruby grinned. "Shit, nobody else will."

Scrappy threw both arms around Ruby and hugged him vigorously. "You sonuvabitch, Ruby! That'll do it! We're fuckin' back in business!"

Toote's recent behavior puzzled Stan Mann; he couldn't figure out the Gents star at all. In Stan's 30-year career as a sportswriter, he had never heard of any professional athlete, much less a member of a team, arranging his own press conference. But such quirkiness appealed to him. From the beginning, athletes had interested him as much for their thought processes off the field as for their physical accomplishments on it. He had claimed as his own the special few who pursued the arts and crafts or otherwise involved themselves in activities besides hunting, boozing, and bimbo chasing, and remained proud of his articles about Dodger second baseman Eddie Basinski playing violin in an upstate New York orchestra, Argentinian tennis ace Guillermo Vilas writing poetry, and Knicks basketball star Phil Jackson, later coach of the Chicago Bulls, studying Zen.

As the taxi sliced uptown through the lunch hour traffic, Stan felt a tremor of excitement. He had no idea what Toote was contemplating, but his instincts told him it would be a bigger story than anyone imagined. And never mind Toote, a big story was what *he* needed.

Lately, instead of setting the pace for his colleagues,

he found himself fighting a rear-guard action, defending and justifying his columns, initially in his own mind and then to his superiors. As contemporaries retired or left the *Post,* he had begun to feel isolated, surrounded by talented and ambitious youngsters ready to work harder, more familiar with current tastes and trends, more imaginative and daring. Increasingly needy of approval now, Stan fearfully conceded that for the first time in his life he was professionally insecure. Everything was changing: he felt the paper had abandoned principle for sensationalism, reporters were better educated but more malleable, the pace was more demanding, the technology too confusing. Everything was changing, he realized, but himself.

He had gotten tired. He found himself getting to the office later and leaving sooner. Anxiety eroded the quality of his work, creating greater anxiety. He had seen it happen to ballplayers during a hitting slump; now it was happening to him. He asked himself if the problem was age, burnout, or both.

But today seemed different. Maybe things could turn around, he thought, as the cab stopped in front of Gallagher's. Stan felt a sense of his old vitality as he entered past the familiar plate glass window stacked with steaks. Gallagher's was his turf, site of scores of press conferences, dozens of interviews. He immediately went upstairs to the private room where today's activity would take place. Like the restaurant downstairs, the dark walls were covered with sports photographs. The long, narrow room was set up with buffet tables loaded with food on one side and tables for the journalists on the other. Most of them were crowding around the bar. Stan felt comfortably at home picking out familiar faces from the New York sports beat: the two sensitive, bearded columnists, George Vecsey of the *Times* and Steve Jacobson of *Newsday;* knowledgeable Peter Gammons of *Sports Illustrated;* the contingent of TV reporters and cameramen, and some radio sports commentators. Stan noted the presence of a few baseball people as well. He jotted down names: Scrappy; Ruby; Al Greene, who was Yankee owner Donald Bigg's "caddy"; a guy from the commish's office. "Hey," Stan muttered. He wasn't alone in suspecting that something important was in the offing.

At the far end of the room, beyond the bar where the newsmen were getting their free drinks, Stan saw a lectern, illuminated by a ceiling spotlight, bearing a dozen or more microphones, that flared out like round-headed pins from a cushion.

At precisely two o'clock Toote emerged from somewhere at the rear of the room and briskly stepped up to the podium. He looked flushed, but whether from excitement or apprehension, Stan couldn't decide.

"I really appreciate your coming," Toote began in a firm voice. "This is something I've been waiting a long time to say. You'll understand why, I'm sure, in a moment. I have a short, a very short, announcement to make and then I'll try to answer your questions. I just ask one thing of you: *Listen* to what I have to say. OK. My announcement consists of three words: I am gay."

"What?"

"What?"

"What the hell did he say?"

"Did you hear him?"

"Repeat that!"

"I can't believe it!"

"What's goin' on?"

"Hey, Toote, cut the crap!"

"Did you hear what the man said? It's incredible."

"It sounded like 'GAY.' Like he said, 'I'm GAY.'"

"Whaddaya crazy? Toote's *gay?*"

Toote leaned toward the mikes again and repeated his announcement. "That's it, guys. I'm gay."

A wire service reporter shouted the first question. "Are you telling us that you're an avowed homosexual?"

Toote shook his head and smiled. "No. We don't have to take vows. We just do what comes naturally."

"Why the hell — I mean what made you decide to be gay?"

"I didn't decide it. I didn't *choose* to be gay. I guess you could say it chose me."

"How long has this been going on, Dick?"

"I honestly don't know. As far back as I can remember. Maybe since I was born."

"How come you're doing this? Why are you making this announcement?"

"Good question. Because I'm sick and tired of pretending. Because I don't think it's anything to be ashamed of. Because it's true and it's time."

"So does the front office know about this?"

"Yeah, how about Scrappy? You tell Scrappy about this?"

"Hey, Jesus, Dick, what about the Gents? You tell your teammates about your, um, *condition?*"

Toote held up the palms of his hands. "Take it easy, now. One at a time. As far as Scrappy's concerned, I think I see him over there by the bar. Why don't you ask him?"

Heads snapped around. Scrappy put down his glass of vodka.

"Look, this here is Dick's show," Scrappy said. "We got anything to say, we'll let you know, like always."

"What about the rest of the team? You tell them, Dick?"

"No," Toote said, shaking his head slowly, "I haven't. They're finding out now, if they're watching, or tomorrow, if they read about it. And I'd like to say something to them. OK, I know this is going to bother a lot of you guys. You probably don't even believe me, or maybe you think I'm crazy. But I want you to know that it's something I had to do. I hope you'll understand that. I'm still the same person I was last season, even yesterday. Nothing about me has changed. I'm looking forward to playing ball this season. I expect to be taking batting practice at spring training, same as always. And I hope you'll all be there, too."

"Dick, you think they'll show up? I mean, what about AIDS?"

"What *about* AIDS?" Toote repeated. It was the question he had anticipated most. "You ought to know by now that every gay man doesn't have the HIV virus. And you ought to know by now how AIDS is transmitted. And how it isn't. I love to play ball. But that doesn't mean I love ballplayers or *make* love to them. They're not in any danger from me. Besides, I tested negative for HIV."

Toote reached into his pocket and pulled out a condom.

"Jeezus."

"Now what?"

Toote resumed. "You know what *this* is? It's a life

preserver. A life preserver in a sea of unsafe sex. Don't be afraid to put it onscreen. Don't be afraid to take a picture of it. Don't be afraid to write about it. And it's not just for gays."

"What about the fans, Toote? You think they're gonna turn out after this?"

"I hope so," Toote said. "And I think they will. Baseball fans are decent people. Fair-minded. They root for underdogs. Yes, I think they'll turn out. And I think they'll support me the same way they always have."

"Are you crazy, Toote? You think the commissioner's going to let you get out on the field and be an example to America's youth? Like Jackie Robinson, Willie Mays, Roberto Clemente? What kind of role model do you think *you'll* make?"

Toote recoiled, then regained his composure. He paused for several seconds before responding. "That's the whole point. I'm what I am, which is the same as what I was. I'm not a criminal, not a gambler, not a druggie or an alcoholic." He smiled weakly, "I don't even smoke. If I was good enough to be a role model yesterday, I'm good enough to be one today. I haven't done anything wrong. Being gay isn't a crime, and gays should not be treated like criminals. Or inferiors. Judge me by how I perform on the field. Or even by how I behave in public. But don't take it further."

"Sure, Dick. But this isn't Utopia; it's America. What about the commissioner? What about the other clubs? The owners? What makes you think they'll even let you out on the field?"

Toote's grimace reflected his concern. This was the issue that had worried him the most. It was a situation, a lawyer friend had pointed out, permeated with politics, one in which having the law on his side, assuming no "moral turpitude" could be shown, might not be enough. The baseball establishment regarded change the way the military viewed treason, and the enshrinement of baseball as the nation's official sport gave its self-proclaimed guardians an almost religious eminence. Toote recalled how the boxing hierarchy had taken Mohammed Ali's heavyweight title away for refusing to serve in the Vietnam War. Besides, the baseball moguls had the resources to tie up the case in court, perhaps for years, while Toote aged himself out of his career.

"I have confidence that the commissioner will uphold the law," he said, with more hope than conviction, as he signaled an end to the conference.

The newspeople rushed from the room to file their stories, uncharacteristically leaving behind almost full glasses of Scotch, bourbon, and vodka.

Following Toote's celebrated press conference, the headline writers of the city's three tabloids relished one of those rare, golden moments of opportunity that compensate for the anonymity of their daily work. Falling as it did to the sports desks, the undertaking evoked the spirit of a journalistic olympiad. The results, while hardly historic, conveyed a certain attitude with clarity as well as brevity.

"TOOTIE FRUITY," said the *Post*. "THE (UN)NATURAL," captioned the *Daily News,* under a full-page photo of the Gents first baseman. *Newsday's* entry was "TOOTE FAIRY."

The articles themselves held largely negative reactions, which, while less overwrought, were essentially just as insensitive. Most of Toote's teammates declined comment, either through loyalty or a reluctance to deal with any subject beyond winning, losing, hitting, and pitching. But the sportswriters found a ready respondent in Donald Bigg, the Yankee owner.

Never one to withhold an opinion, however unformed, Donald savored this occasion with a combination of glee, anger, and vindictiveness. His glee sprang from two sources: Scrappy had been dealt a devastating blow and by prudently postponing a decision on Toote until after the press conference, he had escaped a similar fate. His anger stemmed from his conviction that Scrappy had known in advance of Toote's revelation and consequently had sought to dump the player on him. And his vindictiveness led Donald to swear an unending campaign to destroy Scrappy by banning Toote from baseball.

"Do I have anything to say?" Donald exploded at the first reporter who phoned to seek his reaction. "Does a bear shit in the woods? Do fairies play hide the salami in the shower? You bet your ass I have something to say! I say get that goddam faggot out of baseball! And I say let him take his sleazy, double-crossing manager with him! That's the first thing I have to say. Can you quote me? What the hell do you think I'm talkin' to you for?"

The somewhat bowdlerized version that appeared in the next day's *Times* described Donald as having "urged the banning of Toote and Schwrtznbrgr from baseball as inadequate role models for the nation's youth." The Yankee magnate's opinion was echoed, although less vociferously, by his fellow owners, with the exception, obviously, of Scrappy. The commissioner issued a pusillanimous statement: "We will pursue this matter immediately to determine the potential effect of the Toote announcement on the opportunity of baseball fans to enjoy the sport without fear of any corrupt or subversive influence." In response, a spokesman for the Major League Players Association said, "This organization will make certain that all players' legitimate rights are protected."

Scrappy and Ruby devised a statement that portrayed the Gents management as being reluctantly humanistic. "Dick Toote has been a credit to this team and to baseball. We had no knowledge of his sexual orientation but will do everything possible, regardless of any difficulties, to enable him to continue to use his many skills to make a living, the right of every American."

The next step was more challenging. Ruby wanted to send an anonymous letter to Stan Mann identifying the gay ballplayers whose names Toote had blurted out to Scrappy. "No good," Scrappy said. "This is a helluva story for him and I want him to know who's givin' it. I want to get extra bases with this one. He'll be doing a job for us *and* he'll owe us."

They agreed that getting the information to Mann would be simple. "He's been on my back about Toote for weeks," Scrappy said. "No way he's not gonna be callin'."

Scrappy's intuition was, as usual, unerring. The sports columnist, having correctly anticipated the impact, if not the subject, of the press conference, wanted desperately to lead the pack on the Toote story. Personally, Mann felt supportive of Toote; he admired the ballplayer's courage and sympathized with his distress. Professionally, he was well aware of the *Post's* desire to exploit Toote for all the titillation his story could derive. Once he would have ignored public opinion, backing the declaration of gayness unequivocally and vigorously. Now he wasn't sure: the risk of winding up on the unpopular side was too great. Again Stan felt the pressures of age, of insecurity.

There was, of course, no way he could avoid writing about the Toote situation. It was *the* story: in the papers, on TV, over the radio. In his first column after the announcement, he tried to play it both ways: agonizing

over the impact of the revelation on the kids who idolized Toote, while praising him for his forthrightness.
But he knew he was just buying time. It was a story
aching for exploitation and one that could bring *him*
some much needed attention. His shrinking conscience
wrestled with his battered ego.

"You got any angle on the Toote affair?" Mann's editor
asked. "Boss wants to ride the hell out of this one."
Mann winced. "I'm working on it, I'm working on it," he
replied. "You know, the whole goddam world is covering
this." The editor just shook his head. "The boss doesn't
want excuses. He wants to splash it. Y'know Stan, put
your spin on it." Stan felt the editor's hand on his shoulder. "It could matter," he confided gruffly.

Stan again felt the gnaw of anxiety. It was coming
more frequently these days and lasting longer. Daily he
resented and scorned the enthusiasm of the younger
staffers, dismissing it as playacting for the editors' benefit, forgetting the zeal that had once driven *him*. The
youngsters were threats, coveting his column and his
once-prominent status. Of late, Marti had remarked
on his dourness, but he refused to discuss it. The banter
that had once characterized their relationship was
as rare now as their lovemaking. Everything that had
once held meaning for them seemed to be evaporating.

Stan groped in his mind for the source of their problems. He remembered the arguments that had arisen
from Marti's decision to volunteer with the National
Organization for Women. It wasn't that he opposed
NOW's goals or positions, but he hadn't encouraged
Marti's interest, either. He recalled how disappointed
she had been in his failure to echo her enthusiasm for

the feminist movement. "What's your problem?" she had finally demanded, "Does it threaten you that women need action?" Whereupon, she took on equal rights for women with the same commitment they had shared for civil rights. Finally, she accused him of having abandoned the liberal principles that had been their lodestar.

Stan returned to the business at hand. "Got to get on this!" he told himself as he dialed Scrappy's number. The rasp on the other end of the telephone line indicated he had reached the Gents' owner. "Scrappy," he said, "this is Mann."

Scrappy was elated. "Yeah, man!"

No, Scrappy insisted, he had no intention of folding. He would fight wherever necessary to keep his star on the team and on the field. Sure, it would create problems, Scrappy agreed, but a responsible management assumed responsibility and stood up for its players. No, Scrappy said, he didn't know how it would affect attendance, hadn't even thought about it. Yes, Scrappy imagined, some of the other players would be unhappy, but he was confident that Toote's character and talents would melt any hostility. Speaking of other players, Scrappy said, had Mann heard from any of them? "Any of the, you know, ones like Toote?"

Mann was electrified. "The ones like Toote? What ones like Toote? You mean there are other gay ballplayers?"

Scrappy's voice was calm, didactic, almost scholarly. "You think Toote's the only one? Like they say, maybe 10 percent of men are gay—you know, 1 in 10. You think they're all ballet dancers and hairdressers? With 600, 700 ballplayers in the major leagues, there could be 30, 40, 50 of *them* on the field every day."

Stan couldn't believe what he was hearing. But Scrappy's knowing tone and his logic seemed convincing. Still, he challenged, "You're bullshitting, Scrappy. You don't really know that. You're just blowing smoke."

"Hey, Stan," Scrappy replied. "I got no reason to crap you. Just think about it. It makes sense, don't it? I mean, like, you think there's only one fairy in the majors?"

"Do you know anything, Scrappy? Do you know what you're talkin' about? Do you have any names?"

Scrappy let Mann's questions hang in the air. He hadn't enjoyed talking to a sportswriter so much in 20 years. Especially this one. The one who knew *just* how to get to him. The one who thought he was the conscience of baseball. Let him squirm a little, Scrappy thought. It does *me* good.

Scrappy imposed a few more moments of silence before saying, "How's about Romanski?"

"What're you, crazy, Scrappy? Rhino gay?"

"Look, Mann, you asked, I answered. It don't come with no stamp from a notary public."

"Yeah, but this is dangerous stuff. You can't just throw it out. You got any proof?"

"You mean have I got a picture for you of Romanski giving me a blow job? I got information. I ain't doin' your job for you. You think you can check it out, you do it. If you can't, then I dunno. You get proof for everythin' you put into that rag of yours? I doubt it, Mann. I think you guys go with what your gut tells you is OK. Also, speakin' of 'you guys,' you know there's maybe a hundred sportswriters lookin' to hear this." Scrappy was savoring this conversation.

"All right, Scrappy, so Romanski's gay. Maybe. But

you were talking about thirty, forty, fifty guys. Your information got any others?"

Scrappy and Ruby had decided to drop all the names at once when they got the chance. There was nothing to gain by dragging it out. Besides, they didn't want anyone digging into the story. Get it done quick and easy.

"You got your pencil out?" Scrappy asked rhetorically. "Try Ripp and Jackson and Santiago and Zeeman and Gonzalez and Mike and Johnson and Mayo for starters."

"You're out of your mind!" Stan said, even as he began composing the lead sentence of his column: *Dick Toote is the Gents cleanup hitter. But when it comes to gays in major league baseball, is he just the leadoff man?*

"How could you do something like this?" Marti
asked in anger and disappointment. She thrust the
"Mann to Man" column in her husband's face. "I can't
believe you'd stoop so low."

Stan was shaken. Marti's disgust had never been so
evident. He knew that it wasn't only *what* he had written. She was hurt because he hadn't sought her opinion,
had never even mentioned it to her beforehand. In the
past, in the days when things had been good between
them, he had relied on her reactions, testing his ideas,
often asking her to read his columns before he filed
them. But as they had drifted apart, as Marti's involvement with NOW had given her a purpose aside from
their relationship, Stan had found her less concerned
with his work, less interested in providing advice that
had always been helpful and often wise. And he knew,
too, why he hadn't told her this time, knew that she
would have strongly disapproved of his deviation from
the journalistic high road. But *she* could afford moral
outrage, he told himself. It wasn't her job, her status,
her life that were at stake.

And what was so terrible, anyhow? He was doing his
job the way it was supposed to be done: getting at the

truth for his readers. God knows his editor thought so. "Grand Slam!" were the words he read when he responded to the Message Pending notification on his office word processor.

"Good piece," the writer who covered hockey said as he passed Stan in the hall. "Nice job," said the department secretary, a surefire mirror of her boss's reaction. Puffed up with these encomiums, feeling secure and confident for the first time in months, Stan had been on a high as he entered his apartment.

"What are you so upset about?" Stan replied. "You used to want me to 'tell it like it is.' Well, that's what I did. And that's what I'm supposed to do. It's time you got rid of your romantic notions about the media business. We've never been anointed to change society, you know. That's the job of the politicians we elect. Our job is to find out what's going on and print it. How society handles that is society's problem."

Marti's eyes narrowed. He noticed the crow's feet radiating from their corners and was saddened by the toll the years had collected. What had become of the softness that had been the essence of her beauty? "That's bullshit and you know it!" she raged. "You put the names of these guys in the paper and label them faggots! What right do you have to speculate about their private lives? What is that going to do to them? To their careers, to their families? And you have the nerve to justify it?"

To Stan she sounded out of control. In all the years of their marriage he had never seen her like this. "What has *happened* to you? How could you be so reckless and insensitive? Where is the man who used to deplore Joe McCarthy? *Deplore* him? You've *become* him!"

Marti was conscious of her overreaction. But the pain of seeing her once-perfect liberal knight stoop to supermarket tabloid levels was devastating. To her, Stan's column implying that a number of major-leaguers were homosexual, an article without substantiation, without responses from those identified, was as immoral as the evil they had once fought against together. His descent into sensationalism fed her emerging fear: that marrying Stan had been a terrible error, a dreadful mistake.

The fury of Marti's attack led Stan to consider a new direction. "What's happened to *me?*" he asked sarcastically. "What's happened to *us?* We never talk any more. You're unapproachable." Then he added, "In every way." The sense that she had gone from indifference to outright contempt chilled him.

Marti turned away toward their bedroom. She knew he was right. Their relationship had been deteriorating for months, maybe years, but neither of them had addressed it. He no longer called during the day nor held her reassuringly at night. If he had problems in his work, why hadn't he told her? She missed the intimacy. She felt shut out, unwanted. And now *this*. An act that symbolized a breach in what Marti regarded as the intellectual basis of their marriage: a shared set of progressive values.

His revelations, even based on Scrappy's unsupported statements, did not worry Stan. As unlikely as some of the allegations seemed, Stan reasoned that the Gents' owner would have no purpose in misrepresenting the players. His wording, the newspaper's lawyer had assured the editors, was vague enough to overcome a libel suit, a remote threat at any time. Besides, the ordeal of proving one's sexual orientation in court would doubtless add a substantial obstacle to any legal challenges. If all else failed, Stan believed that the sympathetic tone of his column, which urged that talent alone should determine eligibility, would mitigate any damage.

For some if not most readers of "Mann to Man," however, a different message came through: The majors had been infiltrated by homosexuals; each roster probably included a couple, and among them were some of the leagues' top players; the whole notion of baseball as a "man's" game was being undermined; and this was the worst disaster to befall baseball since, and possibly including, the notorious Black Sox scandal of 1919.

Among those reaching such conclusions were virtually all members of the baseball establishment. Their capacity to deal with Mann's disclosures, coming as they did on the heels of the Toote announcement, was being sorely tested. The news sent a shock wave through the owners and managers, the sponsors and advertisers, the suppliers and vendors, and even the broadcasters and reporters. Each, in his or her own way, had a vested interest in the maintenance of the myth, in the nurturing of the tradition, in the creation of the legends and lore that had transformed a game into a sport, a sport into an institution, and an institution into an industry. The concept that baseball possesses some magical quality that creates virtue through teaching sportsmanship is challenged daily on the nation's playing fields, where deception, hostility, and ill will are regarded as effective strategies that lead to all-important victories. The credo that sports "builds character" has been violated so often that it has been rewritten to state that what it actually does is *reveal* character, usually negatively.

The suspicion that baseball could no longer be equated with masculinity, an implicit aspect of its traditional appeal, was not good for business. The probability that gays had permeated baseball did not seem likely to raise the stock of the national pastime. It figured, then, that something would be done to get rid of them.

In such heartland major league cities as Cincinnati, St. Louis, Houston, Cleveland, Kansas City, and Dallas–Fort Worth, reaction to the news that a number of top-notch players were suspected of being gay was predictable and vigorous. One inventive team publicist even promoted a banner and effigy day with a homophobic theme. But there were exceptions. In San Francisco, the revelation touched off a parade in the Castro district that culminated with a silent tribute to Harvey Milk, the slain city supervisor who had made gay activism not only respectable but politically effective. In Los Angeles, too, demonstrators, largely from West Hollywood, the area's gay enclave, staged a happening that included searchlights, a torchlight procession, and rock music.

In New York, Yankee owner Donald Bigg had barely begun to map out his strategy when Scrappy was on the phone to the targeted owners. They were astounded at Scrappy's interest in their "pariahs," overwhelmed by his offer of "man-for-man" trades. The conversations were brief; the owners too overjoyed to be suspicious. Within hours, Scrappy rewrote baseball history. He put together a totally new lineup, and it was baseball's first gay starting team. Or, as Ruby said, "Far as we know."

The wrath of the baseball establishment, sports fans, the media, the politicians, and most of the nation was unleashed on Scrappy and the Gents. And Donald led the attack. "Out! Get them out! Out of the league! Out of baseball! Out of the country!" he bellowed on every channel's 6 and 11 o'clock news. "Those flaming faggots," he added, adroitly if irrelevantly, "would probably burn the flag!"

The press raged. The story made every front page in New York, including the *Wall Street Journal.* The *Los Angeles Herald Examiner* ran head shots of the nine acquisitions, plus Toote, under the headline: "THE NEW YORK GENTS?" And in Boston, the sassy *Herald,* using the same photographs, trumpeted: "FROOT, FROOT, FROOT FOR THE HOMO TEAM." Even the *New York Times* was roused. In a brief editorial, it solemnly mused over whether "this latest stunt has reduced the national pastime to a midway act."

New York's all-sports radio station had to hire a half dozen telephone answerers to handle calls from irate fans. In reaction to a gay caller who somehow got through to a show host and praised Scrappy as "the best news since Rock Hudson," a man who identified himself as the founder of the Rush Limbaugh and Howard Stern Appreciation Society and Social Club threatened to blow up the studio.

Legislative bodies throughout the nation sprang into action, passing resolutions condemning the Gents and demanding their ouster. In Washington, senators and representatives raced to introduce bills that would keep baseball "unsullied" while taking care not to imperil its exemption from antitrust laws.

As the tornado swirled around and about them,

Scrappy and Ruby strove to remain calm and crafty at its center. Their immediate goal, Scrappy recognized, was to protect their investment. He hadn't even spoken to his new ballplayers, who, he rightly assumed, must be confused, fearful, and hostile. Although spring training was still a few weeks off, Scrappy thought it politic to bring the team together as soon as possible. Abandoning his customary pecuniary habits, he sent them plane fare to New York, along with hotel reservations and a polite summons.

It was not until the plane circled La Guardia Airport that Rhino Romanski realized he was being stared at. The man's face looked vaguely familiar, but Rhino couldn't place it until he noticed the gigantic body jammed into the seat. Mickey Mayo was six-foot-seven, the tallest major leaguer ever to play shortstop. In spite of his towering bulk, Mayo was incredibly swift and graceful.

Like a giraffe, Mayo's long legs gobbled up the infield. His upper body, inclined slightly forward, was always in balance, always ready to adjust to any unpredictable move. His gangling arms gave him an extended reach, enabling his huge hands to snare balls others could merely wave at. But Mayo's most unusual talent was his ability to snatch line drives. Once a power forward for the Georgia Bulldogs, where his muscular thighs and legs had propelled him over basketball players almost a half-foot taller, Mayo's spring now sent him soaring over the infield where, having timed his jump perfectly, he would intercept dozens of potential base hits each season, often trapping disbelieving base runners in double plays.

Mayo held the major league record for participation

in triple plays, most consecutive years, with five. No other player had accomplished that rare feat even in two successive seasons. In an era notable for small, swift, Spanish-speaking shortstops from San Pedro de Macoris in the Dominican Republic, he was a throwback. Sportswriters old enough to have seen Marty Marion, compared Mayo favorably to the tall, slender, esteemed Cardinal infielder of the 1940s. Rhino nodded respectfully to the giant.

Mickey acknowledged Rhino's nod with a wink and, after their plane taxied to a stop, fell in behind him in the aisle. "Some stuff, huh?" Mayo said in his soft Southern accent as they filed through the passageway into the terminal.

"I'm still spinning," Rhino replied. "It's like somebody's pushin' buttons."

Mayo put an enormous hand on Rhino's shoulder. "Let's us get a drink," he said.

With his short, thick-necked bulk, Rhino looked like Sancho Panza beside Mayo's Don Quixote as the two ballplayers walked briskly through the crowd to an elevator that deposited them in the restaurant overlooking the runways. Rhino noticed the stares directed at Mayo and was pleased that Mickey had not acknowledged them. This was not the time to test fan reaction to the news that had convulsed the sports world.

"I'll be a sumbitch," Mayo said, "but I never knew we all had anythin' in common besides playin' the All-Star game."

Rhino grinned. "Y'never know, do you?" He shook his shaggy head.

They ordered beers from a sullen waitress. "Bad, huh?" Rhino asked, anticipating the response.

"Like I'm packing to come to New York," Mayo said. "And my wife's packing for good."

"She didn't know?" Rhino asked without surprise.

"That's what she claimed. Shoot, I don't know. I'm sure she suspected. I'd be, y'know, out late and stuff like that. No real explanation. Maybe she figured it was women. Folks believe what they want." They had gotten married right out of high school, Mayo said, before he'd had a clear sense of his homosexuality. It wasn't until a few years later, in college, that the sexual appeal of his fellow athletes convinced him that he was gay. By then he didn't have the courage to tell his wife. Besides, he admitted to Rhino, he had no difficulty in finding male partners.

Mayo signaled for another round of beers before continuing. "We never really talked about it. We'd make it OK, most of the time." Mayo shook his head and grinned wryly. "Sometimes I'd have to think about some guy I just left."

Rhino, while single, had no problem accepting the fact that gays, men and women, could be married. He had met enough of them. In some of the gay bars, especially in the suburbs, they seemed to be in the majority. He'd be talking to some guy standing next to him and they would be hitting it off pretty well and then when he asked for a phone number the guy would say, "No way. You can't call me at home." And on the way out of the bar he'd slip on his wedding band.

He'd read about the phenomenon. How some gays really believed they were straight or that being married would make them so. Or how they used marriage as a cover. Or how in some cases they truly didn't know *what* they were and so yielded to pressure. So far as he was concerned, people, especially gay people, ought to be allowed to behave as they chose.

"Anyhow," Mayo said, draining his beer, "it doesn't take any great imagination to figure how she'd behave when my picture wound up on the front page of the *Cincinnati Enquirer*. They made it like the biggest thing since Pete Rose. She just held up the paper and asked, 'Is it true?' I couldn't even answer. And then she said, 'You prick!' and started packing. Funny thing is, she always wanted to live in New York."

"Maybe she'll think it over and come back," Rhino offered.

"I don't rightly know," Mayo said. He shrugged. "I don't know if I'd want her. Or if it would work. It's like they stripped all of us naked on national TV. I don't rightly know what's gonna happen to us next. What've you heard?"

They ordered another round. "Me?" Rhino said. "I don't know beans. All I know is I started getting bad vibes when Toote sounded off. You know how the newsies are. Something can be going on for a hundred years right under their noses, they don't even know about it. Then, all of a sudden one of them discovers it, they all go crazy like sharks after blood. Like they didn't know ballplayers did coke till they nailed Hernandez and Gooden and like that. They act like Rose was the only guy ever bet on games.

"Anyways," the bulky catcher continued, "I got this feeling it wouldn't be long before the writers'll be sniffing around, trying to find out who else's gay. Next thing I know I get a call from Phineas Foxx, the guy who covers us, asking me if I want him to print my denial. 'Denial of what?' I says. 'Why that you're a fag,' he says.

'Who says I'm, I'm that?' I says. And Foxx, he says, 'A sportswriter up in New York. Guy named Mann. Used to be big in the business.' I says, 'I know who Stan Mann is.' So Foxx says, 'Well, what about it?' And I says, 'Foxy, if you never before tried to have sexual intercourse with yourself, I suggest that this would be the appropriate moment to try it.' "

Rhino paused for a swig while Mayo roared in appreciation. "I let the phone keep ringing for a day or two, and then I took it off the hook. Next thing I know I get a telegram from the front office saying that I've been traded to the Gents and good luck. So I called New York and got Ruby, who I know for years, and ask him is it true. He says it 'soitinly is' and that I'll be hearin' from Scrappy soon. Then I get a plane ticket in the mail and a reservation at the Hotel Pennsylvania. And that's what I know."

They sat in silence as another round was downed. "So how do y'all think they found us out?" Mayo asked.

"Damn," Rhino said, "I never even thought about that. I guess I always had it in my mind that it would come out some day. But, Mick, that's a good question. Who would've known?"

"Yeah," Mayo added. "And who would've told?"

"Yeah," Rhino said angrily. "Where did Mann get that stuff from?"

"Hey, man, it'll come out one of these days anyhow. It always does."

A new waitress appeared. Evidently they had drunk through the shift. "You guys want more?" she asked.

"Yes'm," Mayo replied. "Bring us a couple each and save yourself steps." She smiled and left.

"Well," Mayo said, emerging from the depths of his thoughts, "it sure looks like we've got one helluva team."

"Y'mean," Rhino said, lifting his glass in a toast, "one helluva *gay* team."

The Pennsylvania, one of New York's more durable
hotels, has catered to several generations of athletes,
tourists, conventioneers, snowbound commuters, and
others attracted by its convenient location, opposite
Madison Square Garden and Penn Station. Its most
glamorous days, or, more specifically, nights, were during the 1940s, when, its Café Rouge was home to the big
bands of the swing era, and its telephone number —
Pennsylvania six-five-oh-oh-oh — even became the title
of a hit song.

Nowadays it serves more mundane functions. But
such was not to be the case on this morning, as Scrappy,
accompanied by Ruby, confronted his potential starting
lineup in a large suite he had reserved for the occasion.

Scrappy had to admit, on looking them over, that the
guys resembled nothing so much as a group of superbly
conditioned young athletes. There wasn't a hint, from
where he stood, that the happening was unprecedented,
that he was facing, at least presumably, the first all-gay
team in the history of major league baseball.

In the few days that had passed since Scrappy ac-
quired his new ballplayers, momentum had built across

the nation to *do something* about this trauma to the American psyche. The baseball establishment, led by Donald Bigg, was in the forefront of the assault, although there were a few, even within the hierarchy, who admitted — off the record, of course — that they doubted anything *could* be done. They ventured that even the Supreme Court, still dominated by Reagan-Bush appointees, would be unlikely to contort itself sufficiently to deprive a legitimate group of citizens of their constitutional rights.

On the record, however, there was little support for the Gents. Voices raised in the team's behalf were few, and the attention they received was limited, and generally snide. The American Civil Liberties Union, in a story downplayed in the nation's press, contended that the right to play baseball was protected by the First Amendment guarantees of freedom of speech and assembly. An ACLU spokesperson cited the "inviolate" entitlement of players to argue with umpires and to congregate at the mound during a pitching change. Although gay activists, as expected, continued to cheer this latest evidence of gay achievement and to bemoan the homophobic reaction, the media did little more than duly note their statements, illustrating them with familiar photographs of Gay Pride Day marchers holding hands. The Gay & Lesbian Task Force got more attention when it demanded priority in obtaining season box seats along the first and third baselines for Gents home games. According to the press, this demand was unnecessary, since, according to unidentified observers: "The stadium will be empty; they'll be able to get any seat in the house."

As the team members chatted with one another, renewing old acquaintanceships or initiating new ones, only Toote seemed visibly upset, his jaw muscles working like pistons. He had accosted Scrappy briefly when the owner-manager entered the suite, muttering, uncharacteristically, "You son of a bitch," but was taken aback when Scrappy snarled, "*You* know where it started, where it all came from."

Now Scrappy was calling for attention by banging a spoon against a glass. "OK, you guys," he said in a commanding voice, "and I want you to know that's what you are to me — guys — I got a few things to say, is why I got you here. First off, I think we got a helluva team. I mean, world champeens. But it ain't gonna be easy. We, I mean, you, are the first *fag* team ever."

Scrappy paused while the words hung in the air. Toote, his face contorted, began to rise, but Scrappy cut him off. "Now I know you don't like to hear that. But you're gonna hear it. And a lot more. You're gonna hear it from the bench and you're gonna hear it from the stands. You're gonna hear it when a pitcher throws at you and when a runner goes to take you out. You're gonna hear it from the umpires, too. And the writers and the coaches and even the batboys. And that's another thing: stay away from them kids.

"You guys been around, so you know there's a lotta red asses out there, a lotta mean bastards who ain't gonna be worryin' about hurtin' your feelings. None of you has run into this kinda thing before. By the time you black guys got up here, it wasn't nothin' special. Not like when Robinson and Campy and Newk and the other ones come up. Ask them how it was. And that's a picnic in the park compared to how it's gonna be for you. At least you wasn't supposed to go after blacks, even if everybody called 'em niggers when they wasn't around. But fags? Hey, gays is still fair game. Well, you know better'n me."

The players looked at each other uncomfortably. A few squirmed in their sofas and armchairs. Scrappy acknowledged their discomfort.

"OK, OK. All's I'm saying is don't expect nobody to back you up or help you out. You're on your own, and you better know it right at the start."

From Scrappy's opening remarks, they clearly seemed convinced of that. For his part, Scrappy apparently felt he had expended enough compassion for the time being.

"Now it's time to talk business," he said. "You guys are here because you was traded. And you was traded because you was gay. It had nothin' to do with the way you played ball. Your old clubs didn't want you around. They was scared of the fans. In the old days it was the same with nig—I mean, with blacks. The clubs said they didn't mind having 'em as players, it was just that the white fans didn't want to sit next to 'em in the stands. Well, I don't give a shit who sits in the stands, long as *somebody's* sittin' in 'em. And when you guys start playin' ball and playin' good, they'll be comin' by the carload. And I mean *everybody,* no matter where they like to put their dicks. That's gonna be good for you. It's gonna be good for me." Scrappy paused and scratched his graying head. And I think it's even gonna be good for baseball."

Scrappy looked around the room, making eye contact with each player. "Now we got a few things to clear up. First thing is that the trades was conditional on you guys bein' healthy. Now we might as well put it straight.

I ain't talkin' about bad knees or rotor cuffs or heel spurs. I'm talkin' AIDS. Any you guys got it, you're outa here. And the way we find out is, you take a test. The test says you got it, that's it. Gone."

Toote was instantly on his feet. "Look, Scrappy, you can forget that! Nobody can make anybody take such a test. Nobody has to and, if I have anything to say about it, nobody's going to."

Scrappy stared at Toote and strutted toward him belligerently, his chest out. It was the way he approached umpires to challenge a call. "Let's get somethin' straight right now," he barked. "You guys work for *me*. Maybe. You don't like the deal, good-bye. But I don't see it any better for you anyplace else. I'm the best thing happened to you and you better believe it. Far as the rules go, forget 'em. They ain't made rules for what we got here. Not yet, anyhow. The trades say 'healthy,' and healthy means no diseases. And no diseases means no AIDS. You take the test or you take a hike."

Rhino Romanski, perched next to Mickey Mayo on the arm of a sofa, pointed a misshapen finger, the victim of scores of foul tips and crossed-up pitches, at Scrappy. "Look, *mister,* maybe you hold our contracts but you don't *own* us. Not now or never. I don't know yet how all this came down, but we didn't get here by no accident. You got us here, so I figure you *want* us. Probably more like *need* us. Anyways, there's somethin' *you* better know. This has been one big ballbreaker for us. Our lives have been turned around and it ain't over yet. Mister, you don't have an idea in the world how we feel right now. So you better just take it easy. You got rights, sure. But we got rights, too. And if we gotta spend the season together, you better wise up and start treatin' us like we mattered. You want somethin', *ask* for it. Like you was dealin' with anyone else."

Grunts of approval sounded. Mayo clapped Rhino on the back. "You tell 'im, man." Toote vigorously shook his head in agreement.

Scrappy turned toward Ruby for help. The little publicist nodded at Romanski. "You're right, Rhino. You soitinly are. Scrappy here gets a little excited sometime so it don't mean anything, it's just his way." He sneaked a look to see how Scrappy was reacting. Satisfied that he hadn't overstepped his bounds, Ruby continued. "It's what makes him a helluva manager. Look, *everybody's* uptight a little. It's natural, seeing what's happening. We all gotta cool down a little, watch ourselves, y'know. Scrappy, he just meant to tell you what the deal calls for. Look, it'll make you feel any better, I'll take the test myself."

Rhino smiled. "Never mind you, Ruby." He aimed a crooked finger at Scrappy. "Let *him* take it." There was a loud murmur of agreement from the players. Scrappy again looked toward Ruby for guidance, and the publicist responded with a quick nod.

"OK, Romanski," Scrappy said. "You got it."

"Hey!" Mayo exulted. "Now we're gettin' somewheres."

Scrappy examined a sheet of paper on which he had scribbled his agenda. Pleased that this major obstacle had been cleared so easily, he had to hope now that all the HIV tests would prove negative. "OK, OK, that's taken care of," he said with relief. "Ruby'll let you know when they're gonna take your blood. Then we gotta wait a coupla weeks to get the news. And like I know it's gonna be good news. Right? Next thing has to do with what goes on off of the field."

There was a stirring among the players. Toote sighed and shook his head, Mayo rolled his eyes, Romanski grunted.

"Now I don't give a shit what you guys do with each other ... or anybody else," Scrappy began. "I mean I myself, in my own mind, y'know what I mean? But we got a team here. And our *team,* it *does* give a shit. A big one. The whole world's gonna be watchin' us this season. Watchin' and waitin'. Waitin' to see you guys play, yeah. But waitin' even more to see you guys foul up. 'Specially if it's for doin' what they think you guys do every chance you get. I don't think I gotta draw pictures for you, y'know what I mean?"

The players shifted uneasily. Gigolo Johnson got up, walked to the window, and looked out at the city.

"Look," Scrappy continued, "it's time you wised up to what people think. I mean, they don't think what you do is terrific, y'know what I mean? Like with some of your boys in Washington, for example. You take your gay congressmen, say. I mean, a guy has the guts to say what he is, there ought to be respect. Respect, hah! They go after them guys like they broke into the Mint. Meanwhile, presidents go around screwin' like jackrabbits, even sneakin' broads into the White House, for Crissakes."

Johnson turned toward Scrappy, bobbed his head slowly from side to side as if weighing his new boss' sincerity, and returned to his seat.

Scrappy went on. "What I'm gettin' to is that now you gotta think of youselves like you was on probation or somethin', like everybody's watchin' your every move. That whatever you do is gonna wind up on the front page. With pictures.

"Like they're all out to nail us. Yeah, us! Because I'm

in this just like you. Maybe more, 'cause I didn't *have* to expose myself, you know what I mean? I wouldn't be surprised if that bastard Donald Bigg puts detectives on you. They get somethin' on you, that's it. They'll throw us outta the league. You know when Jackie Robinson come up to the majors, I know it's before your time, but one of the main reasons Branch Rickey picks 'im is because Robbie had the balls to behave himself no matter what. It takes something special to keep your head when they want you to lose it. Y'know, he played tougher'n nails but he never give nobody no excuses to dump 'im. And believe me, *everyone* was out to nail *him*.

"I'm sayin' that's how you guys gotta think of yourselves. As not givin' no excuses to nobody. OK. Now what that means is no fooling around. Like in the showers. And no screwin' around with kids."

Toote arose, red-faced with anger. "You don't know what the hell you're talking about! You sound like an idiot! You don't even realize who you're talking to! You're talking to people who've spent most of their — our — lives hiding. Not because we did anything wrong, but just because we were ourselves, or tried to be. We don't need any lessons from *you* in how to behave. *We* know what it's like out there. If anyone needs lessons, it's you."

Before Scrappy could retort, Ruby stepped in. "You're right, Dick. We know that. Scrappy's just, you know, being Scrappy. I mean, what the hell would he do with himself if he couldn't sound off?"

The new Gents smiled a little.

"Let's just treat each other like human beings," Toote said, adding, in a good imitation of Scrappy, "OK?"

"Sure, sure," Ruby agreed. "Right, Scrappy?"

Scrappy looked at Ruby with annoyance. "Sure, sure," he mimicked. "Whatever Toote says. Like *he's* the authority."

"The point is," Toote persisted, "we're not freaks. We're not *that* different from everyone else, including *you*. And we don't think about sex 24 hours a day. Or kids, goddamit! So maybe you should just cool it with some of your wisdom and philosophy."

Scrappy swallowed hard. He would have loved to belt Toote. How good it would feel, getting rid of all the pretense that had been building since their first conversation in that queer joint. But this wasn't the time, he cautioned himself. Not now.

"Well," Scrappy said. "I just want you guys to know we got some shit to deal with that we never run into before. And Ruby and me got a few ideas for handling it. So what if it costs a few bucks? And you should realize I ain't talking just a *few* bucks. You know what I mean? Ruby knows some guys can stop Donald and them other bastards from keepin' us off the field and can make you guys the hottest ticket in New York. You just gotta leave all that to me and Ruby. Now, any you guys got questions, spit 'em out."

Mayo was on his feet so quickly he almost knocked Romanski off the sofa. Scrappy involuntarily retreated before the giant shortstop.

"What I want to know," Mayo demanded, "is how that Stan Mann found out about us?"

"Jeezus, Mickey," Scrappy replied with angelic innocence. "Wouldn't we all."

$\infty\mathbf{11}\infty$

In the full-length mirror that hung on the inside of his closet door, Rick Volpino, marketer to politicos, stars, and royals, admired his new ocher shirt. Like virtually everything else in his office, the door was walnut, rich and warm, the way he liked to think of himself. He did not merely *feel* important; he *knew* he was. He had just hung up after a call from the White House; not the president, this time, but a name close enough to the Oval Office to command attention when Rick dropped it casually later in the day.

Name-dropping was part of his game. But it had to be done with tact and skill. If it were too obvious, it would defeat its purpose, which was to suggest the status of the dropper without revealing his need for self-promotion. Name-dropping was accomplished best, Rick had determined over the years, in response to a question. The ultimate example being: "*Who* told you that?"

Rick barely breathed without first considering the consequences. He prided himself on being calculating, delighted that he was a *self-made* man in every sense. Those he dealt with found his seeming indifference to their reactions endearing without realizing how carefully he cultivated the pose. He knew, for instance, that the ocher shirt—he had ordered two dozen to be custom-made—clashed with anything else he could possibly wear. That, in Rick's opinion, was the point, for the bizarre color, which resembled a rotting orange, was simply the latest affectation he had devised to call attention to himself.

He continued to bleach one eyebrow snow white, as he had since getting into the promotion-publicity-marketing-lobbying dodge 30 years ago. That distinction, together with his swarthy complexion, jet-black hair, and thick black mustache and beard, made him difficult to ignore. (Rick grew the mustache and beard, a rival wisecracked, to avoid facing himself in the mirror every morning.) He disdained the likelihood that clients would question his taste; to him, tastelessness and vulgarity were simply qualities, like all others, to be exploited in the interests of acquiring fame and fortune.

Clearly he was right. He and his award-winning firm, Mea Culpa, had become a national phenomenon, first making the cover of *Business Week,* and then of *Time* and *Newsweek*. Its bookings brought in extraordinary amounts of money, even considering the inflated milieu in which it functioned. Its list of clients reflected the leading figures and institutions of the free world, and beyond. Presidents, both of conglomerates and countries, were among Mea Culpa's clients, as were dictators, active and deposed, and more than one royal family. Board chairmen, committee chairmen, and party chairmen sought advice and counsel, along with entertainers, educators, authors, and athletes. In an age when image had become reality, Rick had become indispensable.

Volpino's keen intelligence, unencumbered by scruples, equipped him perfectly for his endeavors. While still in college, he conceived of the brilliant ploy that had launched his career in the occult sphere of public relations, promotion, and marketing. The strategem, credited with re-electing an unpopular governor, became his trademark, and subsequently "my fault," in its Latin form, was adopted as the firm's name. The idea was simplicity itself: convert flaws into assets by not only admitting but also flaunting them.

At first the idea had been ridiculed. Generations of politicians, practiced in deception and subterfuge, greeted the campaign commercials Rick concocted with guffaws. He'd had the governor up there on the screen actually confessing his mistakes, drawing notice to his errors and lapses and failures. With an unforgettable scene of blizzard-stalled traffic on the thruway displayed behind him, the governor said that it was *his* fault the superhighway hadn't been plowed. Pointing next to the indelible photo of an embezzling aide being hauled off to prison in handcuffs, the incumbent admitted that *he* had exercised poor judgment in making the appointment. It had been revolutionary. The approach was so refreshing, the governor seemed so credible, that neither the media nor the electorate ever realized that by acknowledging the political equivalent of adolescent pranks, he had succeeded in concealing what were tantamount to capital crimes. The incumbent, a tremendous longshot before the campaign, had won reelection easily, and the inevitable postmortems made Rick the latest political genius.

He quickly recognized that this idea of "false honesty" had broad applications, politics being just one aspect of contemporary life steeped in deception and chicanery. Within weeks he had set up shop and begun advising and devising. His first clients were drawn from the seedier entrepreneurial ranks — used-car dealers and aluminum-siding jobbers — but his striking innovativeness had soon attracted more notable operators: savings and loan officers, TV evangelists, and Wall Street arbitrageurs. Mea Culpa had endured, then flourished.

Most recently, he had accepted the gratitude of a youthful TV anchorman who, losing his hair with incredible rapidity, almost lost his job as well when, on screen, an ambitious and unscrupulous colleague sent the TV personality's toupee flying with a deftly directed fan blast. The anchorman pleaded for Rick's assistance, and the media wizard came up with a campaign to glorify baldness. "Bald Is Beautiful" was the opening salvo, followed by "Being Bald Means Never Having to Use a Comb." The final full-page ads showed the anchorman with a shaved head. For the next two weeks, according to Nielsen and Arbitron, hardly a New York viewer had watched any other newscast. On the third week, seven other anchors, including three women, shaved themselves bald.

Pleased with the inharmonious effect created by his new ocher shirt, Rick checked out his appointment calendar and noted with satisfaction that Scrappy Schwrtznbrgr and Irwin Rubinstein were due momentarily. Rick liked sports, particularly associating with celebrity athletes. He collected famous people the way others collect stamps or coins, and athletes comprised a significant portion of Rick's name-drop stockpile. So when Rubinstein had made a guarded and, so far as Rick was concerned, unnecessary reference on the phone to the "Gents problem," he was already aware of the problem and welcomed the challenge.

Scrappy and Ruby arrived on time and, at Rick's direction, were purposely kept waiting by the receptionist. Rick never liked to appear readily available. After the compulsory ten-minute delay, Rick buzzed the outer office and the receptionist announced that they could go in, tearing Ruby away from the mass of autographed *Time* and *Newsweek* covers papering the walls and Scrappy from scrutiny of the receptionist's cleavage.

"I guess you know what's goin' down," Scrappy said after the introductions had been completed.

"Oh, yeah," Rick replied, grinning puckishly, "I hear it's your whole team."

"What we want, Volpino," Scrappy continued, as if he had not heard, "is (a) to stay in the league, and (b) to fill them seats. Ruby says you know what you're doin,' so I guess we leave it up to you, y'know what I mean. But, hey, Volpino, we ain't millionaires like Donald, so we gotta talk money."

"I won't bullshit you, Scrappy," Rick said. "I'm interested in the project. I like problems and you've got a big one. I've been thinking about your situation, and I've got some ideas. Good ones. If I take this on, it won't be for the money, it'll be for the fun. I need control, though. I need to be in charge — completely. I do this, you've got to let me go on my own. No checking with you or Ruby or anyone else. You don't see the commercials before they're shown, you don't see the ads before they're printed, you don't see the uniforms until they're made. I get that from you, you get me for nothing. All you pay is costs, not the 15, 20 grand a month I usually get. And I won't even hit you for the commission on commercials and ads."

Scrappy was out of his chair, his hand extended. "Volpino," he said exuberantly, "you got it! And by the way, I really like that shirt."

Scrappy and Ruby were barely out the door before Rick was on the phone to Dore Dupus, his public opinion analyst. Dupus had been something of a mathematical standout at MIT before deciding that the kind of numbers he favored most were preceded by a dollar sign. If there is such a thing as affiliation at first sight, it occurred when Dupus and Volpino met at a Washington cocktail party. They had spent the evening locked in fervid conversation about the potential of polling not simply to reflect public opinion but to shape it.

Dore had explained how he had helped his client, unknown and underfinanced, upset a wealthy incumbent congressman. "We ran a poll in one little part of the district, see," he had told Rick. "Nobody ever heard of our guy, so he gets maybe 20 percent to the other guy's 80. For the next couple of weeks we take every buck we can find and pump it into that area — posters, brochures, buttons, palm cards, phone calls, you name it. But just in those few blocks, see. Then we run another poll. This time, naturally, our guy does better — gets 40 percent. Now, we take the two polls and start going after campaign funds. We say to big-money people, 'Look what this guy did in just two weeks — he doubled his support! Imagine if he had the bucks to keep going!' They're impressed. Who wouldn't be. Of course we don't tell them it was just a couple of hundred people involved. Well, the bucks start pouring in and we win going away."

"Terrific," Rick had said. "What happened to the guy?"

"Well, he kept me on the payroll for one term, then dropped me after I got him reelected," Dore had continued. "Now, I got me a new boy. Can't wait to knock off that other sonuvabitch."

Rick had become so engrossed in Dore's anecdotes and contentions that he had almost forgotten that the reason he had come was to solicit potential clients. Like legendary twins who complete each other's sentences, he and Dupus had found perfect alter egos in each other, sharing thoughts even before they could be articulated.

"Dore," Rick now said excitedly into the phone. "Have I got a job for you!"

Dupus wasted no time in getting to the Mea Culpa offices. He had, in fact, merely to take an elevator to the twenty-third floor of the glistening midtown skyscraper. Rick's terse description had set his nimble mind racing. He loved high-profile projects, work that offered the chance of startling the public and dazzling his peers. He hated mainstream thinking and conventional attitudes, including ethics.

As he huddled with Rick, Dore clearly saw that his mission to enhance the gay team would necessitate a bit of sorcery, some subtle sleight of hand to make the Gents viable, marketable and, just possibly, respectable, although the latter was not expected of him. It was a task for which he was eminently qualified; Dupus was a world-class authority on manipulating opinion by distorting data.

Pollsters, Dupus often told listeners after consuming enough booze to be honest, owed their existence to the media. "Ask your man-on-the-street, assuming he's not being mugged, what he thinks about polls, and he'll tell you that they're full of baloney," Dupus would say. "But the press lives by them. The readers say, 'How can 1500 people represent 240 million?' They're right, of course, for the wrong reason. A valid sample *can* reflect a much larger population. But polls *are* full of baloney. Because the results are based on how the questions are asked. Example: Roper does a poll for the American Jewish Committee in 1992 that finds 1 in 5 Americans doubt the Holocaust happened. Naturally people—especially Jews—get all shook up. Finally, over a year later, they figure out maybe the question was so poorly worded people were answering the opposite of what they thought. So they change the wording and guess what? Only 1 percent say it never happened!

"Now the newspapers and TV really *like* polls. They've even gotten into the business themselves. They like it because it takes the pressure off them. Instead of putting themselves on the line assessing a campaign and maybe coming up with the wrong winner, they run a poll. And to cover themselves further, they throw in a warning, like the surgeon general's, telling readers that the numbers could be off by a few points. As if that's *all* they could be off by. As if the *margin of error* was all you had to worry about."

Dupus, warmed up, could not be stopped. "Hell, let *me* write the questionnaire, I'll get you any results you want. Those stories *ought* to carry a warning: Believing polls is dangerous to your health."

If any listeners inquired further, or, generally, even if they didn't, Dupus would proceed to explain the techniques of question-wording, because it was here that he really earned his six-figure income. He'd demonstrated his skills most dramatically the time he worked both sides of the capital punishment issue — and satisfied both proponents and opponents within a two-week period. Dupus did this by first conducting a poll that asked: "Do you think it is fair or unfair to make a convicted murderer pay the same penalty as his victim?" and subsequently directing another survey that asked: "Do you think it is right or not right for a government to kill its citizens?"

Rick and Dore had quickly determined that the most effective way to solve the "Gents problem" was by avoiding a head-on collision with Donald Bigg and his like-thinking colleagues in the baseball and political arena. Too much power and tradition to deal with there. Instead, they would take the time-tested approach that government leaders follow when confronted by balky legislatures: they would go directly to the people. If they could build a groundswell of support for the Gents, an outpouring of public demand, they were confident they would thwart any efforts by Donald, the baseball establishment, political reactionaries, or religious fundamentalists to keep the gay team off the field.

The first step, they agreed, was to conduct a public opinion survey that would show overwhelming approval of the Gents' right to remain in the major leagues. The results would be leaked piecemeal to one paper after another for a week, to create momentum.

The finale would be a press conference at which Donald would be taunted not only as un-American, for trying to prevent the ballplayers from making a living, but as a coward who sought to undo behind the scenes what he feared facing on the diamond: a superior team.

Dore's assignment, to come up with the appropriate findings in an apparently legitimate way, gave him only momentary pause. After a few minutes' thought, he ordered a batch of reference books and, while awaiting their delivery, began dashing off questions on a yellow pad.

Experience with the media had taught Dupus that few reporters enjoyed more than a superficial familiarity with the polling process, and that such ignorance was even more widespread among their editors. This, of course, made it easier for him and his counterparts to deceive the public. They simply had to satisfy the journalists' concerns about the number of interviews and the distribution of the respondents by gender, age, education, income, religion, and political affiliation to guarantee acceptance of the results.

With this in mind, Dupus realized that "fixing" the Gents poll was simplicity itself: the questions would deal with gay rights, so he would concentrate interviews among the gay population. Since the survey would be conducted by phone, researchers would select exchanges in gay neighborhoods, ensuring a preponderance of sympathetic replies.

Inside of a week, Dore's staff had come up with findings that presented near-unanimous endorsement of the team's continued presence in the major leagues. "It's almost too good," Rick said ecstatically. "You're right," Dupus agreed, erasing an 89 percent response to a key question and penciling in a 79. "Credibility is very important," the pollster said.

Volpino, satisfied with the survey results, decided to leak to the *Daily News* first. "They'll play it big *and* they've got the readers," he explained to Dupus. "The others will pick it up from them. If I go first with the *Post,* nobody's liable to believe it. Although that guy Mann still carries some weight. I'll give it to him next and then *Newsday* and finally the *Times*."

"I thought the *Times* had the most influence," Dupus said.

"You know anybody who reads it for *sports?*" Volpino asked in explanation.

The following day, armed with a sheetful of data, Rick had lunch with a veteran *News* sportswriter he had known for a decade. "You're kidding," the writer said when he was shown the figures. "I was surprised myself," Volpino said, "but I guess people just resent the way Donald tries to push folks around." The responses they were discussing, which dealt with whether the Yankee owner's campaign against the Gents was motivated by self-interest or a concern for the integrity of the sport, had been conditioned by questions relating to examples of Donald's outrageous past behavior.

The next morning's edition, with a tag line identifying the story as a *News* "Exclusive," reported the poll findings under a headline that read: "DONALD TRUMPED, FANS SEE HIM UP TO OLD TRICKS."

At lunch that day, Volpino asked Stan Mann what he would like to drink. "A little of the milk of human kindness," the *Post* columnist said, "after what you handed the *News* yesterday."

"*Moi?*" Rick said, affecting an expression of injured

innocence. "You think I would stoop to leaking to the press?"

"Of course not," Mann said. "It was just another example of imaginative, diligent, painstaking reporting by one of our great urban tabloids. By the way, what are you selling today?"

"Funny you should ask," Rick replied. "I came across a terrific piece of information for you, my friend. Enough to build a column on. It has to do with gay athletes. And *this* time you can attribute it."

"Never mind the sarcasm, Volpino," Mann said. "At least newspapers tell the truth *occasionally*."

"Enough," Rick said, making a T with two fingers to signal a time-out. "Let's get along for an hour or so. It'll do us both good." Reaching into his cowhide briefcase, he pulled out two sets of white sheets containing columns of numbers, and handed one set to Stan. "This is how baseball fans feel about the rights of gays to play baseball, compared with their rights to teach, to practice medicine, to hold public office, and — oh, yes — to write sports columns. Impressive, isn't it?"

By week's end, hardly a living New Yorker was unaware of the tremendous support felt by fellow citizens for the new Gents team, and their deep enmity toward anyone — especially Donald — opposed to its playing. In addition to the stories in the *News, Post, Newsday,* and *Times,* there had been interviews on the morning and afternoon TV shows, and film clips on the 6 and 11 o'clock news. Dupus had appeared several times to explain his findings; Toote had made himself available for a dignified *Nightline* discussion in which he commented, "Let's not abridge the freedom to play baseball," and even Scrappy had participated in a panel with several sports reporters, asking "What's Donald *really* afraid of?"

The effort produced its desired effect. After Scrappy called a news conference to officially announce the poll results and issue a stinging challenge to "let baseball work out its differences on the field, in front of the fans," Donald and his allies decided to hold their fire until the Gents self-destructed. "They'll screw up," Donald assured a political crony. "Scrappy's always been a loser."

"*Waddayuh hear?*" Rhino Romanski asked Mickey Mayo over long distance. The Gents had dispersed around the country after their New York City get-together.

"I reckon I passed," the outsized shortstop drawled. "I got my contract in the mail this morning."

"Congratulations," Romanski said, with a trace of irony. "I guess I did, too. What about the others?"

"Y'got me. Why don't y'all give Ruby a call, then let me know."

Rhino hung up and checked his address book. It was a helluva thing, he thought, finding out if your teammates had AIDS. He shuddered. Like other gays and an increasing number of straights, Rhino had friends who had succumbed to the relentless disease. Girding himself, he phoned.

Ruby laughed when Rhino asked about the results of the blood tests. "We got one positive," the Gents PR man reported.

"That's funny?" Romanski snarled.

Ruby continued chuckling. "You remember, Rhino, you were the one made Scrappy test?"

"You bet I remember."

"Well," Ruby chortled, "he came up positive."

"Bullshit!" Rhino said.

"No," Ruby said. "I swear. Wait'll I tell you. You know how Scrappy is. He says, 'There's no way I'm goin' to any clinic full of faggots. I'll go to my own doctor.' So he goes. And it turns out he's the first guy his doctor ever ran the test on. And he comes up positive, like he's got AIDS for Crissakes. He almost went crazy. I was the only one he could talk to about it, and he's goin' through his whole sex life tryin' to figure out how it could have happened. I told him, 'Look, Scrappy, let's go back to the doctor and try again.' So he goes back and this time the doc sends it out to a lab. Well, Rhino, you know it takes a week to get the results back and Scrappy's off the wall. First off, he starts drinkin', an' I mean major league. He was practically in a coma for a couple a days. Next time I see him, he's up to his ass in books. Yeah, medical books, regular books, all kinds of books, all about AIDS. He starts askin' all these questions, like 'Where the hell did I pick it up?' 'What one of them bitches give it to me?' Then, he starts talkin' about gay people. Not sore or anything, but kind of sympathetic. He even says to me, 'Jeezus, Ruby, now I know what it's gotta be like for these poor fuckers.' Anyhow, the results come back negative. The doc says the first time was what they call a 'false positive.' He said it happens more than anyone thinks."

"I love it," Rhino said. "It couldn't have happened to a nicer prick."

"Yeah," Ruby muttered. "Look, while I got you, there's somethin' else we gotta talk about. I dunno if anybody's been after you, but the reporters have been botherin' me for stories, interviews with you guys. Now, my thinking is, instead of each of you going through all the crap they're gonna throw at you, we decide on one of you, maybe Toote, to be the spokesman. If you guys agree and he's willing, we set up a press conference and let him deal with all the questions. How's that sound, Rhino?"

"To me, it sounds terrific, Ruby. The less I have to do with reporters the better," Romanski said. "You want me to check with the others, I will."

Rhino shared the Scrappy anecdote with Mickey Mayo and each of the other ballplayers. And they shared his willingness to let Toote do their talking. They realized, when their contracts arrived, that they must have tested negative. But three of them, the only new Gents not covered by multiyear agreements, said that Scrappy had offered them 25 percent less than they had been paid the preceding season. They were meeting with their agents, they said, to discuss negotiating strategy.

When Rhino got back to Ruby, the crusty catcher was furious. "That's some line you give me about that prick Scrappy caring. Now he's tryin' to cut salaries. Assholes all over the league who couldn't hit their weight are makin' millions and that sonuvabitch is tryin' to squeeze our guys. And we know it's because they're gay and he figures he can get away with it."

"Easy, Rhino," Ruby said placatingly, "that's the way Scrappy does. It's, y'know, a negotiating move, an opener. He don't mean nuthin' by it."

"Yeah, well you can tell him it means plenty to us," Rhino shouted. "He better stop jerkin' us off this way or he's gonna be lookin' for a new ball club. We're not gonna take this crap. We had to keep our mouths shut in lotsa ways, but no more. It's all out in the open now. We got nothin' to hide now."

"You're right, Rhino," Ruby said, "you're right. He shouldn't have done that. But that's just Scrappy. Look, I'll let him know how you guys feel. Tell me about Toote. Is it OK for him to do the talkin' to the press?"

Rhino, still seething, let the silence build. "How about it?" Ruby persisted, "how about Toote?"

"Yeah," Rhino spat. "It's OK. Just straighten out your boss first."

From the snatches of videotape and the news stories about the press conference and its aftermath, the players were pleased that Toote had represented them. Stan Mann was pleased, too. Considering the dearth of cooperative, articulate athletes, Toote was the answer to a writer's prayer. Makes a helluva role model, Stan thought. He was particularly taken with one of Toote's ripostes, captured in a sound bite and rerun incessantly: "Don't look for our pats, look at our stats."

A week later, over lunch, Mann asked a startled Toote, "How do you feel about spring training in Key West?" Of course Dick Toote was familiar with Key West, Florida. Like Manhattan's Greenwich Village, San Francisco's Castro district and Cape Cod's Provincetown, Key West is a gay haven in an often hostile world. While most of the city's 25,000 year-rounders are prototypically straight merchants, travel agents, fishermen, and Cuban refugees, a lively and self-sufficient homosexual colony flourishes there, the last of the coral islands that trail like raindrops from the Florida peninsula. While its main artery is Duval Street, lined with a tacky collection of T-shirt shops, seashell stands, fast-food joints, and bars, the real gay scene vibrates in the guest houses and hotels, and particularly in the Copa, a throbbing disco with five bars.

It was at one of the five, Toote recalled with a bittersweet rush of memory, that he met Bart, a blond, tanned fisherman who had shared his life for an idyllic week before Toote had to return to his chill, northern apartment. They had talked and danced and strolled through the lush, sultry subtropical breezes to Mallory Dock, where they watched the jugglers and musicians and cat trainers perform before the sun drowned in the sea. Then, back in the inky isolation of Bart's room, they too sank into the press of their bodies and the intensity of their desire.

But Stan Mann's question about Key West caught Toote unawares. Apparently Ruby had fed the information to the columnist without mentioning it to any of the team members. The idea had originated with Rick Volpino, who told Ruby that the "new Gents" marketing concept involved being "totally up-front" about the players' sexual orientation. The choice of Key West as a spring training site was the opening volley in exploiting a gay-identity theme for the club. When Volpino had outlined the plan, Ruby had shrugged, acknowledging the authority that Scrappy had ceded to the promoter. Scrappy only wanted to know how much the spring training venture would cost, and became ecstatic when Volpino said they would be able to use Tommy Roberts Memorial Stadium, the Key West High School sports complex, without charge. They would also get a discount for rooms at the Island House.

In response to Mann, Toote said that it sounded all right to him. "You wouldn't feel uncomfortable there?"

Mann asked. "That depends," Toote replied, "on people like you."

Toote liked the way things were going. The team was beginning to come together, he felt, because of their shared sense of singularity and their continuing distaste for Scrappy. In sports as in life, he thought, hate could be as strong a force as love.

As he counted down the hours to opening day or, as Stan Mann persisted in describing it "Coming Out Day," Scrappy felt better and better about the Gents' prospects for the season. While he had been around too long to place much stock in exhibition games, he felt that this year the Gents' victories really *did* mean something. It was not simply Pollyannaism, he was convinced, but a judgment based on observation. He had never doubted their talent; the Gents were loaded with it. But Scrappy did have some concerns about cohesiveness from players who had never before shared a diamond, except in All-Star competition. And, of course, they were gay, which to Scrappy meant they were likely to be unstable, unreliable, and unstrung.

If he had not known that his players were homosexual, it wouldn't have occurred to Scrappy to consider or even notice their movements and gestures. But once he knew, he couldn't resist looking for indications, however slight, of the effeminacy he equated with their sexual orientation. The fact that such mannerisms never materialized didn't end the matter. "They move pretty good, considerin'," he muttered to Ruby during the first intrasquad game.

"You mean considerin' they're some of the best ball-players in the league?" Ruby replied.

Actually, the team's gayness *was* relevant. And, inevitably perhaps, the players' relationships moved on-field. Scrappy was perplexed initially by Mickey Mayo's delayed throws to second base on double-play balls. It wasn't that the throws were costly: Mayo always got the force-out, and "Speedy" Gonzalez, the second baseman, invariably got the ball to Toote in time to nail the batter. But by the time Mayo's toss got to second, the base runner coming down from first would be almost on top of Gonzalez, compelling him to jump like a jack rabbit to avoid being mashed or spiked. The scenario became clear to Scrappy only when he learned that Mayo and Gonzalez were both dating the right fielder, Chico Santiago.

Scrappy was baffled. He had dealt with hundreds of frictions and feuds and domestic disputes over the years. And it was not unusual for teammates to be involved with one anothers' lives, including one anothers' wives. But it was, as Scrappy put it, "unusual" for *all* the participants to be on the field at the same time. Ruby cautioned patience. "These things don't last, Scrappy," he advised. "These kinda guys, they're like fickle." Ruby's reputation rose immeasurably in Scrappy's eyes a few days later when they saw Santiago coming to and from the ballpark in a Mercedes convertible with a trim, well-dressed companion who was neither Mayo nor Gonzalez. Thereafter, Scrappy noted with satisfaction, Mayo's tosses to Gonzalez seemed to arrive significantly earlier.

Keeping to his agreement with Volpino, the Gents' owner-manager did not involve himself in the marketing plans for the team. He had no idea, therefore, what promotions were afoot or why Olivia Jacob was talking to herself in front of a mirror in a nondescript office in Melville, Long Island.

"Allll right, you fans, this is Ollie Jay coming to you from Gents Stadium on a bee-yoot-ti-full day in early April . . . Naw, not right."

"Hey, you guys. And you gals, too. We don't forget the ladies here at Gents Stadium on Opening Day. Nosirr. I mean, nosirr and no ma'am, Olivia Jacob is here to tell you that you are watching history . . . Oh, crap."

"Okay, baseball fanatics. And you fans, too. Ha, ha. This is your telecaster Lady Jay bringing you the Opening Day festivities at the hottest ticket in New York, Gents Stadium . . . No way."

"You see that grass? You see that diamond? You see those stands? You know what that means? It means another baseball season is under way. And this year, for the first time, the New York Gents are being brought to you by the FNG Cable Network, that's FNG, which stands for 'Fun 'n' Games,' and me, I'm O. J. Cobb . . ."

The office door banged open. "Olivia, I got your mother on the phone. She wants to know how you feel. Talk to her. Please."

"Sure, Dad, sure. In just a second. Dad, I think I got it. I think I got my image, my persona. Even my name. It's O. J. Cobb. O. J., get it? Like Simpson. I know he got into trouble, but that wasn't sports. And Cobb, like Ty Cobb. It's sports all the way. And it's my name, too: Olivia Jacob. Get it? The "O" is for Olivia and the "J" and the "Cobb" are from J-A-C-O-B. It fits. It really fits. This is it. It's gonna work this time, I just feel it."

"OK, honey, that sounds terrific. Really terrific. Just

talk to your mother, will you? She's holding on the phone."

"Mom, hi. You're talking to O. J. Cobb. That's gonna be my professional name, my TV name. How do you like it? . . . Well I know it doesn't sound Jewish. It's not supposed to. You used to listen to Melvin Allen Israel doing the Yankee games, only you thought it was Mel Allen . . . Sure, maybe it would be better if everybody knew he was Jewish, but then maybe he wouldn't have gotten the job in the first place . . . Yeah, I know being Jewish means we have to try harder and so that makes us better. That's what Dad told me when he gave me the job of chief sportscaster at FNG . . . OK, Mom, I know I deserve it, after some of the bad breaks I got. But that's all history. Now my career is in front of me. You're gonna be proud of me, Mom. And Dad, too . . . Sure, Mom, I know maybe he doesn't show it all the time, but he really cares . . . Of course, and about you, also . . . I love you, too, Mom. And folks, that's 30 from O. J. Cobb."

Olivia went back to the mirror and examined what she saw. She practiced smiling, raising her eyebrows in astonishment, looking stern and shaking her head in exasperation. She liked the way her long, straight, dark hair shimmered with movement, and she was glad she hadn't succumbed to the impulse to dye it and become "Red Jacob." That, she felt, had been a sophomoric idea. Literally. It had come to her during her sophomore year at Syracuse, where she had gone to learn the communications business at a school that produced sports reporters with the regularity that its athletic program turned out ranking basketball, football, and lacrosse squads.

In the highly competitive collegiate arena, Olivia's

skills had gotten scant recognition — except from her sorority house roommates, who had tersely critiqued her unsolicited descriptions of imaginary events by urging her to shut up. Similar if less pointed assessments of Olivia's talents followed her after graduation. Taking universal suggestions to go "out of town" for experience, she applied to radio stations in Enid, Oklahoma; Monroe, Louisiana; and Biloxi, Mississippi, without success. Her father, a prosperous sportswear manufacturer, under pressure from Olivia's doting mother, pulled strings to get her a "gofer" job with CBS. But that turned out to be short-lived when Olivia, assigned to work the U.S. Open tennis championships, showed up at the West Side Tennis Club in Forest Hills ten years after the event had moved to the National Tennis Center in Flushing.

Then her father, Morris Jacob, tired of the garment business and harried by his wife to "take care" of their daughter, sold his firm to a Japanese investor, bought a deteriorating warehouse 55 miles out on Long Island, and formed FNG to develop cable TV sports and recreational programs. Olivia, a devotee of George Plimpton, the editor-writer who made a substantial living by thrusting himself into unlikely professional athletic roles and describing the resultant sensations, talked her father into sponsoring a series of events for *her* involvement. Pretending to believe Olivia's contention that viewers would be interested in following her adventures, Morris financed a foxhunt, a caravan, a square-rigger cruise, and a safari, and dispatched a camera crew to record his daughter's experiences.

As FNG checks were dispatched hastily to guides, outfitters, and agents in Virginia, Cairo, Papeete, and

Nairobi, unsettling news of Olivia's exploits kept her anxious parents in suspense back on Long Island. She was thrown repeatedly from her horse at a Middleburg hunt and became desperately lost on the Sahara sands. She was seasick in the South Pacific and immobilized by dysentery in Kenya. The Jacobs were so relieved to have their daughter home alive that they never asked if any of the adventures had been filmed, and Olivia was relieved of the need to report that they hadn't.

With such events in mind, the elder Jacob leaped at the opportunity to televise the Gents home games when his old friend, Ruby Rubinstein, happened to mention that the club had been unable to attract any coverage, even for free. Recalling his past subsidies of his daughter, Morris quickly calculated that any venture that kept Olivia busy would realize a net gain. It would also keep his wife quiet. Morris quickly called Rick Volpino to do lunch and a deal.

Even if it hadn't been Opening Day, April 5, 1996, would have deserved a write-up: New York's steel-gray winter sky had evaporated into a buoyant spring-borne blue, across which puffs of cottony clouds floated like bubbles. The city was bathed in penetrating sunshine, and at Gents Stadium this warmth coaxed a musky promise of renewal from the dormant turf.

Outside the ballpark, Olivia Jacob, in her O. J. Cobb persona, led her ragtag camera crew from the parking lot to the press gate, which, after a brief confrontation with a disbelieving security guard, they were permitted to enter. For Olivia, such challenges to her credibility had become routine. In contrast to the well-placed media who oozed confidence and legitimacy, Olivia was aware she invited disbelief by not only being female, but also by projecting the image of a bumbling impostor. Yet because her response to encounters with petty authority was to radiate a good-natured enthusiasm, she generally disarmed her abusers and achieved her purpose.

Olivia's appearance, like her manner, was decidedly offbeat. Although tall and slim, she lacked coordination to the extent that even the most routine movement was jerky, as if some invisible puppeteer were in control.

Her body language, exaggerated by the swish of her long, black hair, induced sympathy in the way a newborn colt seems to cry out for assistance. Totally unselfconscious, Olivia was oblivious to her innocent appeal. On this special day, she refused to allow the guard's skepticism to mar her upbeat mood. "Remember this face," she said airily, pointing to her unremarkable features, "you'll be seeing a lot of it."

The guard's doubts were not unrealistic. The FNG "team," as Olivia generously identified them, consisted of a single cameraman and a lone sound technician, the latter also serving as producer-director. The security people were used to more substantial operations. For example, at Yankee Stadium and at Shea, FNG's counterparts would be telecasting the action with five cameras. There would be play-by-play announcers and descriptive color men, as well; even a third personality to change the pace. There would be directors and technical directors and lighting directors, producers and production assistants and stage managers, audio men and video men and cameramen, Chyron and Dubner operators and video operators, statisticians to supply instant data, maintenance people to make instant repairs, and runners to provide instant food and drink.

With such an array of operatives and equipment, the networks and major independents would be giving *their* viewers ever-changing perspectives based on the directors' imaginations and inclinations as well as the vagaries of the game. For those watching FNG, the picture would be somewhat different. Olivia, cameraman Phil Pluckey, and soundman Ears Edison would do the pregame show with a minicam, then rush to handle the Gents' opener from the traditional position behind home plate, where their solitary camera was set up.

Olivia was aware of these discrepancies. But she was not dismayed: she was, after all, covering Opening Day in the major leagues, a role that made her feel that she had triumphed over gender and adversity. "I'm in the majors, too," she crowed to herself.

Because they had come through the press gate, Olivia and her associates were unaware of the extraordinary preparations under way to welcome the paying fans. As they made their way through the deserted, labyrinthine interior of the stadium, they could not see the frenetic activities going on at other levels. They were ignorant of the grand scheme that Rick Volpino and his throng of consultants had devised to present and promote the new Gents. They didn't know that vendors were ripping open cardboard cartons to display the pink and lavender purses that Rick Volpino had bought with Scrappy's money but without his knowledge — to give as souvenirs to the first 5,000 ticket holders — male as well as female — who passed through the turnstiles.

The colors were not chosen casually. They were official, selected to adorn the facades of Gents Stadium, designate the seating sections, even cover the bodies of the Gents ballplayers. Carefully chosen and designed by experts in selling tickets, the motif that Mea Culpa had adopted was what Volpino would describe as "bold," and what others would call "gross," "crude," and "flagrant." It incorporated every gay stereotype. Home uniforms were pink with lavender trim; road uniforms were the reverse. The costume was augmented with leather caps, earrings, and robin's-egg blue mitts. The shade of the gloves matched the Gents' caps and spikes.

At the very moment that O. J. and her crew were

approaching the Gents team, the ballplayers discovered their new adornment. Their reaction roared from the clubhouse, through the tunnels and reverberated under the stands. It sounded like a riot. Olivia and her companions hurried toward the source.

"No way!"

"This is total bullshit!"

"Stick it, Scrappy! Shove it!"

"They can all go screw!"

"Never! Never! I'll never wear this crap!"

"What we are, amigos, clowns?"

"I piss on *your* Gents, you Scrappy bastard!"

The clubhouse was in chaos. Pink and lavender uniforms were strewn about the room. Light blue caps and mitts and spikes covered the floor like discarded gift wrapping. Speedy Gonzalez was pounding on the metal door of his locker. Rhino Romanski was beating a tattoo against a wastebasket with his new spikes. As Olivia trotted in, she skidded on some earrings just as Dick Toote stepped onto a bench.

"OK! OK, you guys, hold it down!" Toote yelled.

The racket gradually subsided into a fading echo. "Are you fed up?" he shouted, in his best demonstration-leader style. "Right on!" "Hell, yes!" the players shouted back. "Have you had enough?" Toote roared. "Fuckin' right!" they roared back. "Are you ready to take a walk?" he asked. "We're with you, Dick!" Rhino replied. "All the way!" Mickey Mayo chimed in. "Walk! Walk! Walk!" the players began chanting.

At that point, Scrappy appeared in the doorway of his office. He put a police whistle to his lips and blew an ear-piercing blast. The players' heads snapped around to face him. "What's goin' on here?" he bellowed.

"What the hell do you think?" Toote snarled. He

grabbed Rhino's pale blue spikes and a matching leather cap from Dave Ripp, the Mussolini-jawed third baseman, and held them at arm's length like bags of fetid garbage. "Did you really think we'd wear this nonsense? And these goddam earrings? You must think you got yourself a freak show!"

Scrappy looked astonished. "What is this? Where'd you get it?"

Romanski sneered, "Come off it!" Ripp groaned loudly. Mayo rolled his eyes.

"C'mon, Scrappy, for Crissakes!" Toote replied, "What're you pulling? Don't act surprised. You can forget that routine."

"No, I swear," Scrappy insisted. "I never saw this stuff before. I don't know nothin' about it."

"Sure, sure," Toote said, "you don't know what goes on here. You're only the manager *and* the owner!"

"I know, I know. But I swear I never seen any of it." Scrappy paused a moment to allow a thought in. "Wait a minute, wait a minute. I got an idea of what's goin' on. It must be somethin' Volpino come up with."

"Oh, sure," Toote said. "Some other guy's the owner now."

"No, no, just listen, will you? This Volpino is a marketing guy. I hired 'im to keep us in the league and sell some tickets. He wanted to run the promotion all by himself. I figured I got enough to do, so I let 'im. I figured he knows what he's doin'. He didn't have to check nothin' with me. I swear, Dick, I didn't know nothin' about this till just now."

Toote shook his head in disgust. "Pretty stupid, don't you think? Or maybe you just don't give a damn about us. Well, I can tell you you're really off base. You don't know the first thing about handling *this* ball club. What you've got is a walkout. Opening Day or whatever, nobody's going out on that field looking like trained monkeys."

"OK, OK, you're right, Dick," Scrappy conceded, "I hear you. But we got some problems. I mean, these got to be the only uniforms around here right now. Sure, the earrings are real stupid, even though half the guys in the league wear 'em. Forget *them*. And you guys got your own gloves. But the uniforms, Dick, I don't see what I can do about them right now. Like we only got a couple hours till game time."

"Well, you better start thinking fast then," Toote said.

"Look, Dick, be reasonable. You play today — without the earrings, of course — and I promise I'll straighten this out soon as I can."

Toote faced his teammates. They looked unconvinced. "Leave us alone for a while. We'll talk it over."

Scrappy nodded and walked out of the clubhouse. In the ensuing silence, the only sound was the soft whirring of a minicam. The players turned and for the first time became aware of the FNG crew. Phil Pluckey, the cameraman, immediately stopped videotaping.

"How long you been here?" Romanski asked.

"Only a minute, not even," Pluckey lied. "I was just testin' the equipment."

Olivia and Ears, the sound man, pressed forward to support him. "What's up?" Olivia demanded, shoving herself between Pluckey and Rhino. "What's happening?"

Romanski decided to drop it. "Never mind," he said. "Clear out now. Team meetin'."

"Yeah, sure," Olivia said agreeably, not yet assured

enough to protest. She motioned Pluckey and Edison to follow her out.

When the clubhouse door slammed behind them and they were beyond earshot, Olivia excitedly hugged Pluckey. "Did you get it? Did you get the whole bit?"

Pluckey grinned. "I'm not FNG's top cameraman for nothing."

"Terrifico!" Olivia exulted. "How about you, Ears?"

"Every word," the soundman said. "Even the ones we can't use."

"Great! Great!" Olivia said. "This is sensational stuff. It's more than sports we're into now. It's hot news. The nets will pick it up. FNG will get credited nationwide." She paused to think. She recalled a film about journalists covering a civil war in Latin America. "Give me the tapes," she said. "I'll hide 'em in my briefcase. You know, in case somebody tries to confiscate them."

Pluckey and Edison exchanged amused expressions, shrugged, and handed the tapes to the daughter of the guy who paid their salaries.

"Good, good," Olivia said. "Now, let's wait here and see what happens next."

Behind the closed clubhouse door, the players unanimously named Toote to represent them in dealing with Scrappy. After the initial wave of humiliation and resentment had subsided, they discussed the benefits and liabilities of a protest walkout on Opening Day. Toote made his position very clear.

"Minorities can't depend on goodwill. Or fairness or morality," he said. "The only thing that works is pressure. You need to create fear. Make them realize they've got something to lose."

But as the other players spoke out, the fear that

emerged most clearly was theirs. Mickey Mayo expressed what seemed to be the majority view. "The way I see it," said the towering shortstop, "we're ballplayers first. And ballplayers just don't walk out on Opening Day. We got enough problems as it is without the writers gettin' on our case. And you know they will. No matter who's right, you can bet *we're* gonna be wrong."

When the vote came, only Toote supported the boycott. He shook his head in resignation. "Some day they'll learn," he said to himself, convinced that any compromise would be regarded as weakness. But for now he had lost; now he had to consider how to wrest some value from the surrender.

A few minutes later when he got together with Scrappy, Toote gave a somewhat doctored version of the players' meeting. He said that after a sharp discussion that revealed a deep division, the team had voted to postpone the boycott pending Scrappy's delivery on his promise to supply traditional uniforms and equipment. He stressed that Scrappy's integrity was on the line, adding sarcastically, "and it's not the *bottom* line we're talking about."

With the boycott averted, Scrappy's belligerence returned. "Hey, Dick, I don't need none of this right now, OK? I told you I'd straighten this out and I will. Don't get me pissed, because we're all in this together. Sure, Volpino went too far. But *he* knows we're in show business and *you* better not forget it. Don't pretend that sports ain't entertainment and that athletes ain't rakin' it in these days just because it is."

Scrappy paused to let his point penetrate. "And don't forget to let your friends know that if it's not for me they wouldn't be wearin' *any* uniforms. They'd be playin' volley ball on Fire Island this summer. Now Ruby tells me there's a TV crew waitin' to do an interview. How about we do it together? I'll get Ruby here."

Scrappy felt a twinge of guilt for his sarcasm. He knew that he usually went too far; certainly Ruby was constantly telling him so. But that was the way he had grown up: yell loudest, bluff most convincingly, and if it comes to blows, make sure you land the first punch. Old habits die hard, he thought.

Toote had never heard of FNG, much less Olivia Jacob and her tatty band, so he was understandably suspicious when the three-person cable crew confronted them outside Scrappy's office. But Olivia produced her press credentials so cheerfully, beamed at him so proudly, that Toote had to smile despite his rancorous mood.

"We're covering the Gents this season," Olivia explained to Toote, "and we want to assure you that we'll be doing our usual professional job. I'm O. J. Cobb. This is our top cameraman, Phil Pluckey, and our ace sound-man, Ears Edison.

"How're things goin'?" Olivia continued. "We heard some yelling a while back. What was that all about?"

"None of your bus—" Scrappy began, but Ruby cut him off.

"Just a little enthusiasm," the public relations man said. "You know, new team, new season. Lotta excitement, lotta spirit. You're a lucky gal, O. J., gettin' in on the ground floor with this club. You're talkin' world champions."

"I know, I know," Olivia agreed. "I'm thrilled. So now we'd just like to get a few words from you guys on how the team looks, what kind of problems you expect, what the other teams look like. A season perspective on Opening Day. You know."

"You mean," Scrappy said with a grin, "the usual bullshit." Olivia nodded appreciatively, thinking how proud her parents would be. Scrappy's rough-hewn manner was legendary and now it was embracing her, too. Perhaps she could become as tough as the man she was interviewing, as authentically professional.

••16••

When the routine interview with the Gents management — all clichéd questions and answers — was over, Olivia, Phil Pluckey, and Ears Edison walked out onto the playing field through the dugout. The season's initial view of the bright green sod flooded Olivia with bitter-sweet memories of her first major league game.

She was five or six years old, and, as her father often reminded everyone, his only child FELL ASLEEP DURING THE FIFTH INNING. Still, she could experience it all again now, see herself tightly clasping her father's hand for protection against the crowds. She remembered being lifted over the turnstile, walking up the concrete ramps, and being overwhelmed by the sights and the sounds.

First, they encountered the vendors in white jackets selling programs and scorecards and pencils from booths just inside the entrance, and the souvenir stands displaying caps and T-shirts and toy bats and colorful pennants decorated with cartoonish illustrations of animals and birds and costumed figures. There were tigers, cubs, orioles, cardinals, and blue jays, along with pirates, priests, angels, and lots of Indians. Her father led her past lines of impatient fans waiting to buy hot-dogs and beer and soda and peanuts. When they turned up a narrow ramp there was a sudden blaze of sunlight, and she saw the stadium stretching out before her like the ocean.

It was the greenest field Olivia had ever seen, especially where it met the reddish-brown dirt of the infield. She thought its perfect symmetry was like a drawing in one of her coloring books. Her eyes followed the foul line beyond first base into the outfield until it collided with the right field wall and then continued its climb over the wall until it became one with the foul pole. She traced the other foul line until it disappeared behind a portion of the left field stands.

The outfield wall caught her awed attention with its large white numbers measuring the distance from home plate. Above it there was a huge, black scoreboard crammed with information she couldn't decipher, while below were massive signs promoting all manner of products. It was a world stranger and more wonderful than any she had ever visited: better than the zoo, the circus, even Disneyland. And she wanted desperately to be part of it some day.

Now, some 20 years later, Gents Stadium held Olivia's rapt gaze again. But for a different reason this time. The TV crew stared in astonishment at the stadium's extraordinary transformation, conceived by Volpino's experts. The outfield wall was no longer a dark green. It was lavender. And so were the sections delineating the field boxes. The next level of seats, the loge, was painted pink. Above it, the mezzanine was lavender. And the upper stand was pink. There were none of the familiar signs advertising newspapers and electronic equipment and cigarettes and beer. There was only one: the phone number of the AIDS hotline.

As Olivia took in the striking panorama, the immense video screen in center field blinked into life, revealing a transvestite chorus line sequence from "La Cage aux Folles," the popular French comedy about gay lovers. While the video operator rehearsed the program scripted by Mea Culpa, the public address system began a medley of Judy Garland hits. Olivia was transfixed. No national institution had been so subverted, she thought, since anti–Vietnam War demonstrators burned American flags on the Capitol steps. "Holy cannoli!" she said. "This is historic."

As Olivia mused and Phil and Ears began discussing camera angles, an outrageous figure came out of the Gents' bullpen in right field. Olivia removed a pair of binoculars from the nylon bag slung over her shoulder and trained them on the strange shape making its way in their direction. "Holy fagioli," she said, adding a low whistle, "wait till you grab this." She passed the glasses to Phil Pluckey, who adjusted them vigorously. "I don't believe it!" Pluckey said, handing the binoculars to Ears Edison. "We gotta get *this,* Phil," the sound man said. "We'll make every highlights in the country."

Pluckey zoomed in his minicam on the figure lurching toward the infield in high heels. He gauged the height at a minimum of six feet six inches and the weight at close to 400 pounds. Spike heels supported a body wearing a lavender skirt and a pink blouse emblazoned with a Gents logo, the familiar silhouette of a top-hatted patrician brandishing a baseball bat. A huge red wig topped by a miniature Gents cap completed the outlandish picture. The face, unequivocally masculine, was heavily made up: the eyebrows exaggerated, the cheeks deeply rouged over a shadow of whiskers, the lashes blackened and extended, the lips reddened and shaped in a clownish grimace. When he saw them watching him, the creature minced provocatively, affected a limp-wristed wave, and called shrilly, "Hi, gang! Meet Gentian Violet, your drag-queen mascot."

"Holy Hannah!" Olivia said. "Get that!"

As Phil and Ears turned their equipment on Gentian Violet, Olivia's focused her attention on the dugout and the emerging line of neatly dressed young men wearing white shirts and dark slacks. The men filed onto the playing field, marching casually yet in perfect step, forming an intricate pattern that, when they halted abruptly, was diamond-shaped, a diamond within the diamond. Olivia watched in fascination, then walked out to home plate where the group's apparent leader was stationed.

"Hi!" Olivia said cheerfully, extending her hand, "I'm Cobb of FNG Cable."

The trim man shook her hand. "Ron Fisher. New York Gay Men's Chorus."

"Wow!" Olivia said. "What's up?"

Fisher smiled. "Homophilia, I guess. We've been invited to sing the national anthem."

"Holy cow!" Olivia said. "What next?"

"Check it out," the director said, pointing toward an unmistakable outline waddling in their direction. It was the turnip-shaped profile of the mayor, trailing aides like ducklings in his wake. Olivia, excited over the prospect of an exclusive interview, trotted toward the mayor, whom she had never met.

"Good to see you again, Mister Mayor," she said in her most respectful professional voice. "What brings you out today?"

"Always a pleasure," the mayor said, wondering who this girl was and what she was doing on the ball field. "It's another season, right? It's my town, right? So who else would throw out the first ball?" he chirped. Neither the interviewer nor her subject was aware of the interminable number of calls Rick Volpino had made, personally, before gaining an acceptance. He had exhausted even his list of has-been entertainers and long-forgotten athletes before the mayor, an early choice, had reluctantly agreed to participate.

For the mayor, the decision had not been easy. Public doubt about his sexual orientation, based on his bachelor status well into middle age, had been excuse enough to lead opponents into circulating rumors during his three election campaigns. Now poised on the edge of a fourth run for office, he was urged by his advisers to surround himself with sexy young women and avoid the Gents like AIDS. But the mayor was stubborn. And the prospect of a public appearance, anywhere with anyone, was irresistible.

But, he had scornfully told his political counselors, he was not a *schmuck*. That was when he triumphantly unveiled a huge button that covered almost half his chest. It said: I AM HETEROSEXUAL. It was that button he now had an assistant remove from an attaché case. "Get your cameraman over here, sweetheart," the mayor said jauntily, as he pinned the plastic badge to his suit jacket.

Fifteen minutes into the interview, Pluckey covertly turned off the minicam. He wanted to save enough videotape for whatever else the day might have in store, and the mayor showed no signs of ending his response to Olivia's first question: "Was this good for tourism?" The mayor was so absorbed in his monologue he failed to notice that the telltale red light had gone out. Olivia, also unaware, allowed the mayor to go on. The unrecorded discussion continued for another ten minutes until the mayor's press secretary said, "Hey, you ran out of film."

It's just as well, Olivia thought. The Gay Men's Chorus had dispersed after rehearsing their *a cappella* rendition of "The Star-Spangled Banner," and a few were leaning against the boxes along the third baseline, chatting with Gentian Violet. The morning was fast disappearing when the Gents ballplayers emerged from the dugout and jogged onto the field to take batting and infield practice, shag flies, and run wind sprints.

They were wearing the pink uniforms and robin's-egg-blue spikes and caps designed by Mea Culpa. However, they were carrying their own mitts. No earrings were visible. The warm-up seemed unexceptional. But as Olivia and her crew moved around, singling out players for interviews and action shots, it became evident that it was anything but routine. The players were as nervous as cats at a dog show. "We're human, y'know," Rhino Romanski said. "This is gonna be like nothin' else that's ever been." Even Dick Toote had lost his customary calm. "Who knows about the fans?" he wondered aloud into O. J.'s microphone.

Toote's apprehensiveness was well founded. Fans from throughout the metropolitan area were preparing for the trip to Gents Stadium. It would be an event of major proportions, attracting a more diverse group than a congressional hearing on abortion rights. As Toote spoke, a Long Island chapter of Young Americans for Freedom was waiting for the paint to dry on an outsized banner before heading out to the ballpark. "How does it look?" asked Patrick Henry Turncrank, its creator, confident of the response. "They'll get the message," replied YAF leader Joseph Raymond McCardy with a grin.

At the same time, in the West Village, members of the New York City Gay & Lesbian Antiviolence Project were readying themselves for the confrontations that awaited.

"Faggot!" yelled Hank Minuet in the face of Mike Galliard.

"Homo!" Galliard shouted back.

"Queer!" Minuet screamed.

"Fag!" retorted Galliard.

"Fruit!" bawled Minuet.

Chuck Mazurka stepped between them. "OK, OK, guys, that's cool. If they get violent, kick 'em in the balls."

17

At the **Post,** Stan Mann was getting ready to cover the game. It was, he felt, *his* game. After all, "Mann to Man" *had* helped father the new Gents, even if the players failed to appreciate it. They were, he thought, damned ungrateful. Stan had found it nearly impossible to get any information out of them; they turned their backs or walked away when he approached. Burly Rhino Romanski had made some threatening guttural sounds that Stan interpreted as foreclosing communication.

Nevertheless, Stan's bosses at the paper were still speaking pleasantly to him, although that was hardly the case with Marti. Their marital relationship had plumbed new depths. These days Stan was leaving for work as soon as possible in the morning and stopping for a few drinks before returning home. Alone at the bar, he repeatedly reappraised their marriage in an effort to comprehend its failure, even wondering if their decision not to have children had been a mistake. The strain at home was depressing and incessant, the conversation limited and terse. Since his column identifying the gay ballplayers, Marti's contempt was almost palpable. After a few attempts at justification, he had given up.

When she did speak to him, it was only to reiterate her anger and disappointment. "I thought McCarthy was dead! But I found out I married him." She seemed beyond granting forgiveness.

Stan had no idea how the conflict would be resolved. Marti's rejection of his overtures toward reconciliation filled him with gloom. Perhaps her attitude would change if he redeemed himself, but he didn't know what to do. Intuitively, he sensed he could not win her back.

Believing that the future of their relationship was in Marti's hands, Stan turned to what he had some control over: his work. He found a focus in the extraordinary event about to unfold in Gents Stadium. And so, although burdened personally and professionally, Stan still felt that lightness of spirit that accompanied the start of another baseball season. Since boyhood, he had looked to each spring with the optimism of a gardener, anticipating the excitement of Opening Day, with its virtual guarantee of unexpected events, unfamiliar faces, and unexplored talents. Three decades of sportswriting had not dulled the emotions stirred by the sight of the field and the sound of the crowd. He was ready.

As he put the *National League Green Book* and the Gents press book in his briefcase, Stan heard a chorus of shouts from some of the sportswriters who were huddled by a TV screen. "How about that!" one of them exclaimed, as the others chortled loudly.

"What's up?" Stan asked.

"Take a look, Mann, at what you've wrought," the exclaimer said.

On the screen, Stan saw two tanned, muscular young men sitting on a deserted beach at sunset. They were discussing the Gents, making plans to get season tickets. As they smiled intimately at each other, a familiar logo appeared. It was the profile of an ancient warrior surrounded by the legend, "Spartans," and adorned by what was unmistakably a package of condoms. As the message sank in, a deep male voice intoned, "To be safe at home . . . his or yours."

The scene held for about ten seconds, then faded from the screen to be replaced by the symbol of the FNG Cable network and an advisory that the Gents opening game against the Pittsburgh Pirates would be telecast live in a few hours. "Helluva sponsor for an athletic event," Stan snorted. "Yeah," agreed a copygirl, "nothin' like the good ol' breweries. At least this is good for you."

When Stan arrived at Gents Stadium, long lines already had formed in front of the shuttered ticket windows. Compared with recent season openers, it was astounding; a throwback to earlier decades when the Gents had been pennant contenders. Clearly the 5,000 pink and lavender purses that Volpino had ordered as souvenirs would represent an unnecessary expense; but just as clearly, the reason for their superfluity would bring joy to Scrappy's heart — and cash to his coffers.

Inside the ballpark, as the Pirates tuned up their batting eyes, the vendors did the same for their vocal cords. The Mea Culpa marketers had decided to introduce quiche and white wine to baseball fans, along with the traditional hot dogs and beer. The quiche and wine purveyors, selected on the basis of auditions, were required to shout their wares in falsettos, which they were now practicing at full pitch.

By game time, Gents Stadium was packed. Stan noticed that after all the seats were sold, there were still sizable lines in front of the general admission and bleacher booths. As the ticket sellers shut their windows, the waiting fans turned restive. When they threatened to charge the entrances, the chief of security nervously summoned Ruby Rubinstein, who, after estimating the size of the crowd and noting their temper, offered them standing room at five dollars apiece.

At precisely ten minutes before one o'clock, Stan watched the Gay Men's Chorus file onto the infield to sing "The Star-Spangled Banner." But before they could utter a note, a ferocious fight broke out behind the field boxes along the first baseline. Members of the New York City Gay & Lesbian Antiviolence Project had ripped into Patrick Henry Turncrank and Joseph Raymond McCardy, who were protecting fellow Young Americans for Freedom. The YAF contingent had unfurled a huge banner inscribed "GAYS SUCK."

Stan observed the scene with growing discomfort. Turning to Steve Jacobson of *Newsday,* he muttered, "It's become the national *crass*time."

For Scrappy, the Gents' Opening Day victory over the favored Pirates was a rejuvenating tonic. "Man, Ruby," he chortled to his aide, "it's ten years ago all over again." It had been that long since the Gents had won a season's opener, and longer still since they had won so impressively.

It wasn't simply the 10-1 score, pitcher Tony Mike's complete game, or the three home runs. "I ain't seen that kinda spirit for so long I can't remember," Scrappy continued. "It's like they really *like* to play, y'know play *together*."

"You're right, Scrappy," Ruby agreed enthusiastically. "It's like some of the great ones, like the '69 Mets, the '51 Giants. It's a real team, real teamwork. Like everything fits. And *no* errors! Not a one, and they had to be nervous as hell."

"Yeah," Scrappy nodded. " 'Specially with all that crap goin' on. On *and* off the field. Jeezus, that Volpino's either a genius or the biggest jerk around. I mean that Gentian Violet junk, and the fags singing 'The Star-Spangled Banner.' We're lucky we don't get locked up for treason or somethin'. That ain't baseball, that's just goddam disrespectful."

Scrappy looked anxiously toward his office door as if anticipating a flying squad of FBI agents. But there was no sound from the clubhouse. The players had showered and departed, the reporters had finished their interviews and rushed out to file their copy, and O. J. Cobb and her FNG crew had left to edit their videotapes for feeds to the networks. Scrappy and Ruby were alone.

"It's terrible, terrible," Ruby assented. Actually, he thought it was the best rendition of the national anthem he had heard in at least a decade. "But you got to hand it to Volpino the way he filled the park. I even sold standing room."

"Yeah," Scrappy grinned. "I wonder how Donald is gonna do? I'd like to see his face when he hears the attendance."

"And the score," Ruby added, chuckling.

They would have cherished the sight. Even a Yankee win failed to overcome Donald Bigg's fury as he watched the six o'clock news. "It's a national disgrace," he raged, as Gentian Violet pranced on top of the dugout and the New York Gay Men's Chorus sang the national anthem. He pointed at the screen and shouted to his wife, "That's disgusting, shameful, depraved."

"Easy, Donald," his wife said. "It's just a game."

"Game, nothing," he roared. "They're dishonoring the American heritage. So help me, I'll bring those Gent homos down."

On *their* screens, the Gents saw themselves. And they were furious, too. Watching FNG, what they saw, aside from the festivities and highlights, was the pregame eruption in the clubhouse that Phil Pluckey had secretly filmed. It was immaterial that the videotape showed them standing up to Scrappy, seeking to reject

Volpino's attempts to market their gayness. They felt exposed, violated; victims once again. Once again they were being exploited for their sexual orientation, seen primarily as homosexuals, not as ballplayers or human beings. And at the hands of a two-bit television crew they were yoked to for the season.

"Hey, Mickey," Rhino Romanski said to Mickey Mayo, in front of the screen at Mayo's apartment in Astoria, "we'll have to straighten out that TV jerk."

"I reckon I know how," the lanky shortstop replied.

"How?" Rhino asked.

"Y'all will see," Mickey said enigmatically.

"And those Pirate bastards," Rhino continued. "I mean hearin' a bench sound off is one thing. That's baseball. But I got no use for the way they were carryin' on. Huggin' an' kissin' each other. All that gay-trashing crap."

"I expect we're going to have to get used to it," Mayo said. " 'Cause I think we're going to hear it for a coon's age. We're going to hear it for sure around the league. It's like what the coloreds put up with 50 years back."

"Well, I'll tell you, Mickey, I don't buy it," Rhino said. He smacked a huge fist into his palm as his anger rose. " 'Specially the way they make it like we're sissies or somethin'. And what they were doin' with their bats, pokin' at each others' butts and all. I'm not just gonna sit around for it. And I don't think the rest of the team should, neither."

"Right, man, but what the hell can we do?" Mayo asked.

Rhino narrowed his eyes. "I'll think of somethin'," he warned. "The main thing is we got to assert ourselves. Not just win ball games, which we will. But we got to show these mothers that they can't push us around. We need respect. Let 'em know we're not gonna take it. You know, Mick, it's like when they brush you back at the plate. Your pitcher's got to retaliate, got to protect you. That's what we need here."

At the FNG offices out on Long Island, Morris Jacob pinched the cheek of his leading sportscaster. "Honey," he said, beaming, "you did one terrific job today. I'll bet you got FNG mentioned in every major market in the country. That stuff in the clubhouse with the *faygelehs* was sensational!"

"Thanks a lot, Dad. But I think Pluckey could have done a little more with the camera work. You know, better angles, some indirect lighting."

"Well, you just tell him what you think, honey," Jacob said. "You're in charge out there. And running your staff is really important. Critical, if you want to move up the executive ladder. So you tell him what you want. And I'll back you up a hundred percent. And before I forget, call your mother."

"What should I call her?" Olivia gibed. "Just a joke, Dad."

At his office at the *Post,* Stan checked his notes preparatory to launching another column. It had been an extraordinary day; actually, historic. He wanted to make that point, that baseball was at a crossroads, at another intersection of tradition and progress. He wanted to stress that sports, like all institutions, had responsibilities to society, and could lead or resist change.

Stan bit his lip. He wanted desperately to be once

again in the forefront of his profession, showing the way. Being out in front meant standing alone, using courage and confidence to stake out a controversial position. He had done that often enough in the past. But now, he couldn't get the right words to come. "I'm afraid to write what I believe, afraid of my readers, my editors, the baseball establishment", he agonized. And so he ridiculed the scene at Gents Stadium.

As usual, Rick Volpino was working late. It was his desire, his need. And, as usual, he was alone. That was when he did his best thinking, when he was most effective. He had, of course, been to the ballpark. He always checked out his jobs personally. He had left after the second inning, however, before either team had scored. It was the outcome of his work, not the game, that concerned him.

Nevertheless, he was annoyed. He had seen FNG's coverage of the clubhouse ruckus and the players' angry reactions to Mea Culpa's ideas. Rick Volpino didn't like being abused. "*Some* nerve," he said to the rich, walnut paneling. "But what can you expect from faggots?" Even the fact that there had been standing room only at Gents Stadium failed to ease his vexation.

At Gracie Mansion, the mayor of the world's greatest city asked the five members of his staff clustered with him in front of the TV screen, "Well, what do you think?"

"Terrific!"
"Sensational!"
"Great!"
"Top-notch!"

"A winner!"

The mayor nodded slowly, looked down at the "I AM HETEROSEXUAL" label he still wore, and quizzically raised an eyebrow. "Maybe the button could have been a little bigger."

∘∘𝟏𝟗∘∘

Olivia was still floating on the praise from her father
and the sight of FNG credits on all the sports segments
of the news shows she watched during a few moments of
furious channel-surfing the following night. And so
she was baffled by the icy reception she encountered
when she entered Gents Stadium for the second game
against the Pirates. While the attendants at the press
gate didn't question her credentials or those of her crew
as they had the previous day, their manner made it
apparent that she was unwelcome. When she reached
the clubhouse, where she had hoped to chat with a few
ballplayers or at least share the pleasure of their Opening Day triumph, Mickey Mayo slammed the door in her
face.

"What the heck's going on?" she asked her cameraman and soundman.

"They're probably pissed because we didn't do any
'up-close-and-personals' with 'em," Pluckey volun-
teered.

"Yeah?" Olivia responded uncertainly. "Seems like
there's more to it."

"Well," Edison, the soundman, said. "You know these

guys. Bunch of prima donnas. Like when they kicked us out of the clubhouse yesterday. Who cares?"

"You think *that* could be it?" Olivia asked. "About the footage we got of their meeting?"

"Nah," Edison replied, "look at all the good publicity we gave 'em."

"Right," Pluckey agreed. "They'll come around soon enough. They know who needs who."

"Hey, Olivia, forget it, willya?" Edison said. "Let's set up."

"Try and call me O. J., OK?" Olivia said tartly, recalling her father's advice about authority.

Pluckey looked at Edison and grinned. "OK, O. J.," they chorused.

When the trio got out to the field to install their single camera, the Gents had just begun batting practice. As Olivia watched Pluckey determine the appropriate angle, a ball caromed off the low barrier in front of them.

"That was close," she mused.

Moments later, a second ball cracked against some nearby seats. Olivia noted that Mickey Mayo was up.

"That's weird," she said to Pluckey, "somebody could get hurt."

As another ball sliced off Mayo's bat and narrowly missed them, Pluckey shouted, "You're damned right. That's because they moved the batting cage."

Sure enough, the batting cage, which normally encloses hitters and catchers during batting practice, had been pulled back about a dozen feet, allowing most foul balls to elude its netting. Olivia tried to get the attention of the Gents lounging against the cage, but nobody responded.

Pluckey fumbled with the camera housing as a barrage of adroitly hit balls attacked them. Awkwardly clutching his equipment, he began running in the direction of right field. "Let's get the hell outta here, Olivia!" he yelled.

Struggling to keep pace with her staff under a salvo of balls, Olivia glared at Pluckey as she ran. "I told you," she puffed, "to call me O. J.!"

When they had outdistanced the balls, the FNG crew pondered the situation for a few minutes before deciding where to locate their press booth.

"They'll never reach us here," Olivia said, focusing her binoculars from a distant corner of the right-field stands.

"Jeez, O. J., they look like midgets," Pluckey said, peering through his minicam.

"You mean elves," Edison chuckled. "Y'know, *little* fairies."

"*Very* funny," Olivia said sarcastically. "Let's remember who it is that's buttering our bread."

With the television team out of range, the Gents began batting practice in earnest. Rhino Romanski seemed unusually intense as he stood on the steps of the Gents dugout. Mickey Mayo, wearing a grin as big as his size 12 spikes, ambled over.

"Hey, Rhino, how'd you like the way I got rid of them TV jerks?"

Rhino seemed not to hear.

"Hey, Rhino, you awake?"

"Huh? Oh, Mick. Sorry, I was just thinkin' hard."

"I was sayin'," Mayo drawled slowly, "how'd you like the way I was clipping those fouls?"

"Oh, yeah, terrific."

"Ya could put a little more feeling in it," Mayo continued.

"Look, Mick, I'm just pissed, OK. Like I told you, I've had it with those pricks we're playin'. I don't know about the rest of you, but I'm gonna burn those guys. All I need is a way to do it."

"Well, man, don't sweat it. It'll come to you, Rhino," Mayo said. "When the time's right, you'll come up with somethin'."

Suddenly, Rhino jumped forward so unexpectedly that Mayo thought he had been shot. "Sonuvabitch, Mick, I got it!" he roared.

"Got what, Rhino?"

"Got the way to get us some respect. Watch me today," the burly catcher said. He was whistling as he picked up his bat and entered the batting cage.

Mayo did not have long to wait. When Rhino came to bat for the first time, the Pirates were continuing their homophobic bench jockeying, even intensifying it as their players, resorting to new depths of adolescent humor, tried to top one another. Batting fifth in the lineup, Romanski was leading off the second inning of what was still a scoreless game.

A left-handed batter, Rhino looked directly into the visiting team's dugout as he advanced toward home plate. What he saw made him seethe. A half-dozen Pirates were sitting apart from their teammates. Each was straddling a bat and slowly massaging the handle with his right hand, like members of a well-trained chorus line. All hands moved in unison even as the tempo increased. While Rhino stared, the Pirates rolled their eyes and let their tongues loll out of the corners of their mouths in the universal imitation of male masturbation. Then, daintily waving their left hand at Rhino, they transferred their right hand from their own bat to that of the adjacent player. The message was unmistakable.

Rhino wasted no time. The first pitch was a fastball, low and inside, and with a movement he had rehearsed a hundred times in his mind, Rhino adroitly dragged a bunt that trickled slowly down the first baseline. He let out a short grunt of gratification as he set sail for first base. Leaning forward, he lowered his head and pumped his legs and arms while gathering speed. His eyes were riveted to the foul line about a yard in front of him; he hunched his shoulders forward, thrusting his short, thick neck parallel to the ground and projecting his iron-hard batting helmet ahead like a battering ram. Rhino's timing was precise. He made contact just as the Pirates pitcher bent to pick up the ball and toss it to first base.

The sound of the collision clearly reached the FNG television equipment in deep right field, and through it, the cable channel's audience. The force of the impact sent the pitcher flying through the air until his limp body crunched into the first baseman's midsection, sending them both sprawling into foul territory. Without slackening his speed or even raising his head, Rhino sprinted across the bag and wheeled toward second base. The second baseman, transfixed by the sight of his prostrate teammates, was unaware of the brawny catcher's approach until it was too late to escape. Directly in the baseline, he took Rhino's helmet full in his solar plexus and, pitching backward, went airborne.

And still Romanski sped on. By the time the right fielder overcame his disbelief sufficiently to run down the errant ball, Rhino was churning toward third base. The third baseman, alert to the impending disaster of this one-man wrecking crew, fled toward the Pirates dugout, while the catcher, having dutifully backed up the first baseman, left the plate unprotected. Rhino steamed across without drawing a throw. He had scored an inside-the-park home run on a bunt, and disabled three opponents in the process. Turning toward the Pirates dugout, and accompanied by thundering cheers from the stands, he smiled at his erstwhile tormentors and curtsied.

Out in the right-field stands, Olivia and the guys hugged each other in anticipation of seeing FNG's film make the networks' sports highlights for the second night in a row.

The Gents 12–0 blowout of the demoralized, debilitated Pirates took a backseat to Rhino Romanski's performance. He went three for three, adding a double and a line-drive home run to his phenomenal inside-the-park effort. He also drew two intentional walks, the first from a prudent Pirate relief pitcher who thought better about becoming a target for a rampaging Rhino.

As expected, FNG's coverage made the networks' nightly news. No editor could resist the Romanski sequence, which most sportscasters dubbed a "Rhino charge" and reran several times in slow motion.

Olivia's joy was boundless the next day when she read Stan Isaacs's "TV Sports" column in *Newsday*.

After decades of routine camera work by the regulars, a refreshing imagination has come to baseball telecasting. Its name is O. J. Cobb, the bold new spirit who dares to be different — and succeeds. I'm talking, of course, about the coverage of the Gents, a team deplored and ignored by the big boys of commercial TV because of the sexual orientation of its players.

Well, if you want to see baseball the way it oughta be played, flick on FNG. What you'll see are some of the best players outside the Hall of Fame. And what you'll see them from is a new perspective: right field. Why, you will wonder, did nobody ever think of doing this before? The answer is that O. J. Cobb, the brightest sportscaster to arrive at a New York ballpark since Tim McCarver, has been on the scene for only two games. What's more, guys, O. J. is a she!

One suggestion, O. J. With a monopoly on a team like the Gents, you've got a great opportunity to break ground — sociologically. The sports world ought to be ready to deal with homosexual athletes, and some insightful, discreet interviews with the players could lead the way. And it wouldn't hurt you, either.

Olivia could barely wait to show the column to her father. "Look, Dad, look! I made *Newsday!* And Stan Isaacs, he's big time."

Morris Jacob studied the item, tapped the page with his index finger, and pointed to the columnist's picture. "He's got a nice face, that guy." Morris nodded slowly. "And you, honey, also are lookin' very good. Only make sure you don't tell no one why you're out in right field."

Olivia nodded rapidly. "Gotcha, Dad. And you know, I think he's got something with that suggestion. I could do a postgame show, bring the guys on. Not just ask 'em about the game, though. Ask 'em about their lives and stuff. You know, how it is being gay and all. What do you think?"

Morris pursed his lips and rocked slowly in his desk chair perhaps a dozen times. Then his face broadened into a huge smile. "Honey, I think you got something. It's got possibilities. When you got possibilities, you never can tell what. Who knows, you could be maybe another Oprah? Now, do me a favor and call your mother."

Within the hour, Olivia had assembled Phil Pluckey and Ears Edison for a power lunch at the Sweet Hollow Diner. "You guys read Isaacs today?" she asked, hardly concealing her zeal.

"No, Olivia — I mean, O. J.," Pluckey replied, "I didn't even get to the lottery numbers yet."

"Who needs it?" Edison asked sarcastically. "It's guys writin' about what guys are sayin' about what I'm seein'. If I can see it, I don't need to hear 'em and I certainly don't need to read about 'em."

Olivia shook her head disgustedly. "Too bad. Too bad you guys don't keep up. You don't know what's hot and what's not. No wonder."

"No wonder what?" Pluckey asked as a bored waitress wearily made her way to their booth.

"Forget it," Olivia said, not wanting to become confrontational. "Look, lunch is on me. What kind of burgers you want?"

"Hey, hey," Pluckey enthused. "You hit the lottery or something?" He feigned studying the stained menu. "How is the cuisine today, my good woman? Is it edible or is it the usual?"

The waitress stared at him. "It's a lot like the customers: cheap and greasy."

"Wow!" Pluckey said. "That's terrific! You write Seinfeld's material?"

The waitress, having exhausted either her interest or her repartee, turned to Ears.

"So?" she asked, her pen poised to take his order.

"I'll have the House Extra Super Special. Medium."

"That comes with a pickle," she said.

"I'll take it," Ears said. "And coffee. Black."

"Make that two," Olivia said.

"Make that three, so you won't have to waste your intelligence," Pluckey said.

Olivia extracted copies of the Isaacs column from her purse and handed them to Pluckey and Edison. "Take a look, guys, we're in the public eye."

"What a jerk!" Pluckey said, chafing over the columnist's failure to mention him in connection with the camera work. "He thinks we went to right field on purpose."

"Well, we did, sort of," Olivia said defensively. "But anyhow, that's not the point. The point is, number one, we got mentioned. Number two —"

"*You* got mentioned," Pluckey interrupted.

"Number two," Olivia continued, "he makes a fab suggestion. About the interviews. The way I see it, we start a postgame show. Right away. All we need is a name for it and a place to do the interviews. Then we line up the players."

"Sounds like overtime to me," Pluckey said.

"Me, too," Ears added.

Olivia tried to think like her father. She pursed her lips and began rocking slowly in the booth.

"You OK?" Pluckey asked.

Olivia kept rocking.

"Hey, O. J.," Ears said, "whatsamatter?"

After three more rocks, Olivia drew herself up into what she imagined was an authoritative posture. She smiled broadly. "OK. OT."

Pluckey and Ears smiled, too.

"Now, what we need is a name," Olivia said.

"How about Homers and Homos?" Pluckey offered.

Ears chuckled. "Or Gaze at Gays?" the sound man suggested.

"Not funny," Olivia said. "Isaacs said 'discreet,' remember? Besides, we want to get *our* name into it. Gives it identity."

"What's *our* name?" Pluckey sneered, "Cobb?"

"That's the idea," Olivia said, "something with Cobb. Like, you know, *Kiner's Korner.*" She always watched former Pirates star Ralph Kiner's popular interview show following Mets games.

"I got it," Pluckey said, "Cobb's Closet."

After their tenth consecutive victory, the Gents were relaxing in the clubhouse. Their mood was contentment verging on smugness. Anything else would have been inappropriate. They now led their division by three full games after playing against their three most formidable opponents, albeit at home. They were performing so well that the list of league leaders read like a Gents roster. Pitcher Tony Mike had just notched his third victory with another complete game. Dick Toote, leading the majors with six home runs, was seen as a threat to Roger Maris's season record. Rhino Romanski was flirting with an unbelievable .600 batting average. Mickey Mayo had more putouts than any rival shortstop had assists. Speedy Gonzalez had attempted to steal each time he got on base, and had yet to be caught.

The team was at ease yet spirited, fast and loose, and it didn't take their shrinks to tell them why. Freed from the anxiety of sexual exposure for the first time in their lives, the gay players were finally able to concentrate on baseball.

Now, as they leisurely dressed, the banter turned serious as Romanski said that "that TV gal, whatsername, A. J.?" had asked him about appearing on a post-game show.

"They got a postgame show?" asked Gigolo Johnson, the left fielder. "When's it on?"

"Probably after the game," Mayo said dryly.

"You think so?" Johnson asked.

Mayo shook his head and left.

"What's *his* problem?" Johnson wondered.

"He's an intellectual," said Dave Ripp, the third base-man. "So, Rhino, what about that show?"

"I dunno for sure, Dave. I wasn't payin' much atten-tion."

Ripp caught sight of Ruby Rubinstein leaving Scrappy's office. "Hey, Ruby, got somethin' to ask you," he shouted.

"Ask," Ruby said.

"What's with some kind of TV show about the club?"

"Yeah," the public relations man said. "That little girl, O. J. Cobb, wants to do a postgame show. Y'know, interview guys about the game. You want to be on it, I'll set it up."

"What's in it?" asked Gigolo Johnson.

"You kidding?" Ripp said. "With that outfit, you'll be lucky they don't *charge* you for going on."

"Then you can count me out," Johnson said. "No bread, no Gigolo."

Dick Toote, uncharacteristically elbowed his way into the conversation. "Hold it, Gigolo. Let's talk about this."

"What's to talk about?" Johnson asked. "They want me on TV, they pay me. They're doin' it for money, right?"

"Sure," Toote agreed. "And so are the newspapers. You charge them for interviews?"

"Hey, now you got somethin'," Ripp broke in with

enthusiasm. "The press wants to talk to us, it costs them."

"Sounds right to me," Romanski added. "They want to know why we're winnin', that's a coupla hundred—"

"Yeah," Ripp said, grinning. "And how it feels when I'm in a slump, that's a thou."

Romanski quickly dismissed the fantasy. "Like they'd care that much if they had to pay. What we're talkin' about here's the crap they write when they got nothin' else to print. Think they need to ask you how it feels when you're in a slump? Don't everybody know the answer?" He spat in the direction of a spitoon.

Ripp agreed. "It's like when they ask some guy whose kid just got killed how he feels about it. Some day I wish the guy would say, 'Terrific! It's terrific to find out you just lost your only kid. I recommend it to all your readers.' Hey, how do the papers get away with it?"

Romanski squinted while he considered the question. "It's like their rules," he said. "Sportswriter once tried explaining it to me. They do things a certain way to make the stuff they print more believable. Even though nobody believes it. Like a guy shoots somebody in the middle of Times Square in front of 20 cops and a thousand people. Next day in the paper it says the 'alleged killer.' Alleged, like maybe the guy didn't do it. Like maybe everybody was confused or something, didn't see what they saw.

"Like when that guy shot Lee Harvey Oswald in the police station after Oswald shot Kennedy. It was like on national, hey, *international* TV. Millions, I mean millions of people see what happened. But in the papers, it's 'alleged.' Hey, they think it covers their asses."

Romanski paused. He noticed that perhaps a dozen ballplayers had gathered, crowding in front of the lockers. He didn't mind sounding off; in fact he liked the attention.

He resumed. "So another rule this guy told me is you want to write something you think, you know, your own opinion, you can't do it. Unless you're a columnist. That's to make it look like the paper ain't taking sides. You're a reporter, you got to hang it on someone else, you got to quote somebody. So a reporter gets an idea, what's he do? He runs around looking for somebody thinks the same as him. Then he can quote him and get his own idea in."

"Suppose you can't find nobody?" Gigolo Johnson asked.

"Then," Romanski explained, "they do it another way. They say like 'informed sources' or 'on condition of ano-nymity' or some other bull like that."

"So why didn't they just do that in the first place?" Johnson persisted.

"Because it's their rules, I told you. First they got to try it the right way."

"Still sound like bull," Johnson concluded.

"Sure it is," Romanski continued, "but there's stuff like that all over. How many times you think a first baseman, even Toote here, has his foot on the bag when he gets the throw? You know he comes off too quick. The umps know, too. But they never call it, except maybe one in a thousand. Then everybody gets pissed off. But, man, what did the ump do? He called it right for once. And that's when everybody gets on him. That's bull, ain't it? Bullshit on both sides."

"You want bull," Ripp said, "what about politicians?

What about movies? In that line of work they hire guys to make up lies and call it public relations."

"Hey!" Ruby barked.

"Oh, sorry, Ruby," Ripp apologized. "I don't think of you like that. Y'know, you're diff'rent. You got, uh, class."

"OK, OK," Toote interrupted. "Enough. The point is that what we're talking about isn't the same old crap. This club is different. *We're* different. That's what it's all about. Or at least everybody *thinks* we're different. Maybe that's really what it's all about. For years the only gays people thought about were the queens swishing around. If they were talented enough or kept to themselves, that was OK. But gays in sports? I mean sports like baseball, football, basketball. You kidding? Gays can't do stuff like that.

"Now here we've got a chance to show what kind of bullshit that is. We've got a chance to let people see who we are, what we are."

Johnson sneered. "Oh, hey, what Dick Toote is *really* like!"

Toote ignored him. "And I think we're stupid if we don't take advantage of it. I say we go on whatever program that kid Olivia or O. J. puts together. Free, if we have to. And whenever we can, we say what's on our minds."

Ruby slapped a locker with his palm. It sounded like an explosion. "You got somethin' there, Dick. It's a terrific shot for the Gents, for you guys. Like what they call a photo opportunity. We got a sensational team, everybody knows that. What they *don't* know is what you guys are really like, what you think about off the field, what you do in your spare time. Now don't get me wrong, I'm not sayin' you're weird or such. I'm only saying that the public is real curious. They gotta be. There's never been nothing like you guys in the history of the game. They wanna know your interests, and you got a chance to tell 'em — and, like Toote here says, to show 'em. It's a natural, I'm tellin' you. Take it from me, from Ruby. It'll be worth your whiles."

Toote shook his head rapidly in approval. Rhino nodded thoughtfully. "Right on!" Dave Ripp said. Then he turned to Johnson. "How about you?" he asked. Johnson was impassive. "See how it goes, man," he replied. "Haven't heard nothin' from the TV kid yet. Just you guys."

Ruby took over. "Seeing there's nobody really against it, I'll check it out, let you guys know soon's I can." He couldn't have been more pleased. It had been too long since he had played the PR man's favorite role: negotiating a hot ticket.

"Folks, meet the Gents star left fielder, 'Gigolo' Johnson. Hi, Jig."

"What you call me? You dissin' me, sister?"

"Jig. Jig. You know, short for Gigolo."

"Short for jigaboo, too. Look, gal, you can take that race shit an' run with it. No mother gonna pull that on me. Not on the field, not on the street, nowhere. Y'dig?"

"What's the matter? What'd I say?" Olivia looked pained, bewildered. What was this word "jigaboo"?

"You for real? You never heard jigaboo? Y'heard spade? Y'heard jungle bunny? Y'heard nigger? Well, sister, if you haven't, I've heard 'em enough for both of us!"

"Sure, sure, Jig. I mean, Gig." Olivia felt the sweat collecting under the armpits of her *Cobb's Closet* T-shirt. "How's that if I call you Gig?"

"Sounds stupid, don't it?"

"You think so?"

"Yeah, man."

"I'm not really sure. But, hey, I've got a great idea. Leave it to our audience. Suppose we ask folks to call in and tell us what *they* think. How's that sound to you, er, Mister Johnson?"

"Your show, lady."

Olivia breathed a sigh of relief. This guy was too much.

"Well, folks, you heard it here on *Cobb's Closet*. Another exclusive. Just pick up your phones and call us at area code (718) 367-8268. That's right here at Gents Stadium. (718) 367-8268. Let's get that number up on the screen, Phil."

"Jeezus," Phil Pluckey said, fumbling for the graphic.

"While we're waiting for you fans to call in, let's go to the videotape and look at the way, Jig, er, Gig, er, Mister Johnson, performed in tonight's game against the St. Louis Cardinals. Let's put that on, Phil."

"Yeah, yeah. Sonuvabitch," Pluckey muttered, setting up the tape. Olivia made a mental note to push up the authority lever a notch.

Gigolo Johnson shifted his weight in the uncomfortable chair and wondered why he had agreed to appear on this TV show. And for no bread. Gigolo didn't like putting out without getting paid. Here, this gal's not even a blood sister. He guessed it was because of what Toote had said. About the players showing themselves as they were. As they really were. It wouldn't be easy for him. Not after what he had been through. Not like, say, for Toote. Gigolo had been floored when he saw a film clip of Toote's 'coming out' press conference. How could anybody have the balls to do such a thing? Maybe it was different if you were white. But in the 'hood, being queer was as low as a man could get. And there was no way you would own up to it. His throat felt dry as he contemplated the next few minutes.

For, he, Gigolo Johnson, a Gold Glove left fielder, had gone to elaborate lengths to conceal his gayness and had succeeded until his name appeared in Stan Mann's column. His nickname spelled out just how successful he had been. It always gave him a laugh, the way the world had gone for it. For his pose, his bullshit. When he became certain of his homosexuality, a chance encounter had led to a survival scheme: make it as a "ladies' man." Through self-promotion and flamboyant appearances with countless foxes, he had little difficulty in convincing the homeboys and the newsies that his rep as a stud was warranted.

Despite this achievement, he had never felt secure, guilty about the deception, fearful of discovery. Being black *and* gay had more than doubled his problems. In lighter moments, he recalled a Sammy Davis, Jr., joke about the time the entertainer had gone to play golf and was asked for his handicap. "I'm a skinny, one-eyed, black Jew," he'd supposedly cracked. It was one of the few times Sammy had appealed to Gigolo. Man, the way he kissed Sinatra's ass! And hugging that honky sonuvabitch Nixon. But he couldn't write off Davis's compulsion to make it. Like it or not, whitey's world was *the* world. And when you came down to it, how many of the brothers *didn't* want to get there?

Sure, on the street, black *was* beautiful. But even there, Gigolo pretended. Growing up in south east Washington, D.C., was as beautiful as a bucket of shit. It meant being jammed into a rundown, three-room apartment with two brothers, three sisters, and a mother. No father. But plenty of role models: pimps in their white Caddies, pushers in their gold chains, drunks and druggies and gamblers and hookers. And gangs. And guns. Washington was the nation's capital, and it was also one of America's blackest big cities. For Gigolo, then called by his given name, Kevvon, being poor and black in the District meant living in hell. In the tough, dirty ghetto you grew up under pressure. *Brother* pressure. You were expected to conform: to be mean, to be fast, and to regard Northwest whites and their culture with contempt. It was taken for granted that you were interested in basketball and women. And that you could perform well with both. Being gay was not simply sneered at. It was forbidden. It was "a white thing."

Gigolo didn't know or care that sociologists and psychiatrists, historians and psychologists explained that slavery and racism had emasculated black men, compelling them to assert and prove their manliness through athletics and sexual domination. All Gigolo knew was that he always felt like an outsider, not part of the hood. He couldn't share his classmates' horny hang-ups with women. Or those of his older brothers.

In his fourteenth summer, just before entering high school, he had good reason to wonder. He was alone one afternoon when his oldest brother, Malcolm, a 19-year-old rising dealer, came home unexpectedly and caught him looking at a copy of *Honcho,* a gay picture magazine he had bought at a Dupont Circle stationery store.

"What the fuck you lookin' at?" Malcolm said, ripping the magazine out of his hands.

"Nothin', nothin'. Just found it on the street."

"Booolsheeet," Malcolm said, slowly turning the pages of photos of nude men. "What're you, a fuckin' faggot?"

The word hung in the air, reverberated off the walls

of the cramped apartment. Kevvon flinched. "No! No! Don't call me that!"

"Well ain't that what you are, li'l brother?" Malcolm said, sneering. "My own brother, a fuckin' li'l queer." He shook his head in disgust. "That's no good, li'l bro, no good *attall*. No good for you. No good for me." Malcolm was angry. He made a fist and punched his palm. "For sure no good for *me*," Malcolm said, thinking of his own rep.

Kevvon was frightened. He had always feared Malcolm, never been close to him. His brother's bulk and frequent, unprovoked bursts of violence scared the whole family. But now Kevvon felt menaced. He looked toward the door of his bedroom, but Malcolm anticipated his thoughts. "No, li'l brother, you ain't got no place t'go."

Kevvon inched toward escape. "No way, punk," Malcolm said. "We can't have no queers round this house. We gonna have t'do somethin' about that, li'l faggot. We gonna have to straighten' you out."

Malcolm grabbed him by the shirt and threw him to the floor. "Oh, yeah, we gonna cure this li'l cocksucker." Kevvon shook with fear. There was a wild look on Malcolm's face. "We got a way to take care of you, li'l *sister*." Before Kevvon could protect himself, Malcolm was on top of him, straddling his chest, pinning him down. Kevvon strained helplessly against unyielding weight and strength. "We're gonna cure you good, *sis, sis, sis,*" Malcolm said, unzipping his fly.

The incident was never mentioned by either of them. Kevvon avoided Malcolm as much as possible thereafter, a strategy simplified a few months later when his brother was locked up for selecting an off-duty cop to mug. But the experience hovered over Kevvon like a nightmare. What disturbed him most was the undeniable tingle of pleasure he had felt from Malcolm's cock in his mouth. How could a "man" enjoy what Malcolm had done to him, he wondered. Was he really queer like his brother said? Would he ever enjoy making it with a woman? Could he?

Uncertain of his nature and fearful of detection by streetwise neighborhood kids, he'd sought admission to the sanctuary of sports. To the physical components he possessed — size, strength, endurance, coordination, and quick reflexes — he added flat-out determination. Without knowing why, he chose the most manly sport available: wrestling. He made the freshman squad and soon caught the varsity coach's eye as a future prospect. In the spring, although he had never even played Little League, Kevvon focused on baseball, the sport that symbolized mainstream America. He tried out for the freshman team and survived the initial cut. In midseason, with the squad wracked by injuries, the coach played him in right field, where his game-saving catch of a fading line drive made him a starter in the next game. Kevvon remained in the lineup for the rest of the season, enjoying the popularity that success brought. Encouraged, he worked hard enough during the succeeding years to make all-scholastic and attracted enough attention to earn a tryout with the pros.

Climbing the minor league ladder, Kevvon distinguished himself on each rung with his speed and power. Always comfortable on the field, he hated the clubhouse. The sight of naked male bodies was arousing and frustrating.

At the same time, he discovered he could have his pick of the girl groupies that hung around the ball parks. He easily satisfied them, but their pushiness was a turnoff. Screwing nameless foxes was about as much fun as doing deep knee bends. Eventually, one evening, he drifted into a gay bar around the corner from Capitol Hill. What amazed him most was not that all the patrons were black but that there were so many gay black men in his hometown. He had always thought of himself as the odd man out.

He began to move very cautiously into Washington's gay black world, still fearful of the homophobia among straight brothers. Muslim friends from the Nation of Islam told him that homosexuality was racial treason. When he was with heteros, even though his apparent masculinity was adequate protection, fear induced him to share their antigay sentiments. "One a them muthafuckahs comes near me, I cut his balls off," a black teammate had muttered during one interminable bus trip. "Betcher ass," Kevvon had agreed, hating himself as he spoke.

At first, in the gay bars in the District, Kevvon sat alone sipping beer and watching how the men operated: the way they flirted, made passes, paired off. He was fascinated by the ease with which they accepted their homosexuality and distressed by the possibility that he never would. Although drawn to the gay hangouts and their patrons, his only homosexual experience thus far had been Malcolm's assault, which had left him frightened but titillated. His confusion deterred him from making advances. Kevvon found that if he kept to himself and avoided eye contact he would be left alone. Once, at closing time, a slim, goateed dude he'd noticed on earlier occasions joined him as he walked out the door. "Goin' my way?" the young man asked with a provocative smile. Kevvon considered the invitation for a moment and then shook his head. "Not t'night," he said. The man shrugged. "Always t'morrow," he said as he left.

A few nights later, at the same bar, Kevvon found himself searching for the face with the goatee. After a disappointing hour, he saw the man enter and sliced his way through the crowd directly to him. "Yo," the man said, taking the adjacent barstool and offering a warm hand, "name's Spike." Kevvon nodded. "Johnson, Kevvon Johnson." Spike shook his head. "Don't need any second names, Kevvon," he said, adding with a smile, "y'know, it's safer."

Spike said he worked at a brokerage firm. He had a good job, but nothing more than he deserved, having graduated from Haverford and a Quaker prep school. Nor had he benefited, so far as he knew, from affirmative action or any other policies designed to assist minorities. After all, Spike said matter-of-factly, he had enjoyed a solidly upper-middle-class status: his father was a doctor, his mother a school administrator. He had grown up in Cleveland Park, where his parents owned a townhouse. As Spike and Kevvon talked on into the night, it became obvious that their backgrounds couldn't have been more different. Yet for Kevvon, this was the first chance to speak openly and unashamedly about his fears and fantasies. It created a rapport he never had experienced before. It was this bond, far more than the beer, that led him to accompany Spike to his apartment, to embrace him clumsily, and to make hesitant but unforgettable love.

Their relationship continued for six months, exciting while it lasted, but drained, finally, by the differences in their interests. Kevvon felt relief at being able to resume his concentration on sports and martial arts movies without the need for justification. Spike's insistence on "uplifting" him with visits to museums and art films he'd pretended not only to understand but also to enjoy had made him feel phony.

Yet the episode gave him a sense of confidence and a certainty that he *was* homosexual. With that realization, Kevvon became more aggressive in his pursuit of companionship. He learned his way around the District's gay hangouts, experimented with techniques and roles, even crossed once-sacrosanct racial lines in a brief road-trip fling with a white teammate after both had drunk too much. But greater sexual sophistication did not relieve him of his fear of discovery and probable disaster.

With the passing of time, his apprehension mounted. As his career blossomed, he began to attract increasing media interest and scrutiny. On the brink of making it into the majors, he nearly panicked when a sportswriter doing an in-depth profile pressed him about his personal life.

But, impatient to succeed, Kevvon was delighted one night during the off-season to run into Spike at a Washington bar. Kevvon welcomed the chance to confide his ongoing concerns. It was like old times as he and Spike alternately unburdened themselves, listened patiently, offered suggestions. They talked far into the night, and when they finished shortly before dawn, they had created the "Gigolo" strategy.

The high-pitched voice of O. J. Cobb jolted him out of

his reverie: "Well, there, Mister Johnson, we did get *one* call."

"Oh, yeah," Gigolo said.

"Kind of strange, though. Didn't say he wanted 'Jig' or 'Gig.' Just said to call you 'Sis.' Said you'd know who it was."

··23··

Ruby shaded his eyes against a bright May sun and nodded approvingly toward the center-field stands. "When you're fillin' them bleachers, you ain't got nothin' to worry about."

"You're right, y'ol' sonuvabitch," Scrappy replied affectionately. Feeling so good, he forgot to adopt his customary surliness. He was beyond remembering that his gruff, aggressive personality was his own invention, one he had contrived in childhood to protect himself from the mean Brooklyn streets that his parents, seven-day-a-week slaves to their shabby dry-goods store, had compelled him to deal with alone.

The source of his present delight was clear. The Gents were still on a tear. They had set a major league record for victories out of the gate, winning 19 before dropping one to the Dodgers, then taking another 10 before losing to the Mets. They were so clearly the best in their class that sportswriters, having run out of superlatives, had begun to search for historical opponents, the 1927 Yankees being the most popular. Moreover — and to Scrappy and Ruby, primarily — not only were the Gents a critical success, with leaders in virtually every hitting, pitching, and (had anybody bothered to look) fielding category, but they were also filling every ballpark in which they played.

Many fans were still turning up out of curiosity and, sometimes, antipathy. More than a few showed up to vent their homophobia, especially in some of the more conservative cities, such as Cincinnati, Houston, and Denver. In the former, one Reds supporter appeared on most of the TV network news shows brandishing a poster that read: BETTER A ROTTEN ROSE THAN THESE PANSIES. But there was no disputing that the Gents also were attracting crowds because they were terrific. And that meant money for all the clubs they played. Still, no one seemed to have recognized as yet the full dimensions of what was going on and what was to come.

"Can't remember when we sold out before," Ruby continued. "Have to look that one up. Jeezus, Scrappy, it's really great. Writers buggin' me all the time; guys I ain't seen in years comin' up to me on the street. Really somethin' to have a hit on your hands."

"Hell yes," Scrappy agreed. "You see the stuff they're *writin'* about us? It's like the good ol' days, except we never had no ol' days that was *this* good."

Their euphoria was interrupted by a studious-looking young man who emerged from the Gents dugout to tap Scrappy on the arm. "Phone call for you, Mister Schwrtnzbrgr," he said in a respectful voice.

"What? Who?" Scrappy stammered, not immediately recognizing his own name, or the speaker. The young man was Sherman, the son of Ruby's sister, Goldie — "just give him a try" — hired yesterday to assist with the unprecedented activity engulfing the front office.

In the minutes before game time, Ruby surveyed the

filled bleachers again and smiled with satisfaction before taking the long walk underneath the stadium to the clubhouse. He had barely left the rear of the dugout when Scrappy's booming voice came echoing through the tunnel. "Yeah, sure, *now* you're interested. Where were you the beginnin' of the season?" his boss roared. "Or, you sonuvabitch, now that I think of it, where you been the last few years?"

The caller, Ruby soon determined, was from Fox, the network that had carried, then dropped, the Gents. The decision to discontinue coverage, a *first* in the history of major league baseball, had left the team's home games untelevised for the past decade. That extended event, celebrated derisively by the press, left Scrappy vituperatively bitter. Nor had the passage of time cooled his anger and resentment. As Ruby could savor, Scrappy was getting his full measure of vengeance from the hapless TV executive, who evidently had been reduced to pleading with the Gents' boss for a second chance.

"Y'wanna piece of the action, get yourself a whore," Scrappy gibed gleefully, unconcerned that his behavior was jeopardizing a reconciliation. Consequently he was not surprised when the phone went dead, signaling, perhaps, a similar fate for the team's return to mainstream television.

"Them fuckers may have short mem'ries," Scrappy told Ruby, "but not me."

"You think maybe you hit on him a little too hard?" Ruby asked tactfully.

"No!" Scrappy bellowed. "Them media bastards jump around like fleas in a dog pound. They got no loyalty to nothin' except any buck they can get their mitts on. You think they care about teams and fans and the rest of it? Hell, no! They're the same as J. P. Morgan, the old-timer who said 'Fuck the public,' or somethin' like that."

"I think y'mean Vanderbilt, Scrappy," Ruby interrupted. "Commodore Vanderbilt."

"There's a difference? They're both a couple of gonifs. That's another thing," Scrappy continued. "You can't even tell what nobody *really* said nohow, the way it gets dressed up. Like some writer told me once that the general in World War II that got surrounded by the Nazis, y'know that Irish McSomethin'. Well, this writer told me the general didn't say, 'Nuts!' at all. What he said was, 'Balls!' Go look for that in a history book."

The recorded strains of the "Star-Spangled Banner," a particularly unappealing version sung by another relative of Ruby's, drew Scrappy and his associate back to reality and the ball field. The game was with the Phillies, who, other than the Mets, were geographically closest to the Gents and thus, under the unwritten laws of sports, one of their most intense rivals. And while New York was not exactly brimming with Phillies fans, that visiting team always seemed to bring a sizable rooting section with it, a fact that could account for the near full house.

Although the Phillies normally gave the Gents a tussle, Scrappy's club did not receive his undivided attention that afternoon. The game had barely gotten underway when Sherman, the new assistant, summoned him with the first of the half-dozen "urgent" phone calls he would receive before the final out. Even the Gents' success on the field, where they put away the Philadelphians 6 to 2, did not compare with the momentum that was building beyond the stadium.

Two of the callers represented major American corporations — an automaker and a cereal manufacturer — who were seeking a sit-down to discuss advertising campaigns featuring the Gents. Another was from a network talk show that wanted to book Scrappy and a couple of his ballplayers for later that week. There was a call from a state senator's administrative assistant, who explained that his boss was interested in getting input for gay-rights legislation he planned to introduce during the next legislative session. Three literary agents wanted to work out exclusive deals for paperbacks dealing with the team or a first-person account of the season. A *Newsweek* writer, emphasizing that he was "not from the sports section," was looking for an interview to talk about Scrappy's role in heralding the "phenomenon of gay respectability." And an advertising agency pointed out that a number of its clients would like to buy space on the barren reaches of Gents Stadium.

To each, Scrappy was sneeringly responsive. "I yanked their chains," he told an anxious Ruby, "just enough to make *me* feel good." Then he grinned, "They're still hot for us."

"*Us?*" Ruby repeated.

"Yeah," Scrappy said firmly. "We're a team, y'know. Sure, it ain't exactly like having regular, uh, straight guys, but they're not like I thought they'd be. Now, y'take Toote, for instance. Always thought he was a great ballplayer, a terrific guy. Still is. Still the same guy, right? *He's* no different now that I know he's a fa — uh, that he's gay. Look at some of the others. Y'take Rhino. Hell, nobody could *take* him," Scrappy chuckled. "I mean, in a brawl. Helluva guy. Nobody ever done what he did against the Pirates beginnin' of the season. That home run bunt. Sensational! And Gigolo. He's playin' better'n he ever played in his life. And he's had a life that makes mine look like Easy Street, I'll tell you."

Scrappy nodded vigorously. "Believe me, Ruby, we got ourselves a team. And don't you ever forget we're part of it."

Phil Donahue raced down the studio aisle, microphone in hand, his chalk-white hair bouncing buoyantly. "Yes, yes," he said, leaning past three middle-aged men in satiny baseball jackets to stick the mike in front of a fourth.

"Yeah," the bulky man said, rising awkwardly from the padded chair. "This question's for Scrappy." Waving a thick hand at the Gents seated on the stage alongside their owner-manager, he asked, "You're an old-timer, how can you stand these guys?"

A murmur of dissent burbled through the audience of the *Donahue* show.

"What do you have to say to that, Scrappy?" Phil asked, poker-faced. "Aren't you worried about what happens when your back is turned?"

A few men in the mostly-female audience snickered.

"Well, I'll tell you the truth," Scrappy said. "At the beginnin', maybe I felt a little queasy, y'know. But when I got to know these guys—and I called 'em *guys* right from the start—far as I was concerned there wasn't nuthin' different about them than any team I ever run."

"You sure about that, Scrappy?" Phil persisted. "*No different?*"

"Well," Scrappy declared with a grin, "they're a helluva lot *better*."

The audience applauded loudly.

"And," Scrappy added, "I guess you could say there ain't so many, y'know, *girlie* pictures around."

Another round of applause.

Phil tore up the aisle toward a middle-aged woman who had raised her hand tentatively. "Yes, ma'am," Phil said.

"My question is for that big one there on the end."

"That's Rhino Romanski," Phil said, identifying the burly catcher. "He's leading the league in batting. Hitting about .455 aren't you, Rhino?"

"Close, Phil, you're close," Rhino said hoarsely. "Last time I looked it was .485."

"Sorry," Phil said. "Last time you looked? That must have been what I saw you checking out in the paper just before we went on the air."

Rhino laughed. "Y'got me there, Phil." Actually, he had been admiring the photo of a male model in a Bloomingdale's men's wear ad.

Phil turned back to the questioner. "Yes, dear. You wanted to ask Rhino something?"

"Sure did. I'd like to know what his mother thinks about all this."

Rhino cleared his throat. "It's a funny thing, ma'am, you askin' that question now. If you asked me a week ago, I would've said I sure don't know. 'Cause I didn't. Since the winter when that story come out in the paper, I haven't talked to her. I called but she hung right up. I kept calling an' she kept hanging up. I don't need to tell you how I felt. Then just the other day the phone rang. I picked it up and it was my mom's voice. I couldn't believe it. Y'know, *her* calling *me*. She said she had been thinking things over and had talked to her priest. My dad died a couple of years back, so when she's got somethin' on her mind these days, she talks to the priest. And she said she guessed that whatever God made me was what I hadda be. That now she understood that, and things between us would be back where they used to be."

As the audience roared its approval, and the camera closed in on a gray-haired woman brushing away a tear, Dick Toote debated with himself over describing *his* mother's stony refusal to acknowledge his existence.

"That's great, Rhino," Toote said when the applause faded, "but I don't think it *always* works out that way."

Phil broke in. "How do you mean, Dick Toote?" he asked. "This gentleman, as we mentioned in the introductions, is one of the brightest stars baseball has ever known. He was also the first gay player to come out publicly."

Toote considered the consequences: to himself, to his father, to his mother. "I don't think all parents are as accepting. It's not an easy thing, you know. Parents have expectations about their kids. They expect success, and that means in their careers and in their personal lives. They're looking for the American dream: a good job, a good wife or husband, nice children and grandchildren. Gays don't fit into that picture, and parents have trouble with that. I'm not blaming them, I'm just telling you how it is."

"That's very interesting, Dick," Phil said. "You speaking from personal experience?"

Toote deflected the question. "We've all had problems growing up in a society that considers us outsiders. That's why so many of us are still in the closet. I'm talking about discrimination: in jobs, housing, politics, socially . . . any way you want to look at it."

Phil paused, cocked his head and pounced. "Some people might say that you bring it on *yourselves*. That you create your problems by the way you behave. That you flaunt your sexuality, call attention to yourselves, wind up alienating a lot of your sympathizers. What would you say to them?"

Toote reddened. The studio, far smaller in reality than it appeared on the screen, seemed to shrink still further, enlarging his own presence. He hadn't intended to let himself be baited. He particularly resented it from a self-proclaimed liberal.

"To you, er, I mean, to *them*," Toote said, eliciting a few chuckles from the audience and a professionally appreciative grin from Phil, "I'd say that I can only speak for myself, but I don't think gay men — or lesbians — are looking for any special consideration. We just want justice and fairness. And as far as 'flaunting' is concerned, what you're talking about is a small minority. Every group has its embarrassments. By the way, how do you feel about being lumped with Geraldo?"

Phil winced, then decided to go for laughs. "Well, I wouldn't mind it if it meant getting some of his ratings."

A young man waving energetically got Phil's attention. He raced over, waving the mike. "Yes, yes," he said.

"I wonder," the young man inquired, "how the players feel about the tone of these questions? He gestured toward them. "Does it bother you that nobody is asking anything about baseball?"

Phil stared at the questioner in mock amazement for what seemed like minutes. After the audience turned toward him in anticipation, Phil asked, "How much did you pay to get in here?"

"Well, uh, nothing," the man replied, flustered.

"Then you better behave yourself," Phil said jocularly.

Then, ignoring the question, the talk-show host dashed down the steps toward another young man.

"Let's hear their answer," this man said firmly.

"Well, Scrappy," Phil said, "looks like you guys have some fans here."

Scrappy grinned and nodded. "Got lots of 'em at the ballpark, too. Far as askin' us about baseball, I guess the team feels like we do our talkin' on the field, y'know what I mean? I know what that guy means, but it's gettin' so baseball is the *last* thing anybody asks us about. Well, I'll tell you, Phil, we're gettin' so used to talkin' about the other stuff, it don't matter no more. Y'know what I mean?"

Phil nodded slowly, conveying serious thought. "What you're telling us," he said superfluously, "is that the shock has worn off—that your team is able to talk about themselves, about their homosexuality. Is that correct, Scrappy?"

Scrappy looked to Toote, Romanski, and Gigolo Johnson for guidance.

Gigolo raised his hand and spoke. "Like, man, we are gettin' sick of talkin' about all this gay jazz. I mean it's like you cats think it's the onlyest thing on our minds. We talk about the same things you talk about. We are people before we are gay. Y'dig?"

Phil now nodded vigorously. He wanted to play down the program's sensationalism by stressing its social value. "Of course things can grow out of proportion. But if we bring some of these subjects out in the open — out of the closet, if you'll pardon the expression — everybody becomes a little more comfortable, a little more under-standing."

Phil glanced around and saw the man in the satiny baseball jacket waving for attention, and raced to him.

"Yessir, you again. Up for your second 'at bat.' "

"I still don't get how an old-timer like Scrappy can hang out with these fag — er, kinda guys."

Toote shook his head in frustration and disgust, as he saw that Phil couldn't quite conceal his amusement. But the rumble of disapproval that coursed through the studio restored his resolve.

It took a flying wedge of beefy, blue-uniformed guards to escort the Gents through the mass of television, radio, and print reporters jamming the entrance to the hearing room. The activity was unbecoming to these normally quiet corridors, and such furor would have seemed outrageously out of place in the Gothic confines of the ancient and forbidding New York State Legislature across State Street in Albany. That, no doubt, was why it had been scheduled here in the down-to-earth "LOB," the Legislative Office Building.

"Ain't seen nothin' like this since the death penalty days," one panting security man muttered.

"Or since them abortion-lovin' bitches was up here from New York," another said.

"Yeah, right," the first agreed, adding, with a touch of respect. "Them broads was real tough cookies."

Once inside, the Gents who had consented to testify on behalf of the proposed gay-rights legislation took their seats alongside other prospective witnesses. Toote noted that Dr. Goodkind, once his therapist and, after having moved his practice from the West Coast to New York, his friend, was among them. He exchanged nods with several of the activists he recognized from the rallies he had attended recently. One was a TV personality who had come out a few weeks ago amid a flurry of media coverage.

Things were moving, Toote felt. Far too slowly, but in the right direction. And from the limited exposure to politics he'd gained since his own disclosure, he had come to understand that momentum was critical to progress. Centuries-old traditions could be wiped out virtually overnight if the timing was right. But he knew, too, that when the political pendulum was swinging the other way, justice and those who sought it could sit for decades in the judicial and legislative waiting rooms.

In this case, the measure was an innocuous bill that simply would have added "sexual orientation" to the list of entitities, such as race, religion, gender, age, and physical condition, against which discrimination was prohibited.

Yet as Toote glanced around the hearing room, now filling up with witnesses and their supporters, he saw the perennial opponents as well, and realized that a major conflict loomed. For these were the interest groups that in past years had lobbied successfully to keep similar legislation cooped up in committee or, failing that, to defeat it on the floor. They were not difficult to identify in their cassocks and yarmulkes.

There were others holding Bibles. In recent years, Catholic and Orthodox Jewish forces had been joined by born-again Christians and other zealous components of the religious right. Less recognizable but more demonstrative than their priestly and rabbinical allies, they lined the approaches to the Legislature this day, shouting "Shame!" and falling to their knees before the cameras.

The Gents contingent, Toote, Romanski and Johnson, had been exposed to enough hostility on the diamond to control their responses. "Religious nuts," Rhino said dismissively. Toote, recalling his parents, replied, "Yeah, but what about their kids?"

As politicians know, while legislative hearings rarely change votes, they serve the democratic function of allowing all recognized factions to vent their frustrations in public, occasionally in front of national TV audiences. The expectation that some Gents would be present, a fact impressed on the media by Rick Volpino's extensive groundwork, had guaranteed a full house of spectators and inspired an inordinate list of testifiers.

To reinforce the appearance of fairness, the legislative committee scheduled the witnesses alternately, beginning with a proponent. Volpino, whose prudently rationed pro bono contributions were proffered when publicity was certain, had agreed to orchestrate the gay presentation. His strategy was to cancel out the opposition's clergy at the outset by selecting one from his own stable to lead off. His choice was a Presbyterian minister known to the public for his liberal pronouncements and to the homosexual community for his sizable gay and lesbian congregation. As is true with many other middle-aged bachelors, the Reverend Angus MacWatt's own sexual orientation was a frequent subject of speculation.

The clergyman had a warm, robust manner that contradicted his reedy physique and ascetic face; strangers always seemed to expect peckishness and were pleased to discover affability. Such a persona had served him well in a career devoted largely to challenging the dogma of the church and the inflexibility of many of his superiors.

While many religions and denominations still regarded homosexuality as both sinful and remediable, and thus wicked or even satanic, the Presbyterian Church stood out among those seeking to break down barriers and promote understanding and acceptance. It was a policy that reflected both the interests and the efforts of Angus MacWatt.

When he was called as the first witness, MacWatt advanced to the podium with a walk that bespoke confidence bred from experience. There was no trace of nervousness or concern as he contemplated the packed room, taking in every face, making eye contact with each. After giving testimony for many years, Angus MacWatt truly believed he had been created for just such appearances.

Volpino's Mea Culpa agency had devised a comprehensive strategy to present the case for giving gays and lesbians the kind of protection its adherents believed was, unfortunately, still necessary. As usual, he had put Dore Dupus to work compiling a public opinion survey. And Dupus, as was his custom, had designed a questionnaire and selected a sample of potential respondents to accomplish the desired results. The data, bound in an expensive-looking volume, were among the materials that the Reverend MacWatt now placed rather dramatically on the lectern.

"Fellow citizens . . . fellow human beings," he began, embracing them with his resonant voice. Then he paused for several moments and shook his head forlornly, before adding, "and so we meet yet again." There were many nods; few on either side relished being dragged up here to the state capital, away from the joys of summer, to deal once more with this chestnut.

Artfully blending righteousness and statistics, the clergyman filled his allotted time and his audience's ears with a compelling argument for those who happened to have a different sexual orientation to enjoy the same rights as other citizens. Anticipating opponents' positions, he emphasized that the proposed amendment would neither confer special privileges nor induce "converts."

He dwelt particularly on data that showed a striking rise in *reported* violence against gays since the onset of the AIDS epidemic. The figures, he maintained, grossly understated the reality of the problem. This, he said, was because many if not most of the victims, fearing discrimination from employers, landlords, fellow workers, and neighbors, were unwilling to identify themselves publicly through bringing charges. By enacting this legislation, Reverend MacWatt urged, the state would protect such victims against losing their jobs or apartments, and thus encouraged to report incidents of gay bashing. That, in turn, would lead to police action and, hopefully, a reduction of abuse.

The Gents nodded in agreement. None had been a victim, since in the past their athleticism made them among the least likely to fit the gay stereotype. But each had been warned in gay bars to be alert when leaving, particularly to possible attacks in adjacent parking lots.

After MacWatt concluded by closing his eyes and lowering his head, as if uttering a silent prayer, a claque arranged by Volpino broke into loud and sustained applause until the chairman gaveled it into order. But before the minister could return to his seat, he was almost upended in the aisle by a huge, hurrying man who then made an elaborate gesture of apology.

Standing six-and-one-half feet tall, with close-cropped blond hair, he was unmistakable to sports fans as Donald Bigg, the outspoken owner of the New York Yankees and, in these post-Steinbrenner years, occasional spokesman for right-wing causes and candidates. Bigg acknowledged the hearty applause with his familiar thumbs-up gesture, eliciting still further cheers.

The popular sportsman's presence was not unexpected. He was a fixture at anti-abortion and pro-death-penalty rallies and was considered a potential political office-seeker when he became bored with his business interests. But today's presentation would be far from his customary performance.

Forming a "time out" signal with his forefingers, Donald called for silence just as the ovation was about to die out. Beaming a broad smile, he nodded appreciatively. "Folks," he began, "I'm no speechmaker. And I sure do thank you for your warm welcome, because I'm nothing special. I'm just what you might call one lucky human being." Heads bobbed admiringly at this homey modesty.

"Now you might think I'm talking about my good fortune in baseball or in business, where the good Lord has blessed me with some success. But folks, that's not what I had in mind at all. That's not what I'm here to tell you about. Now, I'd appreciate it if you'd just bear with me and listen carefully, because what I've got to say I've never said before. For sure not in public."

Reporters nudged one another expectantly. Stan Mann, his stomach aching daily over his future with the

Post and with Marti, and having made this unappealing trip in the hope he could wrest a column from the Gents' participation, checked his tape recorder and noted "Donald" on his pad. Clearly something out of the ordinary was in the works.

Donald gestured toward the area where the legislation's proponents, including the gay ballplayers, were seated. "Now those folks are gonna tell you how they didn't have anything to do with what they are. They're gonna try to convince you that the good Lord is the one to *blame,* er, I mean, hold responsible." He grinned at the Gents.

"You see," Donald continued, "the way they put it, they're just like the rest of us, except they've got a yen for their own kind. They'd have you believe that they're *powerless*, they're *helpless*, they're *incapable* of behaving any other way than how they do.

"Now if you buy that, they figure, you got to buy the rest of their line. And what comes next is that if *they* can't help *themselves,* then they need help, *special* help, *your* help, to make them even with the rest of us. So you see, their whole argument is built on one point, what the *intellectuals* would call their *premise*. Take the premise and the rest sort of follows."

Donald paused to let his remarks penetrate. "But suppose, folks, that their premise is *untrue*. Suppose it's not the good Lord that made them what they are. Suppose instead that it's their own doing. Suppose that it's their own warped desires. Well, then, I expect their whole argument falls apart. Because if they're like the rest of us, then they don't need any *special* help, any special *protection*. Think about that for a moment."

Toote wondered where Donald was going with this

line. His point so far was familiar: homosexuals *chose* their sexual orientation, thus were responsible for their behavior and its consequences. Toote had discussed the issue many times with his straight friends. He said that even such generally acceptable terms as "sexual *preference*" implied that being gay involved a conscious decision. And, he contended, there was no scientific basis for that.

Donald did not give him long to ponder. After allowing his audience to consider what he had suggested, the baseball magnate compressed his lips and shook his head from side to side to convey the distress he was encountering. "Folks," he said, with evident discomfort, "I know what *they're* all about because I was *one* of them."

For a second, like the moment that separates the flash of lightning from the roar of thunder, there was silence. Then, with the same inevitability, the hearing room erupted. Everyone, even Donald's own contingent, produced an explosion of sound. Committee members, witnesses, reporters, and spectators shouted their disbelief. Toote, who himself had triggered the same reaction at his unforgettable press conference, could not believe what he had heard. And he saw Dr. Goodkind, normally the essence of gentility and reserve, rise to his feet shouting, "Impossible!"

As the clamor finally began to subside, Donald signaled time-out again. Clearly pleased with the impact he had made, he resumed speaking. "Yep, folks, that *is* the truth. It was when I first went to Penn State. I had an athletic scholarship. It was in the summer at football training camp. And I'll tell you, I was pretty young and *very* innocent."

The only sound was the whirring of the TV cameras as every ear awaited the next word. The hefty tycoon appeared prepared to provide a detailed account.

"Well, they roomed me with this big, husky tackle, and I mean *huge*. Like I said, I was young and inexperienced, fresh out of high school. I didn't know that much about girls, much less the kind of stuff I was going to learn. Well, it didn't take this feller long to let me in on what *he* had in mind. He just started cozying up to me right off the bat. Before I knew what was happening, why he had his big hands all over me. And I mean *all* over. And by the end of that summer, I tell you, I was just as queer as a three-dollar bill."

The room reechoed to sounds of amazement and consternation. Donald's cohorts registered sympathy, disgust, and anger; his opponents expressed incredulity. Dr. Goodkind was shaking his head vigorously and writing notes at a furious pace.

"You're right," Donald said, addressing his supporters and ignoring the others. "It was a terrible time for me, taken advantage of like that. And if it hadn't been for the love of a good woman," he said, looking down at his wife, who returned his adoring gaze from the front row. "I don't know where I would've wound up." Opponents of the proposed legislation rose as one and applauded spiritedly.

This time Donald allowed the cheers to continue until they died out naturally. "The point, my friends," he said with deliberate slowness, "is that these folks do what they do because they want to do it. And they could call a halt sure as I did, if they desired. What they need is not laws; it's backbone. They don't need protection; they need courage. And what we should do is not indulge them, but pray for them." And with that, in imitation of the Reverend MacWatt, he cast his eyes downward.

Within seconds, the press section emptied as reporters raced from their seats to their phones. The committee chairman, recognizing immediately that the proceedings themselves were now shorn of any publicity value, banged his gavel and shouted that the hearings would be recessed until after lunch.

Toote lurched from his seat and ran after Dr. Goodkind. "What's he talking about?" he asked the psychiatrist.

"It's total nonsense!" Dr. Goodkind said heatedly. "Come with me."

Toote followed him out of the hearing chamber to the press room, where dozens of reporters were shouting simultaneously into telephones. Once they had alerted their editors, they formed a horseshoe in front of Toote and Dr. Goodkind and began barking out questions.

"What've you got to say to Bigg, Toote?"

"How come you never tried to change?"

"What's this do to the amendment?"

"You got any comment on Donald, doc?"

Toote mimicked Donald by making an elaborate time-out sign. "Hold it! Hold it, you guys!" he said. "Dr. Goodkind does have a few things to say."

"Indeed I do," the psychiatrist said. "What you heard inside from Donald is without any basis in medical science. While it's true that we're still struggling to determine just what homosexuality is — what the factors may be that determine sexual orientation — there is no evidence that it is simply a matter of choice. People do not change their sexuality the way they change their clothes.

"When circumstances limit usual sexual outlets, as in prison or in lengthy isolation from society, some heterosexual men and women may take part in homosexual behavior. But that is because it becomes the only available means of sexual expression with another human being. But the fact is that when such people leave these circumscribed conditions — say, get out of prison — they resume their heterosexual behavior.

"Clearly, however, that's not what Donald was talking about. He was talking about people in everyday situations who have access to partners of either sex. But you don't have to take my word for it. Speak to anyone who has experience in the field of sexual relations. As far as Donald is concerned, his motivations are quite clear. And, I might add, so are his fantasies."

During the month of June the off-field distractions proliferated. There were dozens of newspaper and magazine spreads, including several in the foreign press, principally Japanese; there were more talk-show appearances, both radio and TV, and there was even filming by a documentary crew, whose director Olivia recognized from her Syracuse communications classes. But the Gents continued to play baseball as well as anyone could remember. And that included the veteran sportswriters and broadcasters, those who could fill an empty column or dead air time with countless colorful and retellable yarns, the myths that reinforce the sport's claim to be the national pastime.

With the All-Star Game break, the traditional midseason milestone still several weeks off, the Gents had compiled the best record in both leagues and were leading their division by 16 games. They were not only good but, more important, they were also lucky. Thus far, the team had been injury free; the pitching staff hadn't complained once of stiff shoulders.

Scrappy and Ruby reveled in this success although, remembering the Gents' deplorable performance over the past decade, wondered when lightning would strike. There was nothing tangible to concern them, just the foreboding that seeps into the psyches of perennial losers. Despite their dazzling achievements, the players, too, were somewhat incredulous. By now, the shock of their involuntary coming out had faded, but they had not forgotten Stan Mann's column, the one that had outed them, and they continued to ostracize him.

For Mann, the situation had become increasingly worrisome. He had gotten one of the most sensational scoops in the annals of baseball, if not in all of sports, but it was proving to be an albatross. The Gents were the biggest news in the country, their unprecedented story spilling out of the sports pages into the nation's consciousness, but he, the journalist responsible for it all, now couldn't get an interview with their bat boy.

The predicament was more than simply damaging to Mann's ego: his editors at the *Post* were running out of patience; the goodwill derived from his extraordinary column was evaporating. Nor did he think he was paranoid to feel that the praise heaped on Mike Tremendo, a bright Columbia Journalism School product recently hired by the sports department, portended a challenge. He recognized the managerial stroking of the latest discovery as the same treatment he had received during the early upward spiral of his own career.

Furthermore, his relationship with Marti, once central to his sense of well-being, had deteriorated so as to seem beyond salvation. Following their blowup over Stan's "outing" column, his wife, had avoided all physical contact with him. Conversation was limited to essentials like, "Here's your dinner" and "Your shirts are on the bed." She spent her evenings riveted to the television. For Stan, the coldness that now enveloped their communications made the once-exciting prospect of going home doubly depressing.

Stan kept believing that what he had done by identifying the closeted gay ballplayers had been not only journalistically appropriate but also morally right. "They've never been happier, for Crissake," he argued. "They're playing better than ever *and* they've been liberated. You're dead wrong, Marti."

She refused to agree. She treated him as if he were a shameless fraud who had bartered his principles for a mere column. "You had no idea what would happen to those guys when you ran their names," she said. "And you didn't give a damn. All you wanted was the story."

To delay the bitter encounters at home and disguise his inability to get to the Gents, Stan lingered at the office, digging into the files and his memory to resurrect the tidbits of baseball lore that seemed to delight his readers and placate his bosses. He was consequently grateful for the approach of the All-Star Game, notable down the years for its lode of anecdotes. Among the most perennially reliable was the 1934 event, which, in his desperation, Stan dredged up and retold. It had been played at the Polo Grounds, home of the then New York Giants. Their ace left-handed pitcher, Carl Hubbell, had successively struck out five of the American League's most fearsome sluggers: Babe Ruth, Lou Gehrig, Jimmie Foxx, Al Simmons, and Joe Cronin.

For his next column on the topic of All-Star Games, he picked another morsel of baseball lore, a memorable game played in 1939 at Yankee Stadium. Six members of the same team — the New York Yankees — graced the American League's starting scorecard: Center fielder Joe DiMaggio, catcher Bill Dickey, second baseman Joe Gordon, third baseman Red Rolfe, right fielder George Selkirk, and starting pitcher Red Ruffing. Stan told his readers that such a lineup was a first in All-Star history. The response was so enthusiastic that he felt hopeful about the market for nostalgia.

Despite the brush-off he was getting from the Gents, Stan kept tracking their fortunes. He attended almost all the home games and watched the others on television. His best source, he had to admit, was that goofy female, O. J. Cobb, who covered the team for FNG Cable. O. J., as she insisted on being called, was flattered by his attention and welcomed all queries about the Gents. "It means a lot to me, Stan, uh, Mister Mann, to be a source for *you*," she said over a postgame beer. "You're a legend in my own time."

It was from O. J. that Stan learned about Toote's new habits. Customarily first in the clubhouse and last to leave, Dick was showing up late for batting practice and occasionally dashing out quickly after the final out. "I don't know what's got into him," O. J. told the sportswriter. "He even turned down a few chances to be on *Cobb's Closet*."

Mann commiserated, "It must be something major."

His newsman's curiosity nagged him. A few days later, as he was leaving the ballpark following an afternoon game, Stan saw Toote jump into a cab. Remembering Cobb's comments, he decided on impulse to follow the ballplayer, even though he knew he was too old to be chasing cabs. "Can you follow that cab?" Stan asked the driver, adding lamely, "I see an old friend in it." The driver peered at his passenger in the rearview mirror before roaring off in pursuit.

To Stan's surprise, Toote's cab took the eastbound entrance to the Long Island Expressway and headed away from the city. Mangled by the rush-hour traffic, Stan's driver barely managed to keep his quarry in sight. They continued for more than half an hour, and Stan began to regret his impulse as the meter clicked beyond $20. Where the hell was Toote headed? Certainly nowhere Stan wanted to go. These days, he thought dolefully, he would have difficulty justifying the trip on his *Post* expense account. Especially if no story resulted.

His concern eased as his driver alertly followed Toote's cab into the slow lane and then off the expressway at Exit 45, identified as Manetto Hill Road. The lead cab accelerated off the ramp, ignored a sign indicating "Plainview," and followed an arrow that pointed toward "Woodbury." They passed a few light industrial plants and shortly were humming through areas pockmarked by Texaco and Gulf gas stations and delicatessens with beckoning Budweiser and Miller signs.

The commercial belt gave way to residential neighborhoods of small ranch-style houses behind whose picture windows Stan imagined unseen families conducting the rituals of suburban living. Kids peering at MTV while their moms peeled potatoes and trimmed steaks in anticipation of the arrival of their husbands. Maybe these days the moms were out on the job, too, Stan thought, working in law offices and schools and hospitals to bring home the bucks that kept the mortgages paid. It was all speculation, all beyond his experience, though. He had no home in the suburbs, no mortgage to pay off, no working wife, no children. Soon, perhaps, he projected, no wife at all, and maybe no work, either.

A few minutes after a sign welcomed them to Huntington, the post–World War II split-levels reverted to an earlier era of turreted Victorian houses with sweeping front porches and cushioned gliders. The town looked unpretentious, old-fashioned. Moments later Stan found himself in a small "downtown," a tree-fringed Main Street lined with banks, boutiques, and jewelry stores, seafood restaurants and pizza parlors. A few turns and the neighborhood became less picturesque, more commercial again. Auto repair shops with yawning garages, weathered second-hand clothing stores, and food markets hawking wares in Spanish stretched along the street. Toote's taxi slowed on New York Avenue and pulled into the driveway of a contemporary two-story building whose striking glass and steel exterior contrasted sharply with its aging neighbors. Stan noted that except for a three-digit number on its facade, the structure bore no identification.

"Keep going, Abdul," Stan said, using the name on the hack license. The driver drove on for several blocks until Stan directed him to double back. As he watched Toote walk to the building's rear entrance, Stan wrote down the address and morosely gave Abdul his own in Manhattan.

"What the hell was Toote up to?" Stan grumbled to himself in anger and frustration. This trip would cost at least 50 bucks, which, given its fruitlessness, he'd be damned lucky to get back from the *Post*. It had taken two hours of his life and produced nothing but a boring ride on the Long Island Expressway. Or had it? Stan's reportorial instincts revved up again. Why had Toote taxied out from the ballpark to Huntington? There had to be a story there. If only he could find it.

At the **Post,** Stan went immediately to what used to be called the morgue in his early days, doubtless because it was the repository of dead news, but was now, in politically correct times, called the library. The library was rumored to be only nanoseconds from being deposed by an "electronic retrieval system" where every story, every statistic, every bit and byte of data and reference material would be stored on computer disks and hard drives. In a corner of the room, where dog-eared volumes were chained to a rack, Stan picked through the heap of source books until he found a well-worn copy of *Cole's Reverse Directory.* Thumbing to Suffolk County, and Huntington, Stan located New York Avenue and then the address he had jotted in his notebook.

"Awlll righttt!" he shouted exuberantly, sending faces swiveling toward him. The address read, "Long Island Association for AIDS Care, Inc."

Stan wasted no time. After calling up the Gents' roster on the screen of his word processor, he quickly phoned Dick Toote at home.

"Gotta talk to you ASAP," he barked after identifying himself.

"You must be confused, Mann," Toote said coldly. "I

don't have anything to say to you. In case you've forgotten why, I can refresh your recollection."

"Look, Toote, let's forget that. If you'd just stop and think about it, you'd realize I helped put your team together. Now, I've come up with something else that concerns you. I'm calling to give you a chance to talk about it, to give your side. If you don't, this column may not be as beneficial as the last one. I think you're making a big mistake, because I'm going to go with it anyhow. Now do you want to talk to me today or read about it tomorrow?"

"Don't try to bully me," Toote snapped. "People like you write what they want regardless of what they're told. Whatever it is, you're just looking for more sensation, not more accuracy. Haven't you done enough damage?" Toote hung up.

"Sonuvabitch!" Stan yelled through the dead telephone line. "Read it and weep." Don't these guys realize how they're hurting themselves when they stonewall, he wondered. He still had his story, but he wanted confirmation from Toote. Stan had wanted Toote to discuss the situation, to give the piece some humanity. Not incidentally, Stan felt, it would make *him* appear more compassionate, maybe even more appealing to Marti. But Toote's response had killed that possibility.

Stan made what he knew would be a futile phone call to the Long Island Association for AIDS Care to find out Toote's involvement. He was told that such information was confidential. Doubly frustrated, he turned to his keyboard and began punching out "Mann to Man."

Is the news that everyone's been waiting for and nobody wants to hear ready to break? We've all watched the Gents make sports and social history. Are they now going to make medical history? After adding

"gays" to baseball's vernacular, are they about to provide still another four-letter word? And is it "AIDS"?
Maybe Dick Toote knows the answer. But somebody
else will have to ask him. He won't talk to me.

Stan read over what he had written, nodded with
satisfaction, and stitched together the remainder of the
next day's column with bits of gossip and trivia. Before
sending it to the copy desk for editing, he muttered,
"That should shake things up a little." Toote's hostility,
his stubborn insistence that he had been wronged by
the press, helped ease any pangs of conscience that Stan
felt about his unverified conclusions. He had given
Toote a sporting chance.

Dick Toote had no illusions about what was in store
for him. If he needed any convincing, his dealings with
the media since that historic press conference six
months earlier had made evident some reporters'
ruthlessness in pursuit of a story. He had heard politicians and celebrities protest how the press abandoned
fairness and accuracy in the heat of a feeding frenzy
over some apparent misdeed or scandal. He had read
false stories about a nonexistent ski mask in the journalistic furor surrounding the O. J. Simpson murder
case. And, a few years earlier, in an American history
course at Stanford, he had listened as a professor lec-
tured about media's irresponsibility in the fifties, when
they'd rushed to air phony charges of disloyalty from a
senator named Joseph McCarthy, and of the conse-
quent destruction of careers and reputations. And now
it had happened to ballplayers whose most precious
right, the right to privacy, had been violated because of
their sexual orientation. He had heard his teammates
anguish over the impact of being outed. How parents,

brothers, sisters, friends, and even, in some cases, wives and children had reacted to learning the players were homosexuals.

Toote bristled when he recalled the nearly universal response of the media to the assemblage of gays on the Gents team—the tasteless headlines, the savage cartoons, the bigoted barbs that had accompanied the news. And he angrily remembered that, with few exceptions, those free to express opinions—the commentators and columnists and editorial writers—had demonstrated equal ridicule and disdain toward the Gents. Mann, whom he had always admired, had joined the pack. Indeed, one of the lessons this season had taught him, Toote felt, was an awareness of how similarly the media reacted to events of any kind. They created heroes and villains quickly and tended to keep assigning those labels despite any new evidence. In the daily press, at least, second thoughts were rare, apologies virtually nonexistent.

He had no idea what Mann was up to, but knew that it was no good. The *Post* columnist's identification of the gay ballplayers, despite the fact that they had combined to become his teammates, in Toote's mind marked Mann as unscrupulous and certainly not to be trusted. But he wondered what he had done now to prompt the phone call and the urgency in Mann's voice. Toote tried to review his recent activities on and off the field through Mann's eyes as a journalist. And then, suddenly, he got it.

Even before the phone began ringing, Dick Toote had reserved the upstairs room at Gallagher's for another press conference. He had briefly considered involving the Gents' management—Scrappy and Ruby—in his plans. But recalling the haranguing that had preceded his "coming out party," he decided instead to retain control and preserve secrecy until ready to make his disclosure. However, he thought Ruby would be useful to inform the media of the time and place. Toote spoke to the public relations man at the ballpark that night.

"Another press conference?" Ruby asked with alarm. The memory of Toote's sensational announcement six months ago still made his guts twist.

"Don't worry," Toote said, reassuringly squeezing Ruby's arm. "I can handle it."

Ruby's insides were still churning when he informed Scrappy.

"Holy shit!" Scrappy bellowed. "What's comin' off now?"

"He won't say," Ruby replied. "Just told me he'd take care of it."

"You don't know nothin'?" Scrappy roared back. "What's goin' on? What's the rumors? What do the others say? You know them guys are closer'n the cheeks on your butt. I need to know what's goin' on. Get me something, for Crissakes. I got a champeenship team here. I don't want nothing screwing it up."

Ruby, taking the onslaught with hunched shoulders, nodded rapidly, like a hen pecking for corn. "Sure, Scrappy, sure," he said, quickly backing away. "Soon's I can."

As the game was about to get under way, Ruby made his way to the right field corner where O. J. Cobb and her two assistants had their television booth. Olivia, as usual, was wearing a pink *Cobb's Closet* T-shirt. She had on black designer jeans and black sneakers. Her long, black hair reflected the stadium floodlights.

"Hey, O. J." the PR man said with a forced smile. "How ya doin'? Boy, oh, boy, was that a good show you put on last night."

"Oh, thanks a lot, Ruby. I guess you mean last week. That's when we had our last *Cobb's Closet.*"

"Yeah, kid," Ruby nodded, "that's what I meant. It stayed with me, y'know what I mean?"

"Well," O. J. said, "coming from *you* that means a lot. You're like a myth to me." She smiled engagingly at the older man. It was a crinkly sort of grin, not flirtatious, but ingenuous and disarming. Olivia, unaware of her charm, didn't think to exploit this advantage.

Ruby smiled back. "Thanks, kid. I been around the bases a few times. Any time I can help you, just let me know."

"Oh, thank *you*, Ruby. And y'know, the same goes for me."

"Well, I appreciate that, O. J.," Ruby said, placing a fatherly hand around the young announcer's shoulder.

"Matter of fact, there is something you might be able to help me with."

"Anything at all," O. J. replied happily.

"Thing is," Ruby continued. "I need to know a little about what's goin' on with Toote. There's all kinda talk floatin' around, y'know?"

"Oh, yeah," O. J. said. "Stan Mann was asking me, too. You mean about the way he's been acting lately. Like getting to the park late and leaving so fast after the games. And looking so worried and all. You'd think he was sick or something."

"Waddayuh mean, sick?" Ruby demanded, just as an executive of the Gay Men's Health Crisis began singing the national anthem.

The Gents had barely taken the field before Ruby found Mann in the press box. "Gotta talk," Ruby gasped, winded from the long walk and high climb. Stan followed the public relations man to the privacy of a temporarily isolated walkway. "What's up, Ruby? You look worried. Is there an empty seat in the house?"

Normally Ruby enjoyed bantering with the sportswriters. He savored the give-and-take and relished their needling. He usually gave as good as he got. But tonight he was in no mood for kibitzing.

"Look, Stan, I ain't got the stomach for that right now. What's doing with Toote?"

Mann gave Ruby a long, appraising look. "Well, he's hittin' about .400, got 30 home runs, 61 RBIs. That's according to the *Post,* of course, so it may be a little off."

"I ain't talkin' stats, Mann. I know his stats. What I'm talkin' is," Ruby had difficulty getting it out, "is his *health*."

"What do *you* hear?" Stan asked suspiciously. So far as he knew, the content of tomorrow's column was known only to his editors.

"Only what that kid, O. J., told me. That you were nosing around about what's botherin' Toote. His personal stuff, like that. If something's up, we gotta know. The guy's a helluva big part of this ball club."

"Tell you what, Ruby," Stan said, confident that his item was still exclusive. "Read me tomorrow."

Ruby was hurt. He had an indisputable reputation for trustworthiness. One of his unofficial roles, in fact, was to serve as a sounding board for reporters' story ideas and even for the stories themselves. He had never violated such a confidence, not even when the target had been the Gents or Scrappy. And here was Mann holding out on him, treating him like some bush leaguer.

"That's bullshit, Mann," he said angrily. As he turned to go, Ruby took aim. "Just in case your buddies forget to tell you, Toote's got a press conference tomorrow. One P.M. at Gallagher's. *You* might learn somethin'."

Gallagher's was packed with a lunchtime crowd when Toote arrived a half hour before his press conference was scheduled to begin. And when he got upstairs to the private room he had reserved, it was chaos. As he pressed his way through the mass of journalists, photographers, and technicians, it was obvious that Mann's item was on everyone's mind and lips.

"There he is!" a radio sportscaster shouted, temporarily abandoning the microphone he was attaching to the lectern. For a moment there was absolute quiet and then a clamor of excited voices and fusillade of flashbulbs exploded in the long, narrow room.

"Hey, Toote, how do ya feel?"

"What's goin' on this time?"

"Is it true?"

"What's the story, Dick?"

In response, Toote just shook his head and forced his way through the unruly crowd. He could have been mistaken, but it seemed as if the reporters opened a path with unusual alacrity. One of those who appeared anxious to avoid physical contact was a local telecaster not noted for his sensitivity. "Hell," the guy muttered with a touch of bewilderment, "he looks pretty healthy to me."

Toote took the two steps up to the lectern in a single stride and whistled sharply into the microphone. Silence replaced the babble, like a TV clicked off. "Thank you," Toote said, "glad you could come." Appraising the huge turnout, he grinned and nodded in the direction of Stan Mann. "I guess the *Post*'s circulation has picked up." Audible chuckles. Stan Isaacs smiled and said to *New York Times* columnist George Vecsey, "Grace under pressure." Isaacs had recently attended a Hemingway symposium.

Toote's expression turned serious. "The last time we were together you had no idea why you were here. Not until I told you something about myself that had never occurred to you. You found it tough to buy, and I imagine you accepted it only because you had just two choices: Either I was gay and stupid for saying so, or straight and crazy for thinking that I wasn't. And it was easier to believe that I was stupid." Vecsey nodded appreciatively.

"This time," Toote continued, "you came with an idea in mind. An idea that you got from Stan Mann. You think I have AIDS. And that's supposed to be news. Back when Magic Johnson announced that he had tested HIV positive, it made *big* news. And Magic became something of a hero. I'm sure you all remember that."

There were murmurs of recollection.

"Well, you may not remember what else was said then," Toote went on. "Or who said it. It was Martina Navratilova. And she said it to the *Post,* the same *Post.*

Toote produced a newspaper clipping and began to

read the tennis legend's words. " 'Like if I had the AIDS virus, if people would be understanding? No, because they'd say I'm gay — I had it coming. That's why they're accepting it with him, because supposedly he got it through heterosexual contact. There have been other athletes who died from AIDS, and they were pushed aside because they either got it from drugs or they were gay.' And she went on to say a few more things, but I'm sure you get the idea."

Toote paused and looked slowly around the room before resuming. "Now get ready, because here comes my announcement: I do *not* have AIDS. I'll repeat that: Dick Toote does *not* have AIDS. I am *not* HIV positive. It so happens that I tested negative this week. That's the second negative in six months, which means that unless I was exposed to the AIDS virus within the past couple of months — which I have *not* been — there is no basis for Mann's charges, accusations, insinuations, suggestions, hints, innuendoes, whatever you want to call them."

The room burst into an uproar. Toote waited a few moments before whistling loudly into the microphone.

"OK. Now, let's go over this together. Magic Johnson, a self-described *heterosexual,* announces that he is going to *stop* playing professional basketball — is ending a brilliant career — because he tested *positive* for the virus that causes AIDS. And sportswriters and columnists and editorial writers fall all over themselves calling him a hero, saying that he's courageous for telling the truth — a truth, by the way, that he might have found *pretty* difficult to conceal.

"Now, here we have Dick Toote, a self-described *homosexual,* being more or less *compelled* to announce

that he is going to *continue* playing professional baseball because he *doesn't* have AIDS."

Toote paused and looked around the room, making
eye contact with the people he knew. "I don't know what
they call that in journalism school, but I call it a double
standard. I call it mudslinging. I call it homophobia. I
call it gay bashing."

Stan flinched. Here was the ultimate confirmation of
Marti's contempt, that for the sake of a sensational
story he had sunk finally to gutter journalism. And he
knew that he deserved that contempt. No amount of
rationalization or sophistry, no contorted moral gym-
nastics, could justify the way he had violated Toote and
perverted his own power. What had he come to? How
had he gotten here? What, he asked himself, had become of the young idealist who had taken to heart the
challenge to "afflict the comfortable and comfort the
afflicted"?

Stan tried to reconstruct the recent past in an effort
to comprehend his decline. But all he could sniff was his
own fear. It was nothing dramatic, he knew, just a slow,
inexorable process. Over the years, aware of the energy
and ambition of his younger colleagues, he had only
dimly recognized that he no longer was consumed with
the same desire. It had been different in the old days.
You went after the story, not the next rung in the corporate ladder. Hell, you gloried in being a reporter. Now,
these J-school graduates can't wait to move on, to become editors, executives. They like the money, the social climbing. They suck around for invitations from
celebrities. What ever became of getting drunk with the
boss after work, swapping absurd stories of derring-do,
getting fired on Friday and rehired on Monday? All that

excitement had gone with his old pals, now mostly retired or dead.

Stan realized the truth. He was not just isolated; he
had stopped caring about his profession, once a prime
source of joy and excitement, of fun. As he removed
himself from Toote's accusatory eye and the sudden
coldness of the room, he made a mental note: "I've got to
survive. I'll do whatever is necessary."

Leaving the press conference without responding to questions gave Toote the opportunity to deal with the press at arm's length — or, more precisely, at phone's length. He could talk to the reporters or publications he preferred and decline interviews with the others. His first choice was Robert Lypstik of the *Times,* a journalist he admired for his sensitivity to mavericks and pariahs. Toote smiled when he thought how this would rankle Stan Mann.

Over lunch at The Velvet Glove in Greenwich Village, and later at his apartment, Toote described for Lypstik the events of the past few months that had culminated with Mann's surmising, publicly and incorrectly, that he had contracted AIDS. He talked openly and at length to his attentive listener, pouring out the feelings that had been simmering so long. Lypstik occasionally interrupted with gentle questions until Toote had fully traced the geographic and emotional route that had begun at a fund-raising benefit in the Hamptons, then led to the Long Island Association for AIDS Care and, ultimately, to Terry.

Based on the experiences Toote described, the *Times* writer constructed a series of articles exploring a broad range of professional and volunteer efforts aimed at mitigating the impact of AIDS. He began where the Gent's star had: with an invitation Toote had received the year before to attend an AIDS fundraiser in East Hampton.

Like many young, well-to-do Manhattan residents, both straight and gay, Toote was no stranger to the area known as the Hamptons at the tip of Long Island. He had swum, partied, and "cruised" the upscale, pleasure-loving precincts whenever the team's schedule and his own permitted. He had discovered the broad beaches and roaring surf, clamorous bars and posh restaurants during his first season with the Gents, and found that even the three-hour drives did not diminish the pleasures of those sybaritic respites. As a recreational tennis player, he eagerly accepted when a friend associated with Guild Hall, East Hampton's cultural center, asked if he would take part in a celebrity tournament to benefit AIDS research.

At a splendid estate, under blue skies, a warming sun, and gentle sea breezes, the function attracted hundreds of curious, moneyed contributors who paid $250 to watch literary, theatrical, and film stars eat lunch and play tennis. They saw Alec Baldwin and Kim Basinger, Kurt Vonnegut and E. L. Doctorow, Lauren Bacall, Alan Alda and Dina Merrill, Kathleen Turner and Joseph Heller. These celebrities were among the many prominent summer people who move their creativity, networking, power tripping, and social consciences out East for a few months each year. Toote's only discomfort, a pang of guilt, came when, regarded as a heterosexual, he had been teamed up with an openly gay food writer against another presumably straight-gay twosome in a Hamptons-style "mixed doubles" match.

Along with the fun, there was some serious business: a pitch for contributions to fight AIDS that included a rundown on what was — and wasn't — being done. It was during this solicitation that Toote's interest was awakened by the enthusiasm of a representative from the Long Island Association for AIDS Care. Later, Toote encountered the young man at the bar and found his forthrightness appealing.

"We call ourselves *Lye-ack*," he said, pronouncing the acronym. "Somebody pointed out that if we changed it to the Long Island *League,* we could call ourselves LILAC."

Toote chuckled. It was refreshing to talk with someone who didn't always take endangered life morbidly. By the time he left East Hampton, he decided to become a volunteer.

Despite his schedule — the Gents schedule, actually — Toote got no dispensation. If he wanted to become a volunteer, he was told by LIAAC, he would be trained like everyone else. LIAAC was firm when it came to regulations. During May and early June, he had been able to put together a split weekend that met the association's requirements.

At an orientation meeting, a staff member described the opportunities open to volunteers. Lawyers and accountants were urged to lend their professional services. Others, like Toote, could answer questions about AIDS over a telephone hotline; speak to school, business, and organization audiences about dealing with the disease and those afflicted by it; deliver meals to shut-ins and transport them for treatment; visit hospitalized clients; and become a "buddy" to someone with AIDS.

Like all LIAAC volunteers, regardless of their roles, Toote had to attend a two-day training session to learn about the disease and its transmission, and he heard how to avoid it, detect it, and cope with it. He heard from doctors, nurses, psychologists, home-care workers, people with AIDS, relatives of those with AIDS, and those whose loved ones had died of AIDS.

He gave Lypstik an anecdote. "One of the training instructors warned us that when you're working the hotline you've got to expect anything. She said a man called her sounding really panicky. He said he had just given a blow job to a guy who *then* told him he had AIDS. He was ready to do something desperate. The man told her, 'I know I'm going to get it, I *know* it.' She asked him why he was so sure, and he said, 'Because I swallowed it, that's why!' "

Toote said the training instructor then explained she was able to tell the caller that oral sex is the least risky type of behavior, especially if there are no mouth sores or cuts or tears. "You see," she told the trainees, "if we hadn't kept chatting that might never have come out. There's just so much ignorance and misinformation out there."

Toote stressed that street language was the rule at LIAAC, and Lypstik shook his head disappointedly, pointing out that he didn't see how the *Times* would publish the anecdote in anything resembling its actual form. "Well," Toote replied, "what's really important is getting the truth out so people can deal with reality."

The Gents star continued. "There were about two dozen people in my class; about half male, half female, almost all either gay men or lesbians. Most were under 30 and had lost a friend or lover or relative to AIDS. There was a middle-aged woman whose son had died from the disease; another was a man who told us that he was HIV positive.

"But, the thing was, nobody was feeling sorry for themselves. Maudlin was definitely out; so were euphemisms. Words like 'sick' and 'dying' were used all the time, used matter-of-factly. I'm telling you, that experience was intense."

Toote had left each of the day-long sessions exhausted but stimulated. It wouldn't be easy to minister to the terminally ill. It was the closest he had come to the scourge of his generation, and he often felt sick and depressed and angry, too. "Angry," he told the *Times* writer, "because for a long time nobody seemed to give a damn so long as it was something they felt was happening only to queers!"

Toote paused for a moment. "I guess it was the anger that made me know I had to get involved. And I mean *really* involved. So I decided to be a 'buddy.' That meant spending a few hours every week with someone who had full-blown AIDS."

The most critical aspect of buddying, he told Lypstik, was the unique character of the relationship. It would be limited in intimacy and length—the former by LIAAC's rules, the latter by the lethal inevitability of the disease. It meant being something other than a friend, servant, companion, or lover. "Dying people are invariably isolated, fearful, and in great need," Toote said soberly. "The emotional demands on the buddy are tremendous. That's why contact is limited to once a week."

The primary goal in matching buddy to client is compatibility. "I chose Terry," Toote said, "because I preferred to be associated with a gay, easygoing man. Did you know," he continued, as the reporter checked his tape recorder, "that contrary to what one might expect on Long Island, the largest category of those with AIDS is heterosexual drug abusers? And there's an unusually high proportion of women."

Toote abruptly halted his recollections. Maybe he had told Lypstik all he needed to know. But the writer looked at him expectantly, and Toote went on. Terry's story, however personal and painful, was essential. Toote explained that his own celebrity status, and even his well-known name, had been withheld from Terry, because LIAAC felt that the success of buddy relationships required that the volunteer and the client enter as equals. But there had been little doubt about Terry's exuberance when, together with a case manager, they met at Terry's apartment in Huntington. "Terry recognized me immediately," Toote recalled.

When he and Terry had shaken hands, Toote found himself assessing Terry's grip, measuring the state of his health. And he had looked at Terry intently, unconsciously searching for evidence of the disease. "Just like everyone else," he told Lypstik, "I was apprehensive." But, he added, there was nothing to see. The havoc to Terry's immune system was invisible. "He said he felt strong and healthy," Toote recalled. "And he looked it."

Considering his words carefully — LIAAC imposed an intractable rule aimed at preserving confidentiality — Toote gave Lypstik a description of Terry. "A husky, brown-haired guy in his early thirties working as a computer programmer for a Long Island electronics manufacturer. Grew up in Little Rock and came to New

York after graduating from the University of Arkansas."

Toote also described how he and Terry had spent their time together in the weeks following their meeting. They had gone for long walks on Long Island's hilly North Shore, along woodsy trails that had thus far escaped suburban development. They drove to Manhattan to visit the Metropolitan Museum of Art and the Museum of Modern Art. They'd spent hours watching the free-roaming big cats and dodging the baby carriages and strollers at the Bronx Zoo. And they went to Gents Stadium: Toote on the field, Terry in the stands. LIAAC's rules were very explicit: no alcohol, no drugs, no sex. But the rules were irrelevant in their case. Toote did not tell Lypstik that he loved Terry like the brother he'd never had.

Lypstik's series drew considerable attention. It was the first time a daily newspaper had plumbed the murky AIDS scene in such detail. The fact that the guide was not only a celebrity but a baseball star even brought in a vast teenage audience. There were, to be sure, critics. Among the most vociferous was Donald Bigg, the Yankees' owner, who took every opportunity to attack Toote, the Gents, gays, those with AIDS, the *Times,* and Lypstik as perverters of youth, America, and, worst of all, baseball.

But neither Bigg's tirades nor similar invective from some of the other owners was sufficient to keep Toote — and the rest of the Gents — from being selected by fans as the National League's starting lineup in the All-Star Game. It was another first, eclipsing the 1939 Yankees' contribution of six starters.

Toote was excited to hear the news, and relieved that Lypstik had handled the material about him and Terry with accuracy and compassion. His only regret was that he hadn't seen Stan Mann's face when the series had appeared in the *Times*.

••31••

The simultaneous appearance of nine gay All Stars on national television triggered a reaction of seismic dimensions. The fact that they powered the National League to an overwhelming 10–1 victory shattered the preconceptions of the sports establishment and baseball fans. In living rooms throughout the country, families watched their TV screens transfixed as stereotypes of effeminacy and deviance evaporated.

Those uninterested in baseball were not spared the revelation. Commentators, columnists, and editorial writers expounded on the social significance of the contest. David Letterman devoted a week of one-liners to the phenomenon. "Some religious leaders were worried about the effect that a great gay baseball team would have on America's young people, so they asked the Vatican for advice. The Vatican said that a homosexual team was OK, so long as it didn't practice."

Pollsters, led by Dore Dupus, recorded an unprecedented reversal of public opinion as adult Americans indicated by huge margins that now they not only tolerated gays but also had come to regard them as desirable colleagues, neighbors, elected officials, and elementary-school teachers. (Dupus, deeming it overkill, quashed a finding that a gay candidate would be preferred for the presidency.) Statistically, it appeared that the great American public had undergone an unprecedented change of mind. The poll results were followed immediately by statements from politicians, including the occupant of the Oval Office, linking the Gents' extraordinary performance to the American way.

T-shirts bearing the Gents logo began to appear in stores from coast to coast. A Footloose Sneakers commercial featured a slogan: "Just Do It. Your Way." Rappers rushed out labels exhorting homosexuality and lesbianism. *Time* put all nine Gents All Stars on its cover. *Newsweek* highlighted a special section entitled "Out Is In."

In New York the response was even more positive — and frenzied. At Gents Stadium, the AIDS hotline number, which had once appeared alone, a solitary beacon in a sea of blank billboards, was now all but obscured by an explosion of advertisements hawking everything from beer to building supplies. The mayor, contending he had stuck by the club from the beginning, wrangled permission to croak "The Star-Spangled Banner" before a sold-out house at a weekend doubleheader. He wore a huge button stating: "I AM NONJUDGMENTAL!"

Scrappy was swamped with proposals for television coverage, including requests from every company he had solicited in vain before the season's opener. Ted Turner enticed him onto his private jet for a lunch with Jane, but even the promise of her presence on demand at any and all games — regardless of the Atlanta Braves' schedule — was unavailing. Scrappy spent the entire flight praising the realism of her performance as a hooker in *Klute,* disclosing only after they landed that the Gents' TV deals were handled by Rick Volpino and Mea Culpa. Volpino, salivating over this unforeseen potential for TV deals, was frantically consulting lawyers in an attempt to break the contract with Morris Jacob and FNG Cable. Morris, after considering staggering offers from Volpino to sell out, had decided that keeping Olivia and his wife occupied and happy was priceless.

O. J.'s exclusive connection with the team had propelled her into media-business stardom: a photo of her in a black miniskirt so short it made her father howl in anguish wound up on the first page of the *Times'* Monday "Business Day" section and, more important to her, in *People* and *New York* magazines. Meanwhile FNG's audience had soared far beyond anything ever recorded by cable anywhere, and was closing in on the local market's Kennedy assassination ratings. The erstwhile ragtag TV team was savoring a new experience — celebrity.

And the Gents continued to win. Endorsement propositions, talk-show invitations, and ghost-written book solicitations occupied so much of their time that they were forced to hire business managers. All was going so well in every way that Scrappy, the inveterate pessimist, steeled himself for what he intuited as some indefinable but inexorable disaster. Yet the only discordant sound he heard was the unremitting carping of Donald Bigg, joined now by Rush Limbaugh. The public relations avalanche roared on.

Toote continued to spend time with Terry, although the team's road games now precluded a weekly arrangement. After a two-week swing to the West Coast against the Padres, Dodgers, and Giants, Dick came home to find Terry suffering from a nagging cough that defied medication. Toote reported the cough to the LIAAC case manager, who set up an appointment for Terry at North Shore University Hospital in Manhasset, one of three Long Island facilities geared for the treatment of AIDS patients. Terry was diagnosed with pneumonia and hospitalized.

In their furor to cover the incredible Gents, the media were virtually ignoring the success of another New York club. In any normal season, the Yankees would be dominating the sports pages. Off to an early lead in the spring, they had opened a 20-game gap over their nearest divisional opponents, the Boston Red Sox, by the beginning of August. In Las Vegas, they were odds-on to win the American League pennant, setting up an all but certain subway series with the Gents.

Unlike their power-propelled dynasties of the past, when long-ball hitting by such legends as Ruth, Gehrig, DiMaggio, Keller, Berra, Mantle, and Maris had brought world championships to Yankee Stadium, the current team was eating up the opposition through speed, guile, defense, and, most importantly, pitching. The ace of the staff was a rookie phenom named Lou Lewe, a tireless fireballer who unfailingly pitched twice a week and had picked up his twentieth victory before July ended. Considered a clear choice for Rookie of the Year, Lulu, as he was called, was also favored to win the Cy Young Award and to become the American League's Most Valuable Player. His most spectacular performance occurred on the Fourth of July, when he started and won both ends of a doubleheader — with shutouts.

Scrappy was hardly unmindful of the way the races were shaping up. "Sonuvabitch, Ruby," he said as the

Gents were stomping the Phillies one August evening, "if we ain't gonna wind up with Donald in October."

Ruby nodded knowingly. "And won't you love to whup his ass."

Scrappy scratched his head to stimulate thought. "No piece of cake, Ruby. He's got a good club. 'Specially that Lulu. Some arm on that kid." An unidentifiable sense of foreboding flicked out of the shadows of Scrappy's mind. "Well, we got a ways to go yet." Ruby nodded empathetically. He started to pat Scrappy on the buttocks as usual, thought better of it, and punched him lightly on the shoulder.

During August and early September an especially astute baseball statistician could have predicted the course of Dick Toote's batting average by following the progress of Terry's battle with AIDS.

And the status of Toote's batting average was of compelling interest. With the season winding down, the Gents star had become the first ballplayer in more than half a century to flirt with .400, commanding the attention of statisticians and fans alike. In the sports sections of newspapers and on the sports segments of the nightly TV news, Toote's game-by-game performance was being compared with that of former Red Sox slugger Ted Williams, who in 1941 hit an incredible .406. Further, the 61-home-run 1961 season of Roger Maris, the late Yankee outfielder, was not out of sight, nor was the Cubs' Hack Wilson's 1930 total of 190 runs batted in.

The pressure was enormous. To maintain his percentage, Toote needed two hits a day, and going two for five—an accomplishment for most players—merely kept him even. The intense scrutiny did not help. Although he was heartened by the overwhelming support of the fans, including those on the road, Toote's recordbreaking bid goaded opposing pitchers to their utmost. They pursued recognition for themselves the way Western gunslingers once challenged Billy the Kid.

Terry's discharge from the hospital, after little more than a week, gave Toote's spirits a tremendous lift; he celebrated by going five for five, hitting two homers and driving in six runs. Visiting Terry at home, Toote was surprised by what he saw. Although he had dropped a few pounds, Terry did not seem any the worse for his encounter with pneumonia. Moreover, his outlook was optimistic, his mood upbeat. He told Toote some amusing hospital anecdotes; they both had a good laugh over an incident in which a drag queen, mistakenly sent to the women's section, had vehemently asserted his masculinity in soprano tones. Terry omitted the fact that two fellow patients had died during his stay.

With the Gents in New York, the two had several opportunities to get together, and Toote was amazed, a week later, at Terry's robustness and apparent total recovery. He had gained back the lost weight, renewed his healthy tan, and looked even more fit than before his confinement. At a LIAAC buddy session, Toote mentioned Terry's remarkable recuperation to the other volunteers, whose own experience with the phenomenon had been similar. "The change can be unbelievable," the group leader agreed, adding, "either way."

The media coverage of Toote now dealt exclusively with his on-field activities. The Lypstik series in the *Times* had been so definitive, both thorough and intimate—although, of course, concealing Terry's identity—that other sportswriters, including Stan Mann, had been deterred from attempting any exploitation of the relationship.

As the Gents were about to take to the road against the Expos, Phillies, and Pirates, Toote got a call from Terry. Could he possibly come by? It was important, and it wouldn't take very long. Toote had a few free hours before the plane's departure for Montreal, and Terry sounded unusually anxious. Toote immediately caught a cab for Long Island.

When he was greeted at the door, Toote had to steel himself to keep from gasping. He needed no explanation: the ugly, purplish blotches on Terry's face told the story. It was Kaposi's sarcoma, an AIDS-related skin cancer that produces lesions all over the body, although it is neither imminently life-threatening nor painful.

"Gorgeous, aren't I?" Terry said derisively. "It's a face not even a mother could love."

"Nonsense," Dick replied briskly. "Pretend you have measles." But he felt clutched. Terry began to cry. Dick embraced him tightly, trying to keep Terry's body from quivering.

"It's got me inside and out now," Terry said through his tears. "Even strangers will know."

When he left, Toote said, "This will be a short trip. I'll call you, and when I get back we'll go catch the Matisse exhibition at the Met." Terry just nodded.

Toote was hitless in the three games against Montreal, dropping his average 12 points. Nonetheless the Gents, who didn't need the victories, won two of the three. Ruby asked Scrappy if he wanted him to have a sit-down with the first baseman, but Scrappy said not yet. "I mean, the guy's entitled to have a coupla bad days. We're only leadin' the division by, what, 25 games?"

One night after a long telephone conversation with Toote, Terry said despairingly, "I'm tired of fighting. What's the use? I'm dying."

Toote phoned the case manager. "I feel so helpless," he said. "Terry's hurting, at least in his mind, and there's nothing I can do. I can't even be with him. He's alone; you know his family's out of it. They're just sitting down there in Arkansas waiting for God knows what." Anticipating the case manager's response, he added, "I know we talked about all this in training, but Terry wasn't a real person then."

"You're doing more than you think," the case manager replied. "He needs you, and you're responding the best way you can. You can't do his suffering for him. Try to keep your mind on the game. See him when you get back."

Toote managed to concentrate for a few days. In Philadelphia, on his first trip to the plate, he caromed a drive off the center field wall and stretched it into a triple when the fielder threw lazily to second base. As usual, there were lots of Gents fans in the stands, and their roaring ovation for his hustle kept him focused for the rest of the game. He would up with four hits, raising his average to .393.

By the time the brief road trip ended, Toote was still within range of the formidable .400 goal, although his characteristic consistency had given way to cold and hot streaks: either hitless "O-fers" or multiple-hit games.

When the plane landed in New York, he immediately took a taxi to Huntington. Terry's appearance had worsened: his eyes seemed sunken; his skin had taken on a pallid cast. It was ashen, translucent, and glistened weakly, like a faint light on a rainswept night. Perhaps most distressing was his insistence on remaining indoors. The skin cancer had made him extremely self-conscious. He rejected Toote's invitation to take in some Gents games. He was not interested in going to any museums or galleries. He spent most of his time watching television, especially *One Life to Live* and *General Hospital*. When Dick remarked on his new interest in soaps, Terry said dryly, "You know what they say about misery and company." Toote sat quietly next to him, lost in popcorn and pity.

Before they knew it Toote was on the road again, this time for an extended period, as the Gents took on their divisional rivals, the Cubs and Cards, then the Reds, Braves, and Astros, before heading out to the Coast for final series with the Padres, Dodgers, and Giants. Terry and Toote hugged when Toote said good-bye. Terry said wistfully, "I guess we both know time is running out."

Toote, bracing himself, phoned after each game. Sometimes Terry was cheerful and their conversation was animated as Toote described a key play. More often Terry was morose, despite Toote's attempts to raise his spirits. One night he got no answer. The LIAAC case manager confirmed his worst fears. Terry had been hospitalized with pneumonia again. "He's very weak," the case manager said.

When Toote learned of Terry's death, he broke down on the phone and had to hang up. He fell into a chair and sobbed. He had played out Terry's ending many times in his mind, but the inoculation against grief had not taken. He felt more alone than when his parents had rejected him.

Toote called the case manager and said he wanted to fly back to New York. But the case manager discouraged him, saying, "Terry's family is taking him to Little Rock for burial." As Toote listened in anguished disbelief, he added, "Dick, I'm sorry, but they've never even heard of you."

In the final week of the regular season, Toote's batting took a nose dive and left him far short of his targets, although still comfortably ahead in all Triple Crown categories. It would now require a superhuman performance to bat .400, hit more than 61 homers, and drive in better than 190 runs. Stan Mann took the opportunity both to lionize Ted Williams for hitting .406 in 1941 and to suggest that perhaps Toote had failed in the clutch through want of resolve.

In anger and bitterness, Toote called Bob Lypstik at the *Times*. "Would you be interested in a follow-up to your series?" he asked the sportswriter. Lypstik, of course, was. At Toote's apartment, they spent several hours talking about Terry's death and Dick's exclusion from the funeral.

"Discrimination even follows homosexuals to the grave," Toote said. Gay relationships have no legal status, so "longtime companions" aren't even entitled to time off for mourning. "During buddy training, they told us that in the United States, the death of a close relative is worth three days off," Toote recalled. "For gay men or lesbians, a companion's death is not worth anything. That tells you what society thinks *you're* worth."

Lypstik wrote another column about Terry and Toote, about dying and grieving, and about bureaucracy's unwillingness to accept the truth. He explained that in Terry and Dick's case, the two men were, evoking memories of the martyred Kennedys, "dedicated brothers." This time, with Toote's approval, he identified Terry by name. It was a funeral of sorts which, this time, included Dick.

Even with the uncertainty surrounding Toote's performance, the Gents, after taking their divisional series with three straight victories over Cincinnati, were prohibitive favorites to win the National League Championship Series against Los Angeles. The Dodgers had exhausted themselves in a five-game series against the wild card Montreal Expos, after a stretch drive that saw them nosing out the San Francisco Giants by half a game to take the West Division title.

For Scrappy and the Gents, who were already pointing toward a climactic World Series confrontation with the Yankees, the prospect of a walkover in the playoffs was a mixed blessing. A minimal four-game series would give their pitching staff time for a full rest, but the lack of competition might leave the team flat rather than keen. "Like that's all you should ever hafta worry about," Ruby said when Scrappy expressed his concern. "Me, I'm wondrin' about Toote. He's the heart of this club."

Ruby's apprehensions evaporated after Toote's initial appearance at the plate in Los Angeles. With two runners on base in the first inning, he drove a fastball over the left field wall. The three-run homer proved sufficient, as the Gents went on to humiliate the Dodgers, 12–0, in the opener. Toote hit another home run and a double in five times at bat.

In *their* opening game against the potent Chicago White Sox, the Yankees, apparently also looking ahead, sailed to an 8–0 victory on the superb pitching of Lulu Lewe. In a postgame interview, Donald Bigg left no doubt of his goal. "I've been waiting all season to show what a bunch of real men will do to that collection of misfits that claim to be 'Gents.'" Donald paused to guffaw. "If ever a team was misnamed, they're it. Well, it won't be long now."

When the media reported Donald's gibes to Scrappy and sought a response, the Gents' boss thought for a moment before replying. "I can't say nothin'. It would be child abuse." That sound bite made the nightly network news.

If the Chisox were annoyed at being ignored by Donald, they didn't convert their anger into aggressiveness in the second game. The Yankees trashed them, 11–3. Meanwhile, on the other coast, Toote continued his hitting rampage against the Dodgers, going three-for-four with another home run, as the Gents coasted to an 8–1 triumph.

With two teams in the playoffs and both favored to make it into the World Series, the New York media — from the *Times* to the *Post,* from the TV network affiliates to the independents to, finally, FNG, sports editors and sports directors — brainstormed daily to come up with "major league" stories and features.

At the *Post,* Stan Mann felt the intense pressure. With the changed attitude toward gays and, particularly, toward the Gents, the mantle of homophobia he had donned was unpopular. Moreover, he hadn't been producing anything about the Gents, while young Mike Tremendo was charming colleagues and editors with his facile style and felicitous personality. Assigned to cover second-rate events, Tremendo was coming up with immensely readable stories about school-yard basketball players and college baseball stars.

In Stan's prime, his confidence high and his career soaring, he had delighted in coaching fledgling reporters, sharing his experience, helping to add depth and polish to their abundant energies and ambition. Secure in his own niche, it had never occurred to him that he might be creating future rivals, jeopardizing his own status. In some instances, the relationships had gone beyond the office. When the young people were particularly bright or interesting, Stan had shared them with Marti, inviting them out or, occasionally, home for dinner. Their marriage had been good then, and Marti had enjoyed participating in that aspect of his life.

But now Stan perceived the presence of Mike Tremendo not as an opportunity but as a threat. Unsure of his own future, he felt envy and resentment toward the newcomer, whose ultimate success already seemed assured. What rankled even more was Tremendo's manner. He was poised, self-possessed, yet without a trace of arrogance or vanity. He seemed as unaware of the impression he created as he was of his boyish good looks. And his warmth and conviviality made him virtually impossible to rebuff.

Almost from the first, Mike had sought Stan out for advice, flattering him with the recollection that Mann's guest lectures at journalism school were still regarded as highlights. Mike quoted Stan's closing line about sportswriting: "When you stop enjoying it, hang up your jock. But be good to yourself. Take it off first." And so, despite his feelings, Stan found himself captivated.

Slowly but inexorably, Stan got caught up in Mike's life. When Mike suggested having a drink after work, Stan felt unable to refuse. They talked easily about newspapering, about sports, about life. Stan's cynicism softened with exposure to the young man's enthusiasm and expectations. Mike reminded him of himself, in those days of breaking a good story, sharing insights with fellow reporters at some smoky bar, feeling his wife's loving body against him in bed. Now, with his marital relationship stretching toward the breaking point because of Marti's belief that he had caved in to sensationalism, spending time with Mike provided Stan with a welcome respite.

When the Gents and Yankees each took their respective pennants with four straight victories, the mayor hurriedly assembled a super show to celebrate New York's first subway series in almost forty years. Wearing a large button that said I AM NEUTRAL, he announced that the celebration would be held in Central Park. Stan invited Mike to join him and Marti for drinks before attending, and both seemed pleased.

Everyone predicted that it would be a World Series to remember and, when it was over, agreed that they had been right. Fifty-five thousand tickets to seven games were sold out within an hour. Psychologists, sociologists, and historians joined thousands of sportswriters and sportscasters—including more than 100 from Japan, seeking "working press" credentials. Officeholders and politicians from throughout the country pulled every string to get box seats. And in an extraordinary gesture of goodwill that was later seen as a turning point in U.S.-Cuban relations, the president invited Fidel Castro to join him for opening day.

CBS won out over its rivals for broadcasting rights in a mammoth bidding war. But the network had to accept a nonexclusive arrangement, because Ruby insisted that FNG Cable, owned by his old friend Morris Jacob, be permitted to continue carrying Gents games into the postseason. Olivia Cobb, now the famous O. J., FNG's chief and only sportscaster, saw the development as a challenge. "Guys," she said to Pluckey and Edison, her two-man crew, "we got to do our usual terrific stuff or we might drop some viewers to CBS." For emphasis, she tossed her red, white, and blue–beribboned ponytail, a hairdo created especially for the series, from one shoulder to the other.

Gents Stadium, the site of the first two games, was resplendent in pink and lavender bunting. Gentian Violet had received a dozen one-of-a-kind designer gowns to enhance his cheerleading efforts. In addition to the customary quiche and white wine proffered by the falsetto-voiced ballpark hawkers, Rick Volpino marketed a new drink called "Gentsquencher," which looked and tasted like pink lemonade.

Aside from the usual "experting," analyses of everything from batting percentages and earned-run averages to family histories and astrology charts, a number of unprecedented elements marked the preseries hoopla. There were Donald Bigg's ongoing homophobic taunting and Scrappy's increasingly indelicate rejoinders. And there was the appeal by Ruby Rubinstein to the commissioner for at least one gay umpire. After consulting with lawyers, the commissioner said that so far as he knew, *all* the umpires might be gay, but he wasn't going to compel them to declare their sexual orientation. But the most heated ruckus concerned the presence of the Cuban leader.

The president's invitation to Castro had been suggested by an ambitious young White House aide and admirer of ex-President Richard Nixon, who, in reading about *that* chief executive's overtures to what used to be called Red China, had encountered references to a series of Ping-Pong matches between American and Chinese that broke the diplomatic ice. "Sports competition breaks down barriers among participants," he asserted in a memo that found its way to the Oval Office. "So why not among spectators?" The memo went on to propose the invitation to Castro, whose fondness for baseball was better known than his contempt for homosexuals.

It was not until the White House leaked the possibility of the Castro invitation to the press, to gauge public reaction before making an official commitment, that the dictator's homophobia came to light. For in addition to the predictable opposition from Cuban refugees and right-wingers and the support from left-wingers, an unforeseen uproar arose from gay activists and AIDS authorities. Citing studies by Harvard and various human rights organizations, they denounced Castro and Cuba for discriminating against homosexuals, imposing mandatory AIDS tests on all citizens, and confining for life anyone found carrying the virus. Newspapers, led by the *New York Times* and the *Washington Post,* editorialized against the administration's decision. The *Times* called it "either another example of ignorance in foreign affairs or a calculated affront to an oppressed minority." The *Post* compared the insensitivity to former President Ronald Reagan's participation in a ceremony at a German military cemetery containing the bodies of Nazi SS troopers. However, after taking a private poll that indicated no political damage, the White House went ahead with its plan.

Moments before the opener was to begin, a huge block of choice box seats along the first baseline began to fill up with some unlikely looking fans. First came a contingent of New York City police outfitted in riot gear. Next was a group of men wearing dark suits, white shirts, conservative ties, and sunglasses. Then came a cigar-smoking complement of bearded, Spanish-speaking soldiers in fatigues. After them, the president and Fidel Castro, accompanied by aides and virtually obscured by bodyguards, made their way to an enclosed, bulletproof cubicle. Finally, a diverse bunch, dressed like tourists but carrying walkie-talkies, sought to drop inconspicuously into seats on the periphery.

The arrival of the two national leaders was greeted with raucous shouts of anger and derision, but it was unclear at whom the insults were directed. The President and Castro, as if they were being acclaimed, waved vigorously to the fans. At that point, several of the Spanish-speaking soldiers unfurled a huge banner inscribed: "YANKEES, SI! MARICÓNES, NO!"

The message sent most of the reporters and telecasters scrambling for a translation. "It means faggots," Phil Pluckey said.

"Well, ladies and gentlemen," O. J. announced with authority, "the Cuban delegation seems to be rooting for the visitors today."

The White House, pressing its diplomatic gambit, honored Castro by asking him to throw out the first ball, a choice that the mayor had strenuously opposed. "Can you imagine?" he asked rhetorically, "they need a lousy hand to throw out a ball, so they look all over the world and find one with a commie on the end of it." He called his police commissioner and told him to tow away any cars used by the Cubans.

As soon as Castro's role was determined, security experts of both nations recognized they would have a problem. The ball-throwing maneuver would require the Cuban leader to abandon the protection of the bulletproof booth. After a 12-hour brainstorming session, which concluded with an expensive dinner and a visit to a topless bar, the specialists agreed to put a porthole in the cubicle.

When the ritual singing of both national anthems was concluded, Castro's arm protruded briefly through the porthole as he whipped a fastball at Gents catcher Rhino Romanski, the designated receiver, who stood less than 30 feet distant. In one of his most athletic movements, Rhino snared the pelvis-high pitch and fired the ball back. As Castro and the president flinched, the ball ricocheted off their booth, and the Gents shouted, "Olé, Rhino!"

From the first pitch that Yankee Lulu Lewe threw, the Gents knew they were in trouble. It was a wicked slider that gave no hint of its destination when it left the rookie's hand and sped toward the plate. It was followed by a 100-miles-an-hour fastball, and then, from the same motion, a tantalizing change-up. After three pitches, the lead-off hitter, second baseman Speedy Gonzalez, was out of there.

And so it went, inning by inning. The Gents didn't move a ball out of the infield until the fourth, didn't register a hit until Gonzalez beat out a bunt in the sixth, and didn't score at all. For his part, Tony Mike, their ace, pitched as well as could have been expected, holding the Yankees to two runs. But that left the Gents two runs shy in losing the series opener.

In the second game, the Gents' bats came to life. Dick Toote blasted a home run and two doubles, Romanski added another homer, and Gigolo Johnson contributed a triple and two singles to the home team's 8–1 victory. For game three, the action moved to Yankee Stadium, where fans watched a squeaker. The Gents continued their hitting spree, but the Yanks kept matching them.

The game wasn't decided until the ninth, when Toote's home run with Gonzalez aboard gave the Gents a 7–6 lead, which they held through the Yankees' final turn at bat.

The Gents' two-to-one advantage did little to still their concerns about the fourth meeting, because they would be facing Lulu again. After two days' rest, the hard-throwing rookie had his usual stuff, and the result was the same. This time the Gents doubled their output of hits, as Lulu allowed them four while gaining his second shutout victory.

With the series tied at two games apiece, the fifth game was a heartbreaker. The Gents led by two runs, 4–2, in the last half of the ninth. But the Yanks loaded the bases with nobody out, and when their cleanup hitter lashed a line drive toward left field that would have brought in at least two runs, Mickey Mayo, the Gents towering shortstop, leaped high into the air in pursuit of his patented triple play. He miraculously snared the ball but rushed his throw to second base, and he watched helplessly as the ball rolled into right center field and all three base runners raced home.

After that dramatic win, the Yankees returned to Gents Stadium for the final game (or games), needing only a split to become World Champions. But if the Gents were dejected, their mood was upbeat compared with that of Stan Mann. With New York enmeshed in perhaps its biggest sports story of the generation, his column was expected to be a major circulation booster. And yet, as his editors continued to point out, Stan was routinely failing to produce the insights and interviews that once had made "Mann to Man" a reading habit.

Time was running out. He could hear the footsteps of

Mike Tremendo coming ever closer, and he now regretted his decision to counsel the youngster, thereby enhancing his innate talents. Further, while it seemed absurd, he was annoyed by the easy familiarity Tremendo had adopted with Marti at the Central Park festival celebrating the subway series. Although their marriage seemed strained beyond repair, Stan could not ignore the jealousy he felt when Marti showed an inordinate interest in a man almost half her age. Stan recognized Marti's intent all too clearly in the way she gently touched the younger man's arm, focused raptly on his eyes when he spoke, and laughed vivaciously at even his weakest quips. He remembered ruefully that she had once behaved that way with him. That Tremendo appeared equally responsive hardly eased Stan's discomfort.

Now, as they shared a cab en route to Gents Stadium to cover what might prove to be the series' final game, Stan found it difficult to conceal the resentment he felt for his young companion. "What do you think, Stan?" Tremendo asked pleasantly. "Will it be over tonight?"

Mann looked out of the taxi window. "If I knew, I wouldn't be going," he snapped. Tremendo gave him a quizzical look and decided to keep quiet.

In the ensuing silence, Stan tried to figure out some way to end the quarantine that the Gents players had imposed on him. Without access to the sports world's hottest personalities, his future looked as dim as theirs seemed brilliant. By the time he and Tremendo reached Gents Stadium he had decided on a bold, new approach: he would tell the truth.

Inside the clubhouse before the pivotal sixth game, Stan banged his fist against a locker to attract attention from the players, in various stages of undress. "Look," he barked, "you guys have been freezing me out all season. I know it's that column I wrote last winter. And I guess you had a right to be pissed. But that's history. You're a thousand percent better off than you were a year ago. You're out of the closet, you're all together on one helluva team, and you've got a good shot at taking the series. OK, I'm not saying that's what I had in mind. But that *is* how it turned out. So whatever problems you might have gotten because of me, well, you're still way ahead of the game."

There was no doubt that Mann had aroused the Gents' interest. Rhino looked at Mickey Mayo and shrugged. "Maybe he's got somethin', Mick."

Mayo shook his head. "I still don't like him."

Stan paused and looked from player to player. "And there's something else," he continued. "I didn't make that column up. You didn't like it, but it was the truth. And it had to come from someone. Well, I've taken enough shit by myself. It's time to get it all out."

Mike Tremendo pulled out his ballpoint and opened his pad. "The source for that story," Stan said, pausing to capture the full attention of his audience. "Was your boss."

The clubhouse exploded in anger and disbelief.

"Not Scrappy!"

"That sonuvabitch!"

"Never trusted that mother."

"I peese on you, you dirty bastard."

Scrappy, who had been in his adjacent office talking to Ruby, suddenly appeared in the doorway. "What the hell's happenin'?" he bellowed.

"You oughta know, you prick," Rhino shouted. "Mann

here says *you* gave him that fuckin' column." All eyes swiveled from Rhino to Scrappy.

Scrappy gave Mann a hard look. Then the trace of a sardonic smile raced across his face. He looked around the room until his gaze fixed on Dick Toote.

"That's right," Scrappy said. "I did. And I'm not sorry. And I'm sure you guys ain't. But that ain't all, is it? Like where did it come from? Like how did I find out you guys were gay? You wanna know? You *really* wanna know? Then how about you ask that noble hero of the sports world, too-good-to-be-true, phony Dick Toote?"

With Scrappy's indictment ringing in his ears, Toote banged a locker with a batting helmet to quiet the furor. "Cool it! Cool it!" he shouted. "Everybody clear out except the players. And that means you, too, Scrappy. This is *our* business!"

Mike Tremendo was already out the door, racing for a phone. He got the *Post*'s sports desk and began dictating a story from his notes: "Minutes before the start of last night *apostrophe ess* pivotal sixth *caps* World *caps* Series game *comma* the *caps* Gents clubhouse erupted into pandemonium when *caps Post* columnist *caps* Stan *caps* Mann identified the team's owner *hyphen* manager *comma caps* Scrappy *caps* Schwrtnzbrgr *that's ess see aitch double-ewe are tee en zee bee are gee are comma* as his source for *quote* outing *enquote* nine gay major league ballplayers *period sentence* Schwrtnzbrgr *that's ess see aitch double-ewe are tee en zee bee are gee are* retorted that *italics* his *end italics* source was Dick *parens* (Rootie) *that's caps are oh oh tee eye ee close parens* Toote *that's tee oh oh tee ee comma* the veteran Gents star who had been the first major leaguer to announce his own homosexuality *period paragraph*."

The young reporter paused momentarily to compose the next sentence. His heart was pounding so fast he had trouble concentrating. This was his first scoop. In six months, Stan Mann would be history.

As Rhino Romanski positioned his considerable bulk beside the clubhouse door to discourage media eavesdroppers, Toote took control of the players' meeting. "First off," he declared, "I plead guilty. Scrappy's right. I *did* tell him you're gay." A loud murmur of resentment surged through the room. "But, and you'll have to take my word for this, it was an accident. I was coming out to him and, as you all know, it wasn't easy. And *believe* me," he said with a chuckle, "*he* wasn't making it any easier.

"OK, he was saying things like, 'You *can't* be a fairy, you're an athlete,' you know the routine. Well, I just got so damn frustrated, I guess. I mean, here I had finally gotten myself together enough to make this *major* statement, and the son of a bitch wouldn't *believe* me. So I just began blurting out whatever names came to mind. I was so worked up, I swear, I didn't even remember what I had said until I saw Mann's column. I figured maybe I was responsible somehow, but things were happening so fast, I don't know, I just kind of put the whole thing out of my mind.

"Anyhow, that's my story. And I apologize, really apologize, to each and every one of you. I hope you know I wouldn't deliberately hurt you or any other gay person. Ever. I mean, we've got enough trouble protecting ourselves from the rest of the world without giving it to each other.

"But Scrappy, that's another story. I'm not sure what all went on, but given his track record on kindness and discretion, I've got to believe *he* knew what *he* was doing. What that leads up to is this: What, if anything, do you want to do about it?"

Mayo was the first to step forward. "I don't know about y'all," he drawled. "But I want to make him remember what he's done. I'm for teaching him a lesson he won't ever forget."

"Mick's right," Rhino agreed. "Forget all that shit we're better off than ever. If I know Scrappy, he was one hundred an' ten percent for himself. He didn't give a damn about us or our families or anything. I say let's burn him good."

There was a roar of approval from the squad. "No mother gets away with dissin' me," Gigolo Johnson growled. "I say we take a hike."

"That's my man," added Rhino. "I'm walkin' with you."

"Hey," said third baseman Dave Ripp, "I got a better way to stick it to him. We play but we lose. That way we show him who's in charge."

Toote banged the batting helmet against the locker again. "OK, OK, hold it, hold it!" he yelled. "I hear you, but let's not get carried away. We're still ballplayers. We're still a team. And this is still the World Series. Now, I've got an idea. And if it works, we'll have some clout *and* we'll play. And maybe we'll even win."

When the Gents took the field a short time later, it was with a new sense of commitment. Toote's strategy seemed as if it could be a vehicle for repudiating Scrappy while giving the team control over its actions.

The scheme was soon underway. With a 3–2 lead in games, Donald sent his rested and reliable veteran, Wee Willie Winkie, to the mound against Gents pitcher Jughead Jackson. Jackson set the visiting Yankees down in order, and in the Gents' half of the first inning, their leadoff man, Speedy Gonzalez, drew three straight balls. Scrappy, relaying instructions through third-base coach "Horse" Hyde, wanted to get Speedy on base and, in hopes of a walk, directed him to lay off the next pitch. Speedy, who had never before rejected a coach's signal, dropped a perfect bunt down the first baseline. The Yankee infielders were so taken by surprise that Speedy, running all the way, wound up on second base.

"Sonuvabitch was supposed to *take*," Scrappy grunted to Ruby.

"Yeah," Ruby replied drily, "and he might have gotten to first."

Scrappy kicked the dugout step. "That ain't the point."

Seeking to get a line on Winkie's normally effective control, Scrappy signaled the Gents second batter, Dave Ripp, to look at a couple of pitches before swinging. But on Wee Willie's first delivery, Speedy took off for third, and Ripp lined a single into right field that brought Gonzalez home in a walk.

As the Gents fans roared their approval, Speedy jogged to the dugout to be greeted by a furious manager. "What're you doin'?" Scrappy raged. "That's twice you missed the signs."

"*No comprendo, señor,*" Gonzalez said politely, scampering to the far end of the bench. Scrappy angrily kicked the water cooler.

Dave Ripp, now on first, was no speedster on the bases. He had earned his second position in the batting order because of his exceptional bat control—his ability to place the ball behind the runner, usually Gonzalez, on hit-and-run plays. As a result, Winkie barely paid him any attention as he threw the first pitch to Gigolo Johnson, who was waving his bat threateningly. But Ripp was off with Winkie's motion and breezed into second base without even drawing a throw from the catcher. It was Ripp's second stolen base in five seasons.

The Yankee infield was looking for power from Gigolo, and so when he bunted the next pitch they—and Scrappy—were unprepared. Ripp, communicating with Gigolo through the signals Toote had worked out, kept running until he scored the Gents' second run.

Scrappy was livid as Ripp trotted to the dugout. "That's a fine!" he bellowed. "Thatsa fine with me, too," Ripp jeered back.

Toote, the cleanup hitter, belted the first pitch over the right field wall to give the Gents a four-run lead they never relinquished.

The victory, tying the series at three games apiece, gave the Gents a sense of satisfaction they had rarely experienced: a feeling of solidarity. They had stood up for themselves and defied management.

Having a few beers after the game, the players roared with laughter at Scrappy's indignation.

"I thought the little crapper would have a heart attack," Rhino chortled.

"When he kicked that water cooler, I reckon he about busted his foot," Mickey Mayo added. The shortstop gave Toote an appreciative slap on the back. "That was some idea of yours, big guy."

"Felt real cool," Gigolo Johnson said, "to win that one on our own *and* bust Scrappy's chops."

They felt good enough not to discuss their crafty strategy with anyone — not with the media and certainly not with Scrappy. As for Scrappy, his anger over his temporary loss of his authority was short-lived. Upon contemplation, he decided that winning was more than a justification for his humiliation; it was a cure.

And being alive in the Series was sufficient elixir to keep Scrappy from going ballistic when he read the next day's *Post*. In an article that filled the back page under Mike Tremendo's byline, the paper described in detail the clubhouse brouhaha that had erupted over the Gents owner-manager's exploitation of the gay ballplayers.

"Now I got a new entry for my shit list," Scrappy fumed. But while the article did little to enhance Scrappy's reputation as a compassionate human being, he recognized it did no damage to his standing among those in the sports hierarchy. As Ruby pointed out, "What it really says is you put together a champeenship team," adding somewhat gratuitously, "like you're some kinda genius."

The main impact of the story was felt at the *Post*. Tremendo's stock, which had been rising for months, skyrocketed on the strength of his newsstand-clearing exclusive. For Stan Mann, being beaten by a colleague on his own story was a mortifying blow, and to his editors, unforgivable. While Stan, a veteran, an experienced columnist, had been involved in some egocentric act of contrition by identifying Scrappy as the source for his "outing" column, a novice, a cub reporter, had the acuity to recognize it as a good story and get it into the paper. Moreover, the *Post*'s latest readership survey showed that "Mann to Man" was now barely edging out the weather map.

"Look, Stan," the sports editor said, calling Mann into his office, where his eyes kept examining his shoes, "things are rough these days and upstairs is looking to cut back any way they can. They call it 'cost containment.' You know, reducing travel, checking expenses closer, stuff like that. And they're also looking to get rid of some of the heavy salaries. Guys who've been around a long time. Well, it's a chance to get a good deal. Call it a buyout or early retirement or whatever, it makes a lot of sense. Hell, I wish they'd offer it to me."

The cramp in Stan's stomach came on so quickly that he bit his lip to keep from vomiting.

"Fired? You're *firing me?*" Stan shouted. "After 30 goddam years of loyalty, of commitment! I can't believe this! What the hell's going on here? Is Mike Tremendo feeding coke to the publisher?"

"Easy, Stan, take it easy", the sports editor said,

edging away from Stan's wrath. "It's not like that. In a month you'll be telling me how great you feel."

"Bullshit!" Stan snorted. "Don't give me that crap. I'm one of the best things that ever happened to this rag. I sell out the newsstands. In the gin mills, guys fight over my column. I'm a goddam institution." He punched the desk. Papers flew into the air.

"Where the hell do you think the Gents story came from? Doesn't that mean anything to you idiots?"

The editor met his eyes. "Come on Stan. Get hold of yourself. It's not the end of the world."

Stan's eyes began to fill up. The editor's face blurred. "Where will I go? What will I do? I've spent my life here, for Crissakes."

The sports editor was looking at him with a mixture of pity and disdain. Stan wanted to belt him. But what was the use? After 35 years, a lifetime of loyalty, Stan Mann was out. It couldn't be happening to him. But of course, it already had.

Few sporting events in America rival the excitement inherent in a seventh and deciding game of a World Series. There is, as sportswriters have contended for generations, no tomorrow. For one team there is, most of all, glory: the honor, after six grueling, tedious months of play, of being recognized as the best among 28 major league teams, and to be so inscribed in baseball history. For many players, winning a World Series ring is the ultimate goal. It means more than batting titles and Most Valuable Player awards. Not incidentally, there is also the money, although in these days of multimillion-dollar salaries, that may merely translate into another Mercedes. For the other team, there is only next year.

As the Gents gathered in a clubhouse quivering with pregame tension, a subdued Scrappy told the squad that they had made their point. "You guys won a big one yesterday," he acknowledged. "You won it for yourselves. An'," he added, nodding slowly, "by yourselves."

He tried to conceal the nervousness that was crackling through his body. This whole cockeyed season had been simply a prelude to what would happen in the next three hours. Scrappy looked around the room, focusing very briefly on each face. They were veterans, they were All Stars, but, he saw clearly, they were as apprehensive as rookies. They were not only terrific ballplayers, but also, Scrappy had to admit, standout men. Real gents. They deserved to be winners. But that didn't get you a World Series ring. The only way you won on the ball field was by scoring more runs than the other guys.

Scrappy cleared his throat and chose his words carefully. "Yeah," he repeated, "you won it by yourselves. But that was yesterday. Nobody knows about tomorrow, or next week, and for sure not next year. All we got here is today. Most players they spend their lives watchin' other players win World Series. If you're lucky, you get a shot, maybe *one* shot, at playin' in one. You guys, together, got that shot the first time outa the chute. You win tonight's game, you can talk about it the rest of your lives. You lose it, well, you'll never forget it."

Scrappy paused, then shook his head. "I ain't gonna bullshit you. It ain't gonna be easy. Donald is throwin' that rookie at us again. I don't have to tell you what he's done to us so far. He's good, *real* good. *Too* good for Donald, the way I look at it. But we can't do nothin' about that. All we can do is our best."

The players looked at each other with surprise; at Scrappy's restraint, at his lack of anger, at his sincerity.

Scrappy looked down at the floor uneasily. "Just one more thing. I gotta tell you guys it's been a helluva year. I mean, no matter what."

Rhino Romanski and Dick Toote exchanged glances. "Scrappy," Rhino said gently, "I think maybe you're not as big a prick as I thought."

* * *

In the visitors' clubhouse, Donald was locked in conversation with Lulu Lewe. There was little strategy to discuss. In his two series appearances against the Gents, Lulu had not yielded a run, had given up a total of only six hits. His talent was beyond question; he was strong and he was ready. There was really nothing for Donald to say, but Donald could never say nothing.

Putting a paternal arm around Lulu's shoulders, Donald exhorted his star. "Kid, I've been with this club a lot of years. We've had just two kinds of seasons: good ones and great ones. And I can remember them all, like they were yesterday. But I want you to know that nothing, *ever*, has meant more to me than beating those wimpy, limp-wristed, degenerate homos!"

Lulu's frame began to tremble as the downy-cheeked young pitcher slid free and turned to face his boss. Tears began to fill his eyes. He struggled to speak. "Boss," he stammered, "there's something I have to tell you."

Donald stared back at him. "What? What, for Crissakes?"

Lulu twisted his cap in his hands. "It's, it's hard for me to say."

"Look, kid, you got to relax," Donald said, beginning to get unnerved himself. "Get it out. Whatever it is, you'll feel better."

The rookie glanced away, unable to look Donald in the eye. "I, I've never told this to anyone before."

The Yankee boss clenched his hands. "What is it, dammit. Spit it out!"

"Mr. Bigg," Lulu said in almost a whisper, "I—I—I think, I think I'm, I'm gay."

"Gay? *Gay!*" Donald roared in pain and disbelief. "You

think you're gay! You're crazy! You can't be gay! You're a ballplayer! You're a star! My God, man, you're a Yankee!"

Lulu recoiled in the face of Donald's outburst. He seemed about to cry. "I'm sorry. I can't help it. I know how you feel about *them*. I mean *us*. But I just couldn't say anything before."

Donald's face contorted. He struggled to control his hands, which seemed eager to encircle Lulu's neck. He felt nauseous. It was only minutes to game time. *The* game. He stared at Lulu in anger and frustration. He couldn't believe what he had heard. Couldn't believe his ears, or his eyes. They're all around us, he thought. They're everywhere. They come in all sizes and shapes. They look like athletes. They perform like athletes. *What's going on?*

Donald looked carefully at the man standing in front of him. He checked his posture, his looks. Nothing about Lulu betrayed his sexuality. He couldn't be one of *them,* Donald thought. Not and throw the way he does. I'd have to be out of my mind not to pitch him. . . . He made his decision.

Lulu was still twisting his cap. His head was bowed. Donald patted Lulu's shoulder, pulling back only a little.

"Go get 'em, kid," he said, seeking to sound enthusiastic.

Dick Toote didn't get his single until the ninth inning, and so Lulu's bid for a no-hitter went almost as far as it could go. The game had been scoreless until the top of the eighth, when the Yanks pushed over the game's only run. And while there is definitely something bittersweet about a one-hit shutout, Lulu was not complaining when he approached Toote in the wild aftermath of the Yankee's 1–0 victory.

"I'd like to talk to you sometime soon," Lulu said. "It's real important to me." Toote nodded admiringly through the pain of defeat. "Any time. Great game, kid."

Lulu forced a smile. "Thanks. Thanks a lot. But there're things more important than baseball. More important than the series, even."

Toote raised his eyebrows. It was strange talk from a rookie who had just made history by pitching his team to a world championship with three shutouts. "Just give me a call," Toote said.

Scrappy avoided Donald in the postgame bedlam, and Donald, who had been waiting all season for this moment of triumph over the Gents, was uncharacteristically restrained. In a television interview with

O. J. Cobb, he omitted praise for Lulu until the sports-caster said, "Hey, what about that pitcher of yours? Isn't he something?"

Donald nodded slowly. "He's something *else*," the Yanks boss agreed.

The Gents were, of course, disappointed. But there were no hangdog looks, no muttered curses. The club-house reflected tranquillity more than the traditional losers' sullenness. Nor were there recriminations or second guesses. They took the loss as philosophically as losing by one run in the seventh game of the World Series could be taken. They were proud of their perfor-mance, glad that the intense, remarkable season was over, pleased with the friendships they had developed, and already talking about what next year would be like.

Standing by his locker in the clubhouse, Dick Toote considered the question posed by Olivia Cobb in her postgame interview. "How do I feel?" he repeated. "I feel real good, O. J., no matter how that sounds. Sure, we *lost* the World Series. And I know I'm supposed to feel all broken up. But to tell the truth, so many bigger things have happened to me this season that's not how I feel. I'm not saying I didn't want us to win. Or that I'm not sorry we lost. We did the best we could, believe me. And we lost to a better team. Make that to a super pitcher. Nobody's ever done what Lulu did.

"What I want to say is that I feel real good because for the first time in my life I feel like I belong. And I think the rest of the team feels the same way. One way or another, we wound up being ourselves and being proud of it. Proud to be gay, but more than that, really, proud to be out. As far as the Gents are concerned, just wait 'til next year. 'Cause you've got to believe that we can hardly wait."

Toote leaned against his locker and looked past the telecaster, beyond the clubhouse. "There's something else, too," he said softly. "I learned a little bit about life this season. And a lot about death. One thing I'm sure of. Baseball may be big business, and it *is* my career. But it's still a game, or it ought to be. I think it gets taken a lot too seriously. By everybody."

On his way out of the ballpark with some sixty thousand others, Stan Mann felt a hand on his shoulder. It was Rick Volpino, the marketer. Stan, who had avoided familiar faces, particularly in the press box and the ordeal of interrogation and condescension that follows bad news, returned Volpino's tap with a lame smile. "Give me a ring," the publicist said. "Got something to talk about. Like make it tomorrow."

When Stan arrived at Mea Culpa the following day, the receptionist motioned him to a comfortable chair while she buzzed Volpino. "Send him in in ten," Volpino directed, pulling a copy of Penthouse from a desk drawer.

"He'll be with you in a few minutes," the receptionist murmured. Stan admired the rich wood paneling until she told him that he could go in.

Volpino, wearing an ocher shirt, waved him to a leather sofa. "Heard about it," Volpino said briskly. "Who needed that pissant operation, anyhow?" he asked rhetorically. "Look, Stan, I'll be honest with you. I got an offer *you* can't afford to refuse. Lighten up; that's sort of a joke. Anyhow, what I've got is a new client and a great idea. The client is the biggest tobacco company in America, OK? And the idea is we put baseball cards in packs of cigarettes. It came to me after I read a survey that said Joe Camel was the second best-recognized cartoon character among schoolkids. The first was Mickey Mouse, and somebody said they're surprised Reynolds hadn't thought of using *him*.

"Anyway, what do you think? Is that a way to tap that, um, *undergraduate* market, or what? So it's a terrifico idea, right? And you want to know where you fit in? You've been on the sports scene what, 40 years? You know every guy who's ever put on a jock, right? Well, you line up the ballplayers to go on the cards in the cigarette packs. Figure we start with baseball, cause that's, you know, the national pastime or whatever. Then it depends. My man, Dore Dupus, will run some polls. We want to go inner city, we go for the basketball guys. Or maybe football. In the prep schools we could go hockey, maybe even soccer. What the hell, the possibilities are endless. I can see you like. So let's shake."

Stan couldn't believe what he was hearing. He was *wanted* again. Somebody recognized his possibilities, saw him as useful once more. There'd be money, too. It hadn't been mentioned yet, but that's the way guys like Volpino operated. That's why so many of his colleagues had left newspaper work for public relations and promotion. Sure, he had put them down when they left. Even called them sellouts. But part of that had been envy. And *this* was something interesting. It was connected to sports. Volpino had said he knew them all, could talk to them, get them involved in this hot project.

Volpino was smiling at him expectantly. He thrust his hand out and Stan clutched it. "Deal," Stan said.

As Stan left amid visions of a new career, Rick Vol

pino complimented himself. "It didn't even cost me a lunch."

When Stan got home he was pleased to find Marti there. He was also pleased that he had decided to withhold from her the news of his departure from the *Post*. Now that ignominy would be overridden by this latest development. But as he described his meeting with Volpino and explained his role in this exciting new venture, Stan sensed that Marti was not sharing his enthusiasm. By the time he finished, she was on her feet, an expression of revulsion on her face.

"You *what?*" she cried. "You're going to flack for a *tobacco* company? You're going to push cigarettes to *schoolchildren?* Have you lost your mind or just your self-respect? What's happened to you? What's happened to the man I fell in love with and married?"

Her body began to tremble. She put her hands over her ears as if trying to blot out what she had heard. "Oh, Stan," she wailed. "What's happened to *us?* Why can't we be the way we were?"

Stan came forward to comfort her. He gently put his hand on her shoulder. Marti recoiled. "Marti, I—" he began. "I didn't know what else to do. I got *fired,* for God's sake. Fired, at my age, after all these years."

"No. It's no good," she sobbed. "I don't want to hear about it. It's over. I can't live with you. Not with a man who's gotten so far off the track. So far off he doesn't even know it."

Stan just stood silently, watching her body quiver. He wasn't surprised. It had been coming for so long. Why do pleasures have such a short shelf life, he wondered. One by one he had seen them fall away, his influence, his skills, his marriage. Like a pitcher who has lost his fastball or an outfielder his speed, his life had become one of diminished possibilities.

Stan felt old and sad as he contemplated the loss of Marti. But as he turned to the bedroom to pack his bags, he knew he wasn't ready to quit. He had a new job and, in time, perhaps he could win Marti back. He'd work hard on both fronts. Looking for his socks and wondering if he'd have to take up smoking, Stan told himself it wasn't over yet. In spite of his jokes, he still had time before he hung up his jock.

Gents Stadium was quiet on the morning after. Later, the grounds crews and maintenance men and concessionaires would begin the annual task of closing down the baseball operation and starting preparations for the football season. But now, for the moment, all was deserted — except in the office of the owner-manager, deep within the recesses of the sports complex.

In the serenity that follows episodes of high drama and excitement, Scrappy and Ruby were relaxing, contemplating the past and anticipating the future. As always in sports, somebody had won and somebody had lost, but this time it was not altogether clear which was which or who was who.

"Ruby, we give Donald a pretty good run for his money," Scrappy said, violating his rule of no drinks before noon by pulling a bottle of vodka out of the refrigerator.

Ruby waved off the glass twice before taking a drink. "You did mor'n that, boss. Y'set baseball on its ass."

Scrappy smiled contentedly and scratched his crotch. So much had happened during the past ten months that had never occurred before. He had been caught up in the stream of events without having the time to savor or deplore what was going on around him. Until now. And even now he wasn't sure how he felt about himself and what he had done.

"Y'know Ruby, less'n a year ago things were so bad that if I took a good crap in the mornin' it was the best thing that happened all day long. Now look. We made a little bitta history and a whole load of money. We had a helluva lotta fun, and the franchise is gotta be worth 10, 20 times more."

Ruby nodded in agreement. "We, uh, you were, well, sorta like a pioneer, you know. Comin' up with the idea of gettin' those, um, gays together on one team."

"Ruby, that was something for sure," Scrappy said, taking a long swig of the ice-cold drink. "We mighta lost the big one, but there's always next year."

"You're certainly right, boss," Ruby said. "You're lookin' terrific for next year."

"Right on! Who knows? We pick up another starter, there ain't nobody gonna beat us, *includin'* Donald. Hey, talkin' about starters, ain't that Lulu really somethin'?"

Ruby took another sip. "Terrific, terrific. An' I think you may be gettin' a little surprise there."

Scrappy looked up sharply. He had had enough surprises. "What're you talkin'?"

"I dunno exactly," Ruby said. "Just a feelin' I got on account of somethin' Toote said."

"Like what?"

"Oh, like, how d'ya think that kid would look in a *Gents* uniform?"

"Y'think something's goin' down?" Scrappy asked.

"Well," Ruby replied, "if there is, you got about six

months 'til next season to find out. But y'know what the secret is?"

"What's the secret?"

"The secret, Scrappy, is keepin' yourself open to new ideas. You gotta go with change, maybe sometimes even make it yourself."

"Well, you're right, Ruby. If I hadn't thought of gettin' them fag—uh, them gays, y'know where I'd be?"

"Yeah," Ruby said, sensing that he had forever lost credit for the scheme that had turned the Gents around. "Yeah, you'd be back to your one good crap in th' mornin'."

Scrappy guffawed, took another drink and lapsed into contemplative silence.

"Y'know, Ruby, I thought I just wanted t'retire 'n' take it easy. But that's not me. Not anymore."

Ruby eyed his boss. "Well, I guess you're a man likes challenges."

"Betcher ass, Ruby, bring 'em on."

As they sat quietly sipping their drinks and thinking their thoughts, the stillness was pierced by the ring of the telephone. Scrappy fumbled for the receiver and put it to his ear. It was one of the guards in the security office.

"Somebody here wants to see you, Mister Schwartz-errr—" the guard's voice trailed off.

Scrappy's mood was expansive. "Send 'em down," he said.

After a few minutes, they heard footsteps echoing along the passageway, and then there was a knock.

"OK," Scrappy said, as the door opened to reveal O. J. Cobb, dressed in lavender jeans and a pink *Cobb's Closet* T-shirt. She was trailed by a gangling girl in her late teens. The girl wore a baseball uniform inscribed "Jake's Hardware" and was twirling a mitt.

O. J. waved casually at the Gents' boss and his aide. "Hi, Scrappy, Ruby," she said. "I'd like you to meet my cousin Natalie. Nat's got a helluva good arm. And I've got a great idea for you."